Cameo
Lake

ALSO BY SUSAN WILSON

Hawke's Cove

Published by POCKET BOOKS

Cameo Lake

Susan Wilson

POCKET BOOKS
New York   London   Toronto   Sydney   Singapore

POCKET BOOKS, a division of Simon & Schuster, Inc.
1230 Avenue of the Americas, New York, NY 10020

Library of Congress Cataloging-in-Publication Data

Wilson, Susan, 1951-
    Cameo Lake / Susan Wilson.
        p. cm.
    ISBN 0-7434-1276-1
        1. Women authors—Fiction.   2. Married women—Fiction.
    3. New Hampshire—Fiction.   4. Adultery—Fiction.   I. Title.
    PS3573.I47533 C35 2001
    813'.54—dc21   2001021831 √

First Pocket Books hardcover printing July 2001

10 9 8 7 6 5 4 3 2 1

POCKET and colophon are registered trademarks of Simon & Schuster, Inc.

Designed by Christine Weathersbee

Printed in the U.S.A.

*Dedicated with love to family and friends
without whose support this and everything else
I do would be impossible.*

In memory of Meredith

And with enormous appreciation for their labors, I wish to thank my editor, Caroline Tolley, who mid-wifed my literary baby even as she was delivering her own real one; Lauren McKenna, her stalwart associate, and Ed Cohen, whose line editing seemed like conversation. Thanks, as always, to Andrea Cirillo and the Jane Rotrosen team. Lastly, for her cheerful technical advice, grateful thanks to Barbara Stelle, M.D.

Cameo
Lake

Prologue

The small concert hall is beginning to fill up. I know we're here very early, but I was anxious and ready to go. I like sitting here, watching the people file in, find their seats, greet acquaintances with little waves, the women in silk, good jewelry glittering, the men in dark suits. I smooth down the silk of my own dress and dislike the moisture on my palms. I am not a performer, I am here to listen. I am audience. Yet I am nervous and I wish Grace would hurry up. Whenever we go to the theater or concerts, she always seems to time it so that she sees everyone she knows before she climbs into her seat. Finally she arrives and places herself to my right, between Lily and Tim, who are sitting with uncharacteristic stillness.

Though I haven't yet opened the evening's program, I already know they'll be playing Mahler's Fifth Symphony as their first piece. That's not why we're here. Tonight will be the premiere of a highly anticipated new concerto for flute. A famous flautist will play it. As the orchestra files in, I turn around in my seat to see if I see him, the composer. To see if he's looking for me.

One

The sun dappled the track in front of me, strobing brilliant to black, dazzling my eyes and making me squint. I maneuvered my borrowed four-by-four into the ruts I couldn't go around, the groaning of the behemoth vehicle condemning my inexperience.

Just the good side of mud season, the track was only vestigially wet in the deeper grooves, uncomfortable but not impassable. Heavy tire marks ahead of me guided my way when I would have packed it in otherwise. After the lonely three-and-a-half-hour drive from Providence, it wouldn't have taken much else to turn me back from committing myself to this exile in the New Hampshire woods.

Grace's instructions had been precise. I found the turnoff to the cabin easily: third left beyond the abandoned fruit stand, watch for the faded blue sign CAMEO LAKE at the head of the mile-long private way. Before going any further I paused, checked my watch, and picked up the mobile phone plugged into the lighter. Grace had warned me that the cabin lay in a dead zone for microwaves and the car phone would only work at the top of the drive. Once down the road, I was lost to all outside communication. A fact which had made the offer to borrow her cabin that much more appealing.

"McCarthy." Sean's voice was abrupt.

"Hey, I'm here."

"You made good time."

"Under four hours. One stop."

"Good. Good." I knew Sean must have a client with him, his half of the dialogue was shaded with preoccupation.

"I'll call you at home."

"Fine. Wait. I've got a dinner tonight. Call late."

"Never mind, I'll call tomorrow." I repressed my annoyance that he couldn't spend this first night of my being away at home with the kids. Sean had been remarkably agreeable, if not precisely enthusiastic, about my making this working retreat. Putting a good face on it. Every time I mentioned some aspect of the upcoming retreat, Sean would carefully arrange his broad Irish face into a cheerful, benign expression, admirably illustrating the aphorism.

"Hey. Cleo. I'm glad you got there safely."

The track suddenly opened up into a good-sized yard, edged by a semicircle of pine and birch. The late-afternoon sun made golden the yellowish grass and patched the cabin roof between the long shadows. "Plain and simple" was how Grace described this lakefront family camp. Plain and simple it was. Rustic bordering on primitive: a two-circuit electrical system, limited hot water, and no phone. The one concession to environmental responsibility was the recent addition of a flush toilet and a tight tank.

"It's exactly what you need." Grace had taken my unfinished manuscript as her responsibility. "You need to get away from every-one—every distraction." She meant my inability to say no to anyone: PTA, church, community activities. The phone rang and my Pavlov-ian response was to say yes.

Grace, of course, was my biggest distraction, the one who kept signing me up for things—"It'll only be once a month . . . year . . . day." That's not fair. Grace was my one legitimate distraction, apart from my husband and kids. My best friend.

I sat for a long time staring at my future. Would I really find my abandoning muse in this peaceful, if lonely, place? A cardinal flitted in the bramble bush, cast himself into the air, and landed on the tin chimney. He called to the world, "Mate wanted, apply here," with a sharp call, like someone whistling up their dog. I waited. The cardinal dashed off to another, higher, place. Again he whistled his low-high notes. The breeze riffled through the pine trees and I heard a duck, though the lake wasn't visible from the driveway. Finally I moved, climbing down out of the car. I couldn't feel the writing urge come on me like the Spirit over the Twelve. The magic release from daily commitment hadn't kicked in yet. Instead, surveying my new uncluttered surroundings, I felt only the urge to climb back up into that ridiculous vehicle and barrel home to my known quantities and useful excuses. I didn't feel the writing urge; instead, I felt the bitter loss of my anger, that generalized anger that built up when there were too many things which kept me from working, the anger at myself for using those disruptions as an excuse.

Fish or cut bait. I think I said it aloud. I'm standing in my skeleton—all protection gone. Gone the protective coloration of car pools and calling lists. No need to drop everything and run. I had arrived.

There isn't much in Cameo. A green denuded of big trees by storms, a pharmacy, and a pizza joint. In the last few years various rural artisans have set up shops and galleries, but nothing would open until July, which was still ten days away.

The next town over has the Big G grocery store, so I made due this first night with a slice of pizza from the pizza place and a quart of milk bought at the gas station convenience store. I had brought the necessities: coffee and cereal, and wine bought at the New Hampshire State Liquor store. The rest of my supplies could wait. My willingness to shrug off the responsibility of meals and good nutrition came as a pleasant surprise.

The private drive seemed shorter the second time in and I negotiated it more effectively. When Grace offered her family's cabin to me for the summer, I carried the offer in my mind for a long time before broaching the idea to Sean. Even with Sean's mother living on the street behind us, I knew Sean would feel put-upon being left with total child-care responsibility. Not that the kids needed much hands-on. At almost ten and eight, Lily and Tim were pretty independent and reliable. This was their golden time—*post* total dependence and *pre* adolescence—that lovely juncture of age and maturity when they needed only minimal supervision. I could hear his objections before he voiced them: I have to work. I can't blow off clients. What if I have to travel? Subtext: This is *your* job.

Then there was the other thing. The thing which must never be mentioned because I had forgiven him, but which would forever taint our relationship. The thing even Grace didn't know about because it had happened so long ago—yet the pain of Sean's infidelity had the power to occasionally stop me in my tracks.

"So, when are you going to talk to Sean about going?" Grace, friend, confidante, pain in the behind, pressed me for an answer.

"I hate setting myself up for an argument."

"Why should he argue against productivity? Isn't that what he's always talking about in his job?"

"Oh, Grace. Okay. I'll talk to Sean."

"Good girl."

Grace stage-managed the situation, as ably as she stage-managed the community theater where we first met. A few years ago, I had toyed with playwriting. Grace, an associate professor of English at Brown, turned one of my scripts into a respectably received production in a weekend of one-act plays by unknowns acted by students. But, as she knew right from the start, it was the long form, the novel, I really wanted to write. The play never saw the light of day again, but Grace and I remained close friends. I achieved a moderate success at novel writing and it was my fourth book that I was finding it hard to pay attention to.

Memorial Day Weekend, a picnic at Grace and her partner Joanie's flat on the East Side of Providence. Grace had Sean backed into a corner, amber bottle of beer in his one hand, the other hand balancing a paper plate heaped with chicken and salad, defenseless against her charm. "Sean, has Cleo told you about my offer?"

Grace always intimidated Sean by her sheer presence. Showman meets insurance man. Large, with masses of long curly hair, and built on the style of Rubens's vision of femininity, Grace fitted her name, every movement fluid, pouring herself over people, filling their space with her voice and gesture. I watched Sean back away a step. He once said she was the only woman who intimidated him physically while turning him on, evidently a contradiction in his mind.

"What offer, Grace?"

"To finish her damned manuscript at my New Hampshire cabin. To get off by herself for as long as it takes."

Sean's sharp blue eyes met mine. "Sounds like a good idea. When were you thinking?" He could have been speaking to me or to Grace.

"Soon. Tomorrow if she'd go." Grace closed the space between them with an arm around Sean's shoulder. "She's not even done with the first half—are you, Cleo?"

"No."

Sean smiled his insurance smile, practiced and smooth. "It's a great idea."

I knew it would be an interesting ride home and already I rehearsed my rationale, seeking the palatable compromise.

"Then it's settled." Grace squeezed Sean's shoulder and nodded like a well-pleased god.

We walked to the car, parked halfway down the block. The streets were a little shiny now with headlight shimmers. It wasn't too late, maybe ten o'clock. The kids walked ahead of us, the truce of the moment evident in the proximity they kept with one another. Not quite touching, skipping over sidewalk cracks. Tim's blue ball cap on backwards in a rakish imitation of current style, Lily unkempt, her hair pushed into a ratty ponytail. Had I made her brush her hair before we left the house or had she gone to Grace's that way?

"Do you mean to be gone all summer?" Sean and I walked in a large-sized duplication of the kids, close but not touching, stepping carefully over the cracks.

"I need the time, Sean. I need the solitude."

"Are we that bad? You've managed before."

"It's not you. It's me. I'm not as good as I once was at shutting everything out." Even as I said it, the specter of old conflict, Hamlet's ghost, was raised and I remembered how successful I had once been at ignoring things.

Sean took my hand and slowed our pace down enough to fall behind the kids a little bit. "I love you."

"Sean, it's not a matter of love."

"Yes, it is. I love you enough to say, 'Go, write, thrive.' We'll be fine." His hand tightened on mine. "I'll be fine." The promise.

I squeezed his hand back and smiled. "It'll be all right. Once I can spend whole days working, it won't be long at all. Besides, the kids have been pestering to go to camp. Maybe this is the year."

"Absolutely." Then, "When will you go?"

"Not before school lets out. I don't want to miss the end-of-year activities. Mid-June, maybe. Kids get out around the twentieth."

"It's settled, then. A retreat."

"It's not impossible for you and the kids to come up on weekends."

Sean had slipped his hand out of mine to scratch at a mosquito bite. "Hmmm? Yeah, of course, weekends."

Hamlet's ghost hovered in the back of my mind and suddenly I was afraid.

What have I done?

The whole leave-taking was almost derailed when the timing belt in my ten-year-old minivan went. Grace, as always, to the rescue. "Take my SUV. I don't want the summer students renting our place to have it, it's no good to me in Italy, and I would love to know you have a good, reliable car up there. No if, ands, or buts, Cleo. No excuses not to go." I wondered what she would have said had I told her about Sean. But I kept my eyes looking forward and turned my back on history.

It was dark now and I chided myself for not leaving a light on in the cabin. I clumped up the steps, instinctively warning any predator of my arrival. I knew a light chain dangled from somewhere near the

center of the kitchen space, I swung my hands in unintentional mock-
ery of the blind before I could see the faint glow of a tiny luminous
Scottie dog suspended in midair. One sixty-watt bulb, nestled in a
blue cardboard shade, warmed the room. The pervasive smell of
mold seemed more pronounced than when I had first come in that
afternoon, the night's dampness raising the ante. Of the cabin's three
rooms, the kitchen/living room space was biggest. The two bedrooms, originally one room now halved by particle board, were only
large enough for two camp beds in the one and a three-quarter bed in
the other. Both held only one three-drawer bureau into which a summer's worth of clothing had to be crammed. The recent addition of a
bathroom, a lavatory really, encroached on the porch. The only
shower, lake-water-supplied, was outside. The walls were painted
pine, mostly shades of tan, varying where each summer's painting
began and ended. The pine floor was dark brown, and here and there
scatter rugs covered the worst of the gaps in the floorboards. An
island counter separated the sitting area from the half-size stove and
gas-powered fridge. The other attempt at modernization, a picture
window, took up half of one wall; in the dark it was a black mirror,
but in the day I knew that it overlooked the lake and the little islands
rising out of it. The White Mountains served as backdrop. A screened
porch jutted off the side of the cabin, precariously balanced on stilts.

I opened the windows against the musty inside air, letting in a
chill early-summer breeze. So quiet. I pulled on a sweater and went
out onto the porch. No, I was mistaken, it wasn't silent at all. I
breathed in the fresh lake air and listened. The night sounds of bullfrog and cicada pierced the gloom. I strained to listen over it. Not one
human-made sound. I stared out into the dark. Trees loomed more
darkly than the night sky. They ringed the lake, massive pines hush-
ing gently in the light breeze. From the porch it was clear-cut to the
lake's edge. Unlike the ocean, the lake was still and made no noise
except for the occasional splash of a jumping fish. Ungentrified, rustic, it was perfect.

Directly across from where I stood there suddenly appeared a soft
yellow light, flickering slightly, as if not made of stable electricity.

The screeck of a screen door carried across the water from the small island opposite my shore. So, I was not entirely alone. Sipping warm chardonnay—my single glass of indulgence—I stared at the beacon, thinking of Jay Gatsby longing after Daisy.

Random thoughts flickered like the light across the water. I wondered for the first time if this sabbatical might be as much time out from marriage as it was from everyday stress. A little separation to renew the faltering romance of a busy and distracted relationship. I poked at the thought a little to see if I could make it flame. The specter of past conflict was there, it was never entirely absent in our marriage. I loved my husband, but I couldn't entirely trust him. I never had any doubt that he loved me, but, like his father before him, Sean couldn't stop himself from flirting. I remembered the first time Sean brought me home to his family. We were new lovers, besotted with one another, keeping no less than a fingertip's distance, and yet, immediately, I felt the flattery of Francis McCarthy's attention. "Come sit by me, young lady," blue eyes so like Sean's glittering under shaggy brows, "tell me about yourself." Lacking a father, even while he was alive, I felt charmed and somehow *selected* by Francis McCarthy's interest in me. I thought it unfair of Sean to pull me away as he so quickly did.

"Bred in the bone," Alice McCarthy said when I complained to her about Sean's compulsion to flirt. "Pay it no mind or you'll never be happy." It was advice I shouldn't have taken.

A drift of piano music floated across the still water toward the screened porch where I sat, mired in old memories. The music was almost a perfect backdrop to the conflicted emotions I had pressed into being by allowing myself to dwell on what was supposed to have been past. The piano chords were a rising, inharmonic progression leading toward a natural resolution. They stopped before they touched the chord which would have put them into sense, leaving me with an auditory frustration not unlike missing the last rung of a ladder.

Eventually the porch light from across the water went out, and I went inside.

Two

I slept later than I had intended. Already my resolution to be up with the dawn, coffee in hand and laptop humming, was dented. I consoled myself, there was always tomorrow and tomorrow beyond that, extending for ten blessed weeks, interrupted only by the two weeks at the beginning of July when my family would join me. Tim would make us crazy wanting to use the canoe lodged now beneath the porch, Lily would explore the riches of the woods. I pictured family picnics down by the lake, board games by the dim kitchen light. No TV, no radio, we'd be forced to enjoy each other's company. I had ten days to get enough done that I could prove to Sean I was making good use of this sabbatical, but not so much done he would wonder why I stayed behind as they drove back to Providence without me.

The lake was quiet in the morning; a robin deep in the woods called and, in the farthest distance, a chain saw buzzed, the only attention-grabbing sounds. I was surprised to feel the mild air when I opened the porch door. After last night's chill, I hadn't expected to find summer outside. The lake looked a lot bigger in broad daylight, the three little islands much smaller.

A raft lay equidistant from my shore and the island opposite. I judged it to be just at the midpoint of my swimming ability, perhaps three hundred feet. The lake was so still I couldn't detect any rocking, it was as motionless as something sitting on ice.

Still in my T-shirt and boxers, I set up my laptop on a table on the porch. I'd let the old-fashioned range-top percolator go too long and my coffee tasted a little burned, but with enough kick to get me started.

Open file: novel. Page 26. I'd led even Grace astray. This book wasn't just unfinished, it was bloody well unstarted. I paged backwards, reading paragraphs, hunting down clues to my plot. Protagonist Karen's description was something like my own. I usually had short heroines, but some urge made Karen tall, thin, and dark-haired like me, except her hair was long and straight while mine was short and wavy. I hadn't yet given her an eye color, but would probably default to green. Do we always make our characters doppelgangers of ourselves? Or just what we wish we could be? Karen at twenty-eight was ten years my junior, single, childless, and clever. And in twenty-six pages she hadn't yet met the man who would become the object of her desire.

I stood up to pour out my cold coffee and refresh the cup. Across the water I could see my only neighbor. He was hanging a load of wash on a single line strung between two trees and occupying the sole sunlit patch of yard near his cabin. Shirtless, he wore a khaki-colored baseball cap and jeans. As his arms rose and fell in the process of pegging the various articles of clothing, I admired the flex of his long back and shoulders. When he turned to pick up the basket, I was grateful for the shadows of the screen hiding my blatant observation. At first I thought he must be a young camper, but when he took his cap off to run a hand through his dark hair, I could see a little tonsure of baldness at the crown, signifying a grown man.

A pair of bird-watcher's binoculars hung on a peg near the sink and I casually took them out to the porch, as if simply interested in the lake's rampant bird life. My neighbor was still out there, hanging the wash in the odd way of men, using clothespins profligately, never clipping things together end to end to conserve them, instead single socks pinned side by side. I tested the binoculars, drawing the far shore, beyond the island, into focus. Then, slowly like a spy in a trench, I lowered the glasses toward my target.

Sharp features softened only a little by middle age, his nose quite high-bridged and prominent between high cheekbones. He turned back toward his cabin before I could see more. A gentle face, I would call it. A face we would call good-looking, not handsome. A nice face, my mother-in-law would say of men like this.

I studied his wash. White V-neck T-shirts and colored boxers, two pair of faded blue jeans, khaki shorts, and a pair of tan chinos. Fully half the line was filled with freshly washed polo shirts, white and mauve and blue and navy. Two odd garments fluttered in the breeze, they might have been men's dress shirts, but they were collarless and short-sleeved, I could pick out strings hanging from either side and I realized that they were faded hospital johnnies.

I lowered the binoculars and turned my attention back to my work.

Within a day or two a pattern evolved. A wind-up alarm clock prevented any more wasted time. By seven-thirty I was on my porch, coffee in hand, laptop functioning. When the coffee pot was empty, I'd go for a run before lunch, a luxurious stretching run. Following well-trod trails up and down the pitch of the slope, between trees and rocks, I found the soft humus-packed track a delight for my pavement-conditioned feet. I thought I could run forever. Even in late June, the water was still a little too cold for me to plunge into, so after my run, a lake-water shower heated by the inadequate hot-water heater. Then I'd make a peanut-butter sandwich and go back out onto the porch and eat it while watching my neighbor do the same. Most times he tossed bits of meat to the cats. I had to smile, watching him as he casually twisted Oreo cookies apart and licked the icing off before fitting the two halves back together and popping the whole thing into his mouth. Clearly he thought himself safe from observation.

I'd work until the late-afternoon sun was in my eyes, drawing down the long day as it lowered behind the mountains in the distance. In the first shadows, my neighbor's light went on first. The porch light across the way putting paid to my solitude. Sometimes I would watch him light it, lifting the chimney off the base and touching the wick with a match. Spending a moment adjusting the flame to a smokeless level and then setting the glass chimney back on. I supposed he didn't have electricity out on the island.

In those first few days I enjoyed watching him split wood and stack it, building a lovely wooden wall between opposing pines. Obscured by my fine-mesh screening, I watched as he set the wedge and swung the maul. Little rivulets of perspiration caught the sunlight . The sound of the maul hitting the wedge echoed off the hills, a split second's delay from the observable strike. Two echoes, metallic but dull, tickled the pressure in my ears.

A cat kept coming up to him and rubbing against his legs. He'd stop and swing the gray striped tiger into his arms, ruffling its fur and scratching it under the chin, then set it at a safe distance, only to repeat the action a few minutes later, when the persistent cat wove its way around his legs for more attention.

To justify my binocular-aided spying, I worked it into my story. My protagonist's love interest, Jay, burns off frustration and anger at Karen by chopping wood. His aim clear and steady, muscles rippling in the sun. Thus I consoled my conscience, voyeurism is a legitimate tool of writers.

By prearrangement, every evening, just at seven-thirty, I drove the four-by-four along the rutted drive until I reached the point where the cell phone would work. Every night it was the same, I listened patiently to Lily's recital of complaints about her brother. Tim, oblivious to the griping, was only interested in asking when I'd be coming home. Once I got him talking about his skateboard accomplishments, the whining stopped. Love you's and kiss-kisses said, they would turn the phone over to their father.

"Hey, Clee, how're the woods?" Sean would ask every night.

"Wild. Lions and tigers and bears." There was so little I could share with Sean at this point. I never spoke of my works-in-progress, a superstitious sense that to tell my ideas out loud would corrupt them. Besides, Sean wasn't all that interested. The writing process, amorphous and somewhat undignified, made him uncomfortable. Sean liked quantifiables. Numbers, action plans, and goals.

We met our last year of college. It was, we often said, something of a miracle we ever met at all. Our paths being so divergent. I had spent too long meeting with my advisor and was at the wrong end of the campus to get to my usual dining hall before they started breaking down for the night. The dining halls were supposed to serve until seven, but inevitably they started clearing out at six thirty. I glanced at the clock tower and grimaced. Somehow, eating at Hope Hall dining commons was like invading someone's private space. It felt wrong. I had only a yogurt sitting on my dorm windowsill and I was far too hungry for that. Looking around, the only familiar face I saw was Sean's. I couldn't quite place him, but with his distinctive red hair I knew that we had probably been in a class together at some point. He was sitting alone at the only otherwise unoccupied table.

"May I?" My shoulder ached from the weight of my canvas bag full of books and notebooks.

"Please, of course." And, unbelievably, he stood to pull the chair out for me, tall enough to lean across without having to leave his side of the table. "Sean McCarthy."

"Cleo Grayson."

"The pork roast is really good tonight."

"Is that what it is?"

Sean laughed around a mouthful. "Weren't you in my macroeconomics class?"

"Not a chance. I've avoided anything with the word *economics* in it. How about Professor Fisher's survey course?"

"Survey of what?"

"English lit, from Shakespeare to Joyce."

Sean mimicked a shudder, "Not a chance there, either."

Our hunt took us through dinner, and we lingered a while, or at least until the dining commons staff began to make clear our presence was an annoyance and we belonged on the other side of the twin sets of double doors. Having discovered that we both lived at the southern end of the campus, it was natural that we walk back together.

"I always eat in Hope on Mondays and Wednesdays because its closer to my last class."

As good as an invitation.

* * *

I didn't tell Sean much more than it was going well. That it was very quiet and a bit lonely, but necessary. Nothing that wasn't true.

And he told me that's great. We're fine here. We'll see you soon.

One morning I woke just as the sky was brightening, the first glimmer of dawn silvering the light in my unshaded room. Fighting the need to pee, and thus leave my warm bed for the early-morning chill, I lay awake to hear the first call of the earliest bird. The dawn sounds were of another key and tune than the harmonics of the night. Bullfrogs quieted, day birds tuned up. Losing the battle, I got out of bed and trooped to the lavette. Coming back, I looked out of my big picture window and saw my neighbor facing my cabin. As I enjoyed the nightly spectacle of sunset backlighting his place, now he seemed to be admiring the sunrise over mine on the opposite shore. By now the sun was streaming through the open room and I was quite visible standing there, framed by the window. I couldn't be sure he saw me, but I waved anyway, lest he think ill of me; assuming he had never noticed my spying. He either didn't see me or he chose not to respond. Then I realized his eyes were neither on my cabin nor on the sunrise behind it but on a pair of swans gliding toward him. As I watched, my neighbor pulled open a plastic bag and began feeding the swans. He had the technique of long experience, knowing just when to let go of the bread before the aggressive white birds closed on his fingers. He didn't attempt to touch them, keeping to his place and letting them come to him. I was amazed at the size of the two birds. The larger one's head reached nearly to the man's waist, and when it stretched its wings back in a little warning to its mate I was reminded of "Leda and the Swan." No wonder they evoked so many classical allusions. Eagles evoked power, crows mischief, but swans portrayed mystery, beauty, and sex, obscuring the hidden viciousness of their natures.

My neighbor stepped back toward the shoreline and dumped the crumbs into the water. A little flock of ducks scrambled toward the debris. It was then that he saw me watching him. A little embarrassed, I waved again. This time he lifted his empty hand in a brief gesture, not exactly a greeting, but certainly an acknowledgment.

"Okay, Timmy, put Dad on now."

"Can't, he's not home yet." Lily, on the other extension sounded put out.

"Late meeting?"

"I don't know. He's always got a late meeting." She sounded like a future henpecker. "He ordered us pizza but he got mushrooms on it. I hate mushrooms." Lily was all set to rehash the whole debacle, mushroom by mushroom, when I cut her off. "Who's home with you?"

"Gramma."

"Good." It was all right for the kids to be home a little while during the day without supervision, but by suppertime I wanted somebody there. "Mind her, now." My kids were past masters at avoiding toothbrushing.

"Want to talk with her?"

My inclination was to say no, but in the interest of relations, I said yes.

"Cleo?"

"Alice."

"Kids are fine. Seannie bought them pizza." I could tell by the tone of her voice her approval of this fast-food dinner was extremely tenuous. "I would have been happy to make them something. He didn't need to do that."

"Well, he probably thought on such short notice . . ."

"But it wasn't short notice, Cleo. He asked me two days ago to sit tonight with the kids."

"Well, thank you for doing it."

Alice muffled the phone as she directed the kids to start cleaning up. "So. How are you, dear?"

"Great." Then I wondered if that was an impolitic response to one's mother-in-law. "The work goes well. But I miss everyone."

To her everlasting credit Alice didn't respond by telling me how much everyone missed me, or how things were going to hell in my house. A widow, a veteran of raising six kids, this woman understood solitude is not a bad or necessarily selfish thing.

My parents are but a vague memory of distance. Mother, precisely manicured and coiffed, her club activities and tennis dates providing her with a daily structure. Father, tall and rail thin, thin combed-back hair of indeterminant faded brown washed with gray, his rheumy eyes equally colorless, like the eyes of a fish. He favored brown suits, always double-breasted, and, as if to make up for his colorlessness, sported bright ties, snubbing the old school tie of his prep school but falling back on his Yale tie for solemn occasions. He seemed not to know what to do about me. I'd appeared late in my parents' well-ordered life together, a wholly unexpected child.

Sometimes I blamed myself for their "problem," as I overheard it called. Assuming that if I hadn't come along, they would have still loved each other. Their one shared passion, after the years had driven out all the rest, was alcohol.

They were the worst type of drinkers. Silent and refined. Only the exceedingly slow and articulated way they spoke gave them away to me. Father and Mother—never Mom and Dad—enjoyed their cocktail before dinner, their wine with, and their postprandial cordial after. Then their nightcap. Scotch in ever larger tumblers, no ice, no water. I remember sipping from my mother's glass when she had stepped from the room. I spit the harsh scotch out onto the parquet floor of the living room, just missing the oriental rug. I knelt down and tried to mop it up with the hem of my private-school uniform. It was one of those days when my mother had been out all afternoon at her club, and she never even noticed the puddle or the wet edge of my skirt.

"Cleo is quite the young lady, isn't she?" I might have been twelve, just entering that peculiar hell of adolescence, when any reference to my ungainly and sudden height and tender breasts was enough to make me cry. Mr. Ramsey was the husband of a fellow club woman, and he and his wife were frequent dinner guests. They all seemed to know one another very well, but I had never heard my parents refer to them by their first names in front of me.

"Yes, she's growing up very fast." My mother said this as if I couldn't grow up fast enough for her. She plucked at my blouse to straighten it, instantly drawing attention to my unformed breasts, at least in my mind, and, by self-conscious assumption, in Mr. Ramsey's. She then put a harsh thumb to my cheek as if to rub out the obvious zit there. Now I realize these might have been construed as touches of affection, but I knew they were the same sort of touch once gives objects one is a little disappointed in. Maybe if I turn this vase in this direction I'll like it better.

When I met Sean I liked him right away. He had that effect on people, on women. When I met his family, I fell in love. Here were people who were loud and cranky and funny and teasing and, most intriguing to me, physical. They touched each other, quick embraces, slaps at hands reaching impolitely across the table. The girls played with each other's hair, they hugged their father, and Sean picked up their mother as a joke. It surprised me when Sean's mother—Ma they all called her, incessantly vying for her attention—gave me a hug after my first visit. She put me to work peeling potatoes on the second, and joked about sex on the third. They were earthy in that "salt of the earth" way. The McCarthys absorbed me into their family and I did my best to imitate their boisterous extroversion, but it never felt natural to me.

"Hey, Ma, thanks again for staying with the rugrats." I didn't always call her that, but sometimes it just seemed fitting.

"Cleo, they're my grandbabies."

"Is Sean okay?"

"Yes, Cleo. Everything's fine. Don't worry about anything."

I rang off and sat for a few minutes in the big car, the mobile phone still in my hand. I hadn't meant to ask that last question in

quite the tone of voice I had. I knew that Alice took the right interpretation and her assurances carried the double meaning I needed.
Sean was behaving himself. She was being vigilant.

My need for conversation unquenched, I did the next best thing
and punched Grace's number into the keypad.

"Hey, have I told you how grateful I am you made me do this?"

"Once or twice, but not since you've been there. How the hell are
you?"

"Great. Working well. Getting in some good runs."

"Weather been okay?"

"Better than okay. I went for my first swim today."

"Out to the raft?"

"Not yet. Just a quick in and out." Mention of the raft brought my
neighbor to mind. "By the way, Grace, who's the guy who lives across
the lake from your cabin? The tall skinny guy with the cats?"

"Oh. Ben Turner." There was a downturn in Grace's voice, a
tinge of disgust or dismissal, I couldn't decide.

"Who is he?"

"A loner. Keeps to himself." There was hiccup in the line, not a
noise but the absence of noise, and Grace excused herself. "Sorry,
Cleo, I've got to take this call. Call me tomorrow. No, wait, we leave
tomorrow. I'll call you when we get home."

Sitting there with the disconnected phone in my right hand, I
wondered whether my absence was working out too well for everyone else. Who has not, in childhood, thought . . . they'll miss me when
I'm dead. That'll show 'em. I sat there in Grace's car and wondered if
I was being shown just exactly how unmissed I'd be. Life certainly
goes on.

Day six and Karen and Jay were shaping up nicely. With my Discman
providing background music, this day heavily Dvořák, I advanced
Karen's falling in love with Jay, who remained aloof or oblivious to
her feelings. I hadn't quite defined his motivation or conflict yet, it
would come out as I got to know him better. I had given him a nifty

occupation—restaurateur. And, with Karen being a food critic pathologically afraid of gaining weight, I had opened up a whole world of potential conflict. I got hungry as I devised a menu for Jay's restaurant and gave up mid-entrée. My Spartan diet was getting boring and I decided a pork chop was exactly what I wanted. It was late enough in the day to call it quits, anyway.

He stood in the checkout line just ahead of me in the Big G supermarket. I watched his choices as they rode the conveyor belt to the cashier, who popped her gum and chatted relentlessly with the teenage bag boy. Milk, eggs, whole-wheat bread, and cheese; canned soup, five pounds of sugar, a hand-picked bag of baking potatoes; cold cuts, a two-pack of chicken breasts, and a tiny, one-person pot roast. His array looked almost like mine, except I'd chosen pork chops instead of beef. The one concession to temptation, in his case was a two-pound bag of Oreos; in mine, Fig Newtons. He'd picked up a copy of *George,* I'd snagged *Vanity Fair.*

It crossed my mind that our menu plans were similar because we were single people living in a world which put things in six-packs. I had never experienced having to buy groceries in such limited quantities before and never realized how difficult it was if you wanted to avoid eating the same thing over and over. I had a notion to comment on our groceries, something about how if we combined our resources we could have more choice and still be economical. But, of course, I didn't. I didn't speak. After all, we really didn't know each other.

He turned toward me as he fished his wallet out of his back pocket. He smiled with that little "You look familiar" smile. Civility. I smiled back with a little nod of, yes we do sort of know each other. He picked up his bags—paper, not plastic—and walked out.

The gum popper looked at me long enough to ask my bag preference, then continued her conversation. I stared after my neighbor until he was obscured by the display of beach balls blocking the store's windows. I could see only the top of his head with its tan baseball cap, then he was gone. In the one split second of eye contact my interest in my neighbor moved from mild to more.

. . . He had the most mild eyes of any I had ever looked into. Full deep brown, they revealed a man incapable of hurting anyone but himself . . .

"Thirty-nine twenty-seven, please." The cashier's gum-muffled voice startled me and I knew I'd been writing description in my head. Those collie eyes would suit Jay perfectly. I wrote that line on the back of my receipt and stuck it in the back pocket of my shorts.

I maneuvered the big car around my bicycle-riding neighbor, pedaling with determined pace on his twelve-speed trek bike, its panniers filled with his groceries. This far into the White Mountains, there is no flat, just up or down, and he was working hard. I left him in my rearview mirror as I turned into the parking lot of the local library. For such an outpost, the Cameo Lake Public Library is well endowed, and I took a leisurely time registering as a patron and picking out a couple of quick reads. I never like to read anything too good when I'm working for fear I'll give up when faced with superior writers.

Chiding myself for leaving off work for so long, I was going a little fast along the narrow secondary road which looped around the lake. Ahead I saw something on the side of the road which quickly resolved into my neighbor squatting next to his bike. I was a full twenty yards beyond him when I stopped and, in neighborly determination, reversed to where he stood. I buzzed down the passenger side window. "Need some help?"

He was slow to come alongside of the car, almost as if he thought I might hit the gas pedal and take off. He stood off a little from the passenger side of the car and looked in to see who it was who had stopped. "Thanks. I could use a lift. Flat tire." He gestured toward the now supine bicycle. "I live on the lake."

I restrained myself from saying "Yes, I know" and simply popped the release for the back door. "I think it'll fit inside. This car is so big I think you could slip a full-sized motorcycle in without trouble."

I pulled a little farther off the narrow road, aware suddenly of the danger from cars just like this one speeding past. Bike settled, my neighbor climbed in. "I'm Benson Turner." For a moment, it almost seemed as if he expected me to react.

"Cleo Grayson." He took my hand in the briefest of greetings, but long enough for me to get a sense of warmth and long fingers, a little callused.

"I live on one of the islands, so you can drop me at the road to the boat ramp. I'll be fine from there. It'll be less out of your way."

"It's not out of my way. I live across from you in Grace Chichetti's cabin."

"Oh." Ben pressed the palms of both hands against his knees. "I didn't realize that was you. I've seen you running." He seemed a little uncomfortable with that admission, but I couldn't make myself leaven the tension with an admission of my own voyeurism in watching him chop wood. However, as nominal hostess in this situation, I felt compelled to find small talk. The mile to the access road loomed interminably. "I hope you didn't break any eggs."

"Eggs? Oh, no. Fortunately I didn't fall off. I hit a broken beer bottle. I wasn't looking where I was going. Lost in thought as usual. A failing of mine." I had my eyes on the road so I couldn't see if he was smiling in self-deprecation or not.

"Should we drop the bike off somewhere?"

"No. No, this is good. I'll take care of it. I usually fix them myself." Another tenth of a mile. Then two more silent tenths. I was about to fall back on the traditional weather gambit when Ben spoke. "So, how do you like the lake?"

"Oh, I love it. So peaceful."

"Won't be in another week. Once July hits, the lake gets pretty busy."

"Grace told me there's a pretty active social circuit here."

"I suppose there is. I pretty much keep away from it."

Grace had called him a loner. "Well, I imagine that I will, too. I came up here to get away from those kinds of distractions. Besides"— and at this point I arrived at the access road—"I don't know anybody here to socialize with."

I drove him down to the boat ramp, where he had a canoe tied up. Ben climbed out of the SUV and fetched his bike and groceries from the back. "Thanks for the rescue, Mrs. Grayson."

"Please. Call me Cleo. Mrs. Grayson was my mother."

He smiled, "Well, Cleo, now you do know someone. Even if it is just me." He held out a hand and once again I looked into those mild brown eyes. "By the way, you know that you can use the raft?"

"I will."

When I looked out the picture window of Grace's cabin, I could see Ben paddling a green Old Town canoe from the direction of the boat ramp. Lashed across the bow was the bicycle. The only moving object on the still lake, the canoe left a mild etching of wake behind as the sharp prow neatly pushed through the dark water.

He paddled with slow strokes, coaxing the canoe, not forcing it, across the expanse of lake toward his landing. I watched until he made landfall, stepping neatly from boat to beach, pulling the canoe, with the bike still athwart, securely onto the shore. The screek of his screen door pierced the quiet dusk.

A self-described shy person, I am quick to recognize that characteristic in others. Sometimes our reserve as shy people comes across as snobbery, sometimes as being quiet, or standoffish people. Sometimes our shyness is inbred, sometimes it's learned. My mother used to say of me, "Still waters run deep." I suppose to explain to her friends why I wasn't talkative in their company, to excuse my failing to be witty in their midst.

Benson Turner seemed to be a shy person. Not shy as if he had been born that way, but shy as if he'd become that way. As if he was recovering from an illness and needed all of his strength to get well.

Three

The next day was unnaturally hot. When I woke up it was already stifling in the cabin, the night air had given no hint of this surprise change in the heretofore temperate June weather. I opened all the windows and, fighting a little with the expandable screen inserts, no matter how I pushed or pulled, there remained a mosquito-wide gap between the top of the screen and the bottom of the window.

The breeze off the water kept the shaded screen porch cool enough that I was fooled into thinking it would be perfect for taking my noontime run. Even before I had gotten up the initial slope of my track, I was drenched in sweat. The air was dense but I kept going, enjoying the sense of a hard workout without the hard work. The heat loosened my muscles and eventually I reached that silken flow of stride and breath which keeps runners running. The rhythmic pum pum pum of my feet against the humus in time with the music on my Discman, a steady quarter-note motif. All the way around I held the cool thought of plunging into the lake at the end of my run. I made the turn for home and sprinted for about a hundred yards. Halfway back I began to downshift until I came to a pulse-slowing jog for the last thirty yards. I might be eager for my swim, but not for a heart attack—the water was still ice cold. At the water's edge I balanced on first one foot and then the other to pull off my running shoes and socks, dropping them next to the Discman.

I yelped as I hit the water. The shock was mildly pleasant in a masochistic sort of way. I stood up in the waist-deep water, then plunged again, striking out for the raft anchored halfway between my shore and Ben's. The redwood surface of the raft was lasciviously warm in the afternoon sun. I lay my chilled, exhausted body flat against the wood, luxuriating in the palpable waves of heat already drying my nylon tank top and running shorts.

Lulled half asleep as the noon sun sucked the chill out of my wet clothes and the raft rocked ever so slightly, I was slow to become aware of piano music until it stopped. And then started, and then stopped again, each time the same few notes, varying a little in rhythm. I listened casually, without lifting my head, letting the tinkering drift in and out of my consciousness. Then the notes began to coalesce into a recognizable new theme, new chords embroidering it until what drifted to the raft from Ben's cabin really was music. Music which stopped abruptly with an irreverent "shave and a haircut, two bits."

I rolled over to bake my still damp nether end. In the distance I heard a screen door slam and a soft splash accompanied by mild swearing in acknowledgment of the lake's chill. Just as I flipped onto my back, Ben's head crested the edge of the raft. The startled look in his eyes was clear evidence he had no idea I was out there. His surprise forced us both into quick, unnecessary apologies and laughter at ourselves.

"I'm sorry, I didn't know you were here."

"Hey, there's plenty of room for both of us." To demonstrate, I slid over another board-width.

Ben hauled himself up without using the ladder, arriving aboard with a cascade of lake water. "Forgot your bathing suit?" He gestured at my odd swimming attire.

"Running."

Ben thumped the raft to scare away a big water spider.

"Was that you? Playing just now?"

Ben nodded without looking at me.

"It was lovely. Except perhaps for the bit at the end. A little trite, don't you think?"

Ben laughed, a nice amused chuckle. "You've just been treated to the new theme for some car coming out in the fall. I forget which one. Luxury sport utility. Oxymoronic, if you ask me."

"So, then. You're a composer."

Ben laughed again, but this time the amusement was derisive. "Sort of. I write commercial music. You know, advertising jingles."

"Would I know any?"

He named a potato chip and an adult dietary supplement. I recalled both products and their TV commercials, but no music came to mind.

"It's subliminal. You really aren't supposed to be aware of it. Sometimes it's pseudo-rock and sometimes it's pseudo-classical. Not like the old days, when ad jingles had words . . ."

"Oh, you mean like the Toyota theme?" Unusually unabashed, I sang the little ditty I associated with Toyota commercials for years.

"Something like that. I don't write lyrics, just music."

"It's funny but such things are so much a part of our culture. I mean, who can't sing the 'I'll wonder where the yellow went when I brush my teeth with Pepsodent.' "

"You'll."

"What?"

"You'll wonder where the yellow went . . ."

"Right. Well, generally speaking, people do remember those things, like cigarette slogans, long after the products disappear, or evolve." I stood up. "You're part of the American subconscious, Ben."

"More like the American unconscious. Anyway. I promised myself a swim when I got that piece of Americana out of the way, and now I must go tackle a breakfast cereal. Something incredibly sweet and garishly colored. They sent me a carton of it for inspiration." He named the cereal.

"I have to admit, that one's my kids' favorite."

A stillness dropped between us, a slight wedge whose provenance I thought was the mention of kids, maybe a little surprise that I was there without family. He quickly broke through the pause, "By the way, I've read all your books." It came out as if he had had to steel himself to make such a personal remark. "You're a good writer, Cleo."

"Thank you, Ben. I have a good editor. But, you know, it's funny, I don't usually introduce myself as Cleo Grayson. That was like introducing my alter ego. McCarthy is my married name. I don't know why I did that."

"Maybe because while you're here, you are Cleo Grayson." Ben stood up, dry already in the baking sun.

"Thanks for the company, Ben. I hope I didn't intrude on your privacy."

"No. Not at all. I've been pretty solitary lately and a little company is nice."

He poised himself at the edge of the raft facing north, which puzzled me for a minute as his cabin was due west. Then he stepped back and gestured to the west side of the square raft as if aware of my thought. "Cleo, you should know that it's really dangerous to jump off that side of the raft. There's a submerged boulder and it's hard to judge where it is as the raft tends to swing a little."

"Thanks for the heads up."

"I keep meaning to paint a warning on the edge, but I'm the only one out here. I mean, usually."

"I'll make sure my family knows that when they come."

Somehow he didn't seem convinced by my answer and repeated, "Remember, never jump off that side."

"I won't, Ben. I promise."

That seemed to satisfy him. Ben dived then, a graceful arc of lithe body, entering the water with only a slight splash. In twenty strokes he'd curved back toward his own shoreline.

I dived off the east side of the raft a moment later, though with much less grace. I arrived, breathless, on my shore and bent to retrieve my shoes and Discman. When I stood up I could see Ben on his shore, one hand raised in friendly salute, as if acknowledging my successful return to shore. I waved and went back to work.

Four

The nocturnal music of bullfrogs and crickets, a rare owl, and myriad other night sounds surrounded me. Breaking through my random thoughts, another sound. The light music of a breezy piano piece, Mozart, I thought, not being musically confident enough to be sure. A sweet sound competing equally with the natural sounds of the lake. The only human sound until next week, when the other cottages would fill the air with televisions and radios, and two-cycle motors on fishing skiffs. But for now, Ben's music was the only human-derived sound, wafted to me on a breeze which riffled through the trees, carrying on it also the promise of a storm.

I was awakened sometime after midnight by the first volley of thunder. The surrounding peaks echoed with the sound and the blackness was riven with lightening. I lay in my bed and watched, thrilled by the storm, electrically charged by its bright intensity, no other light invading. Even my little digital alarm clock was blank, the power out now. I pulled the blankets to my chin and enjoyed the event.

The storm rolled off the lake like a lover, leaving the area with only sporadic rumbles followed by a hissing sound. It took a moment for it to register, then I recognized the sound of hard rain falling on the water. It was as dark with my eyes open as it was with them shut. Just knowing the electric pump wouldn't work was enough to make me need to pee. I was enough of a girl scout to have a flashlight ready, and the little ecology couplet came to me, "If it's yellow, let it mellow."

On my way back to bed I glanced through the picture window. The dark ridges of the hills stood out against the darker sky. The only light was Ben's little porch light. Gatsby's kerosene beacon.

The morning sun betrayed no vestige of the night's storm except the resolutely blank face of my electric clock. I was grateful for the gas stove and brought my morning mug out to the porch to start work. My laptop's battery ran out within half an hour and I wished I had someone else to blame for not recharging it when I should have.

I pushed myself away from the table and flopped down on the old porch glider, making it swing with a slightly on-the-water sensation. Unexpectedly without the focus of my solitude, I felt truly alone. If this had happened at home I would almost without thinking have pulled on my shoes and headed over to Alice's for a cup of tea. Or I might have piled the kids in the car and headed to Roger Williams Park Zoo for the afternoon. I would have taken advantage of the situation. Here I was, where I boldly proclaimed I needed to be, yet, without my raison d'être, I was at a loss, and lonely. There seemed nothing left to do but go for a swim.

I paddled around for a little while close to shore, enjoying the smooth, silky feeling of the brownish water, yet feeling less buoyant than when I swam in salt water. We usually spent a week at Narragansett in July, Sean and the kids and I along with one or another of the other McCarthy families. We rented the same place annually, a cottage not too far from Watch Hill. The beach there brilliant white in the hot July sunshine, the waves sometimes aggressive, and the salt water tangy against my skin.

Narragansett. Despite the eight years since it happened, despite wonderful family vacations, the name still had the power to raise the memory of Sean's betrayal. The time we never spoke about aloud, somehow leaving responsibility for keeping the peace on my shoul-

ders because I told him I forgave him. But I never went there without him again. Not until now, coming to Cameo Lake, had I left
the door open so wide. By leaving him home, I implied a trust I was
uncertain I felt. I dived under the surface of the still water and,
rising, made for the raft. With every stroke I told myself, of course I
trust him. He was younger then, he's a different man now. He is not
his father.

Ben was already on the raft when I got there. "You're early."

I hauled myself up onto the deck. "I'm neglectful, no juice in the
battery."

"Well, I'm just being lazy today. I had a couple of late phone calls
and somehow all my juice ran out."

I looked at him, sitting with long legs dangling over the side,
aware of a note in his voice which clanged a little against his flip
words. "Is everything all right?"

Ben looked at me with a little glance of surprise at my blunt question. "Yeah, fine."

I could see the psychological hand held up, holding my natural
concern at bay. Don't intrude, I told myself.

"But thank you for asking."

So, I thought, there was something going on. He was a little like
Tim. When Tim had his feelings hurt, he clammed up. A little tight
quahog which needed, wanted, a little steam to open.

"You just sounded a little sad."

"You have a very good ear."

I let it drop then, as I would with Tim. In his own time, I thought,
and then wondered why I had such curiosity. I really didn't know him
well enough to be so invested in caring. Except that every night I could
hear his music, not the jingle stuff, real music, float toward me across
the expanse of the lake. Music so evocative it made me think I knew
him.

We lay down, not talking, just enjoying the subtle rock of the ten-
by-ten raft in the slightly choppy lake.

"Cleo, assuming the electricity stays out for a long time, would you like to take a hike?"

"Are you telling me to take a hike, mister?"

Ben rolled over and propped his head on his hand, "No, a hike up that hill," and he pointed north. I would probably call what he pointed to a mountain, but I know that in New Hampshire they have different standards than we Rhode Islanders do about elevation.

"Love to."

"It's a good day's hike."

"It's a good day for it."

It was only about nine-thirty when we met on the raft, so we planned to meet at the boat ramp at ten. I put together a knapsack of clean socks, bottled water, and Band-Aids. We'd agreed to buy sandwiches on the drive there, so the trip began to look like a picnic. I was unaccountably excited. I thought maybe because it felt kind of like a snow day. But there was a different tang to the excitement than just that. I was excited about being friends with Ben. Pals. Sean and I had a lot of couple friends, and I was blessed with terrific girlfriends in my sisters-in-law. And Grace, queen of best friends. But I'd seldom been friends with boys. Girls' schools, a girl-filled neighborhood, no cousins. I guess that Sean was my first boy friend, and, soon after, boyfriend. I remembered so clearly that first flush of excitement at making that friend, of hanging out together and the slow evolution to love. Of course, that wasn't what was happening now. With Benson Turner I'd just have the first part of that journey. The fun part.

I was actually surprised to see the number of cars in the trailhead parking lot, somehow it had seemed like a unique idea to spend a June Wednesday climbing a hill. We got out of my car and shouldered our packs, my schoolgirlish Eastpak a poor cousin to the big L.L. Bean on Ben's back. "I thought this was a day trip, Ben."

"My scoutmaster instilled the rules of 'be prepared' in me a long time ago." I caught the little glint of mischief in the corners of his mouth.

"Somehow I think you're telling me the truth."

"Always truthful. After you, ma'am."

"That would be the 'courteous' rule, right?"

"No, the self-protective rule. There's bears up there, lady. You go first."

The banter was so easy, so comfortable and natural, it seemed as though we knew each other from long association. I kept getting the feeling that we were like passengers on a commuter bus, habitually sharing a seat, sharing a little banter, but knowing very little about each other. I couldn't express what that bus was or where it was going, but I latched on to the sensation and gave over to it. I'd find out where we were going soon enough, and whether we had more than a bus seat in common.

Initially, the trek was pretty easy, a slow graduation in elevation, easy on the thighs, comfortable on calves. We chatted along the way, our pace fast enough to pass other hikers taking more leisurely walks. I don't think our quick pace was intentional, more a result of Ben's long stride and my natural tendency to move quickly. We winded ourselves pretty soon, just as the trail narrowed and we were forced to climb up a series of natural steps created out of roots and rocks. The mosquitoes and the deer flies began to torment us as we began to sweat.

"Hold up for a minute, Cleo. Reach into my pack and find the bug spray."

He squatted a little so that I could reach deep into the outside pocket of the blue knapsack, a curiously intimate act. My hand found the can of repellent. I handed the can to him, but instead of spraying himself, he started on me, spraying my neck and the back of my legs, then handed the can to me to finish the job. I did the same for him, and when we were both done, I replaced the can.

"You need a hat, there's an extra in the main section of the knapsack, reach down deep."

I fished around until I pulled up a worn baseball cap. "The Yankees? Really, Ben?"

"I'm from New Jersey."

"I'm not sure I can wear this, I'm a loyal Red Sox fan."

"Sure you can, it was my wife's and she was from Boston."

Just by the way he said it, I knew that the past tense was not due to ordinary circumstances like divorce or separation. That simple declarative sentence creaked with old aches. I put the hat on and wondered why he had brought it with him, or had it simply remained in his knapsack from some long-ago hike. But it fit pretty well and I was glad of the protection, even if it was a Yankees cap.

Our conversation petered out as the elevation steepened. I tried to pay attention to the magnificent forest on either side of the path, but the various hazards along the way and my increasing tiredness made me keep my eyes on the trail. Ben led, holding overhanging branches out of my way, calling out a warning at a particularly slippery spot. The storm-cleared sky was obscured by the pines and birches above our heads. I heard the loud call of a warbler but couldn't find the bird with my eyes. Just as I thought I was going to have to give in and beg for a rest, Ben held up a pausing hand and pointed toward a small clearing where a three-sided lean-to had been erected and the remnants of campfires indicated an authorized rest stop. With great relief, I shrugged off the knapsack, which by this time was cutting into my bare shoulders, and flopped down on the bench inside the lean-to.

Ben off-loaded his own knapsack and sat on the floor. "We can't sit long, or we'll stiffen up."

"Okay, *Kommandant,* but can we eat?"

"*Jawohl.*"

"*Bitte danke, Herr Turner.*" I pulled my sandwich and bottle of water out of my bag and commenced to eat. The air around us was cool, much cooler than at the base of the mountain. I shivered a little and wished that I had brought another shirt. The sweat on my tank top was drying, adding to a general feeling of discomfort. Ben wordlessly reached into his bag and, like some kind of magician or den mother, hauled out a flannel shirt and handed it to me.

"Thanks. You really are prepared, aren't you?"

"I do this a lot." He amended himself quickly. "I did this a lot."

"You and your wife?"

"Yeah." He turned his attention to his sandwich, not looking at me but out toward the amazing vista open before the clearing. "It was one of the few things besides music we both loved equally. I haven't done it in a long time."

"Can I ask how long she's been gone?"

"Almost a year." Abruptly Ben stood up and swung his pack onto his shoulders. "We'd better head back, down is almost as tough as up." With that he squelched any further questions I might naturally have asked.

The day before my family arrived it rained nonstop, making it easy to stay put and work. After lunch I tidied up, running a dust mop across the ceiling boards to knock down the worst of the spiderwebs. Lily wouldn't come inside if she thought there was any danger of being touched by a spider.

At seven-thirty I dashed to the car, already late for our nightly call. I wanted to talk about my hike up the mountain, but the kids were full of their own story. "We went to the zoo!" They were in the kitchen with the speakerphone and the echo chamber effect made me nervous but at least we could all talk like a family.

"And how's Alice the elephant today?"

"She's fine." Tim's voice conjured his little map-of-Ireland face in my mind. "Eleanor didn't know she was named Alice."

"Who?"

"Eleanor . . . Daddy's, you know . . ." Lily was looking for the noun which would describe Eleanor's role in Sean's life.

"Secretary." I offered.

"Administer." Lily countered

"Administrative Assistant." Her predecessors were all secretaries but the term had fallen out of favor recently. A secretary by any other name.

"What-everrr," this in Valley Girl dialect. "She and Daddy surprised us."

Tim launched into every detail of their trip to the Roger Williams Park Zoo, including the ice cream before lunch and the penguin key chains Eleanor bought for them at the gift shop. It was easy to make the appropriate exclamations without concentrating on their every word.

Finally I saw an opening in the litany, "Is Daddy there?"

"No. He's making up lost time."

Sean's expression. Whenever we co-opted any of his work time he'd say, "Cleo, I've got to make up the lost time." As if it weren't his own business. If I pulled him away for a school conference or a long weekend, it was the same. It was as if he felt that a moment's inattention would bring down the business his father had built. Francis McCarthy had never taken a day off, either, until his first heart attack.

Sometimes I pointed that fact out to Sean, but he'd just tell me he wasn't his father. He wasn't a hard drinker, or a smoker, and he kept his cholesterol down. He knew that in one colossal way he did resemble his father, but we did not speak of it. However, a trip to Roger Williams Park Zoo with his secretary was a red flag to me that Francis's DNA was acting up in the son.

"Well, when is he coming home?"

"Dunno." Lily was chewing something and her voice was thick, "Gramma's here."

Alice immediately took me off speaker. "Seannie's been crazed trying to get ready to take his vacation." Alice offered this even before I commented on yet another late night.

"Well, he's awfully lucky to have you to fall back on."

"I enjoy it. You know that, Cleo."

"I do. I'm lucky, too."

"So tell me about this trip to the zoo."

"They went, that's all I know."

"Alice . . . Ma, should I come home?"

"Don't be silly, it was a trip to the zoo with the kids."

After I hung up I sat for a long time gripping the steering wheel as if guiding the parked car. Although I trusted Alice's judgment, I decided I would call Eleanor tomorrow and thank her personally for giving up her afternoon for my family. Emphasis on the *my*. Then I laughed out loud. If this were a first-draft novel, I'd be embarrassed at the absolute banality. This was life and life can be stale, but I wouldn't let my professionally overactive imagination stereotype me. Yet I would have a word with Sean when he arrived. A delicately balanced word. It was critical I avoid any hint of mistrust—the other thing he inherited from his father was his anger.

Five

After backing up all the work I had done onto a floppy disk, I packed my laptop away. A couple of weeks away from Karen and Jay wouldn't be a bad thing. I kept my notebook handy to jot those thoughts and brilliant bits of dialogue which would come to me during the weeks off, so as not to lose them. I spent an hour grocery shopping at the Big G, raising the eyebrow of my usual gum-chewing clerk at the profligate array of snack foods and quantities so at variance with my usual habits. "Family's coming today," I felt compelled to explain as if embarrassed at my wanton spending. As if the kid cared.

Just saying it aloud tweaked my excitement at seeing my kids again. It had been less than ten days, but I felt that I hadn't seen them since forever. At the same time, I knew that the solitude had been productive and necessary. Still, I couldn't wait to see my babies, imagining that they had somehow grown up in my absence.

After unloading the groceries from the car I skipped lunch and changed into my running gear. The thunderstorm on Tuesday night had cleared the unnaturally hot weather but had left behind true summer. Each morning a light mist hovered over the warming water, ethereal and reminiscent of Arthurian legend. I couldn't see Ben's cabin until the mist dissipated, but the fog amplified simple sounds, a cough, bird song, the repeated measures of a new motif Ben was working on early in the day. As the mist lifted, the sounds weakened and we were again separated by the flat, shiny expanse of water.

Running along the wooded path, I saw signs of arrival in several of the lake cottages; cushions left out in the sun to air, a dinghy pulled down to the water's edge which wasn't there yesterday, voices calling instructions to spouses and kids. I saw evidence of children and imagined my two chumming with others, exploring the lake and having the experiences which they would carry into adulthood as "When we went to the lake...do you remember?..." Sometimes I felt as though I wasn't giving my children enough memories. Sean and his sisters had hours of stories from their childhood, everyday moments turned, by some McCarthy magic, into spun gold. "Remember when we had that rabbit and convinced Colleen that it talked?" "Remember the time Dad took us all to Rocky Point and we all put on English accents, pretending not to know what clam cakes were?... Remember finding shapes in the clam cakes like clouds?"

For the life of me I couldn't raise memories like that. I remembered asking for a pet, and the dismissal of the idea out of hand by my mother. "Pets are a nuisance, Cleo. A nuisance." My parents traveled. At least early in my life I know they traveled to New York and Boston. I have a vague memory of going to some city with them, but not of where, or why I was there. Only a shadow of memory of a hotel lobby and the odd little cap the bellboy wore.

Certainly there would be childish memories of Narragansett, of spending time with the cousins and making sandcastles at Watch Hill, of riding the ancient carousel there. Certainly Sean and I had given them those memories to treasure. They would never know about that one terrible summer, and so the place would remain precious to them.

I grimaced against the sudden stitch in my side as I made the turn for home. I was running faster than I should, my pace evidence of how anxious I was to see my kids and watch them record memories for themselves. Running faster, as if to make the time move. Still breathing hard, I peeled off my shorts and top, revealing my tank suit, pulled my running shoes off while still in motion and plunged into the lake. Conditioning and thermal warming had lessened the shock but I still gasped aloud.

Ben was already on the raft. He had been on the raft long enough for his skin to dry. Only a slight gleam in his gray-threaded dark hair and the dampness of his baggy swim trunks remained of his swim. "Is your family here yet?"

I had told him of their imminent arrival, partially as a head's up, his raft solitude would be under attack, and partially because I was excited. "Not yet. Sean's leaving this evening after work. He doesn't want to lose an extra day." I rolled over to sun my back, resting my cheek against my arm. "I liked what I heard this morning."

Ben blushed a little under his tan, a tiny pleased reddening on his sharp cheekbones. "Thanks." He, too, rolled over to rest his cheek on his arm.

"I'm beginning to recognize it so I guess you've been working on it for a while."

He didn't say anything, but his fingers against the deck tapped out invisible notes.

"So, what's it for?"

"It's not for anything." He pushed himself up and went to sit on the edge of the raft, his back to me, his fingers still tapping.

"Then what is it?"

"Just something I've been noodling around with for a while now."

I got up and sat beside him. Once again the grown man made me think of my little boy. Yet I sensed a willingness to be pressed into telling me more. "I don't mean to be nosy, I just like it and wondered what it was."

Ben stared across the lake as he spoke, his fingers suddenly still, gripping the coaming of the raft. "A concerto for flute."

I dangled my legs over the edge beside him. "Sounds like an ambitious project."

"My wife was a flautist."

"What a lovely idea, Ben. A wonderful gift." I didn't say "memorial," I didn't know enough.

"Thank you." Ben looked at me, his eyes holding my natural questions at bay. "I haven't gotten to the solo part yet. I keep going back to the orchestral parts."

"Maybe you're not ready." I don't know what prompted me to make such an observation and I wished I hadn't. It wasn't mildness which made Benson Turner's eyes so striking in an ordinary face, it was grief and I had trespassed on it.

Ben looked down at his moving fingers and shrugged. "I may never be ready."

I felt as if somehow my curiosity had prodded this revelation out of Ben at a cost to him and I wished I'd kept my mouth shut. We sat quietly for a few more minutes, then stood up and dived off our different sides of the raft.

The headlights of Sean's car broadcast their arrival late that evening. I dashed out to help carry in sleepy children. Lily and Tim revived long enough to argue about going to bed, then caved in. Sean and I chose to leave most of the stuff in the car until morning, when we could see. The Volvo was filled to capacity with what the kids deemed essentials, half of which I knew no one would use. Clearly the kid's had had carte blanche in packing.

"Leave it and come sit with me on the porch." I handed Sean a bottle of locally brewed beer and picked up my own glass of wine. "The best part of this place is this porch."

Sean followed me outside. We sat quietly for a few minutes on the old metal glider with its musty cushions, Sean letting the buzz from the long drive subside. It was well near midnight and I felt the long day's end in the heaviness of my limbs and the grit in my eyes. I'd been up since six, eager for their arrival. Now I just wanted my bed, but I knew that we'd make love. I expected it, should have wanted it, but, at midnight, the anticipation had dropped with my energy. I shouldn't have run so far today, or maybe should have taken a nap. Certainly not be drinking wine, with its soporific effect on me.

"So, how was the drive up?" I nestled in beside Sean and he put an arm across my shoulders.

"Fine. Long. Kids slept only after we crossed into New Hampshire. Traffic around Boston was a bitch." Sean went on in this vein, by rote, as if he'd taken the trip a thousand times. As if he wasn't engaged in his surroundings and the experience. "Look, Cleo, I'm really exhausted. I've been working a lot of extra hours to clear my desk. Would you mind awfully if I just went to bed?"

I tried to keep the relief out of my voice. "I'm beat, too. Let me just finish my wine and I'll join you."

"Kids sleep late." The implication.

"I'm sure they will." The agreement. Though I had my doubts they would, I chose not to argue the point.

At some point in the night I heard Sean get up. Not long after I heard the toilet flush, I felt him return to bed.

"You awake?" His breath in my ear tickled. I could hear the first birds of the day.

"Yeah."

Sean nuzzled my neck and pressed against my back, his right hand finding my breast. Slowly I moved into his rhythm and we made love. The light was just brightening to full when we parted. Sean was asleep again in seconds. I lay fully awake, already missing my solitude.

Even before breakfast the kids were in the water. Longtime YMCA swimmers, they were strong and confident, making for the raft without hesitation. I didn't worry too much, the raft wasn't terribly distant for kids used to laps, and it was only over their heads toward the middle. Still, I made them promise not to swim unless Sean or I was within sight and I made them promise to jump off only facing Grace's cottage. A request which effectively kept us together outside or separated while one of us did time elsewhere.

Thus our days fell into routine. Breakfast, swim, hike, lunch, swim, break up afternoon squabbles, supper, shower, and bed. Kids began showing up to play with Lily and Tim. The air was filled with screechy giggles to harmonize with the rusty bedspring notes of the red-winged blackbird. I tried to keep the kids off the raft at noontime, planning lunch and an activity so Ben could have the raft to himself. I hadn't seen Ben except from a distance since our last conversation on the raft, and I had the lingering bad taste of having said the wrong thing to him.

Sean stuck his cell phone into his shirt pocket. "I'm going to take a little walk."

"Don't be long, lunch will be ready in a little bit." I was shredding lettuce for Caesar salad.

"Half an hour, tops. You okay to watch the kids?"

It was overcast this morning and the kids had stayed in on the porch, playing Monopoly with the neighbor boy. Through the kitchen window which looked out on the porch, I could see three curly heads bobbing, two copper-red and one, the neighbor boy, jet black.

"Of course." I had my hands full of lettuce. Sean pecked my cheek and bolted through the door as if he had an appointment. Watching him disappear up the well-worn path, I had to smile at Sean's inability to vacation. Not smile in amusement, but in resignation. He hadn't always been this way. Only in the last couple of years, as his client base had grown from individuals looking for protection for their cars and homes to corporate clients looking for protection against liability should their products do harm or their employees see harassment in a dirty joke. I dumped the shredded lettuce into a glass bowl and stuck it in the refrigerator. "Can I play?" I asked the kids who made room for me to sit and handed me the little car token.

Sean had been supportive of my need to come to the lake to do my work. I could hardly complain if he thought he needed to do his.

Tim pulled over his head a T-shirt I'd never seen before. It flaunted a status logo of which I highly disapproved. I did not like my ten-year-old son wearing status-symbol clothing. "Whose shirt is that?"

"Mine." Tim held the bottom of the oversized shirt down. "Eleanor bought it for me."

Eleanor. I never had called to thank her for her taking the time to take the kids to the zoo. Now she was buying Tim clothes.

"You know how I feel, Tim."

"But Mom, it was a present and I would have been rude to say no." Tim let go of the hem. "Besides, I'm not in a gang. It's just a shirt."

"Fine. You can wear it here, but not to school."

"Mom," Tim said in that wonderful rationalizing tone of children, "by the time school starts, it'll be too small."

I pressed his face to my chest in a quick, stolen hug. But Eleanor's innocuous act of kindness nagged at me. I felt my antennae quiver and I forced myself to let it go. I would not give in to it because I needed to trust Sean. He hadn't given me any cause for concern since that time—between Lily and Tim—that time when I thought my world was going to fall apart and somehow we glued it back together.

I knew that Sean was often the object of crushes among the young women in his office. One or two had told me so. He had told me so. His easy charm and brotherly teasing often led them to imagine things. It wasn't the first time one of them had overstepped her bounds in little ways. Those crushes were not threatening because Sean did not respond to them. It hadn't been a schoolgirl crush which caused him to betray our marriage. No, that had been quite different.

I tried conscientiously to keep Lily and Tim off the raft when I thought Ben might be there. I tried to be sensitive to a childless person's privacy, keeping my kids at bay around folks who might not understand or appreciate the totally invasive quality of a young child's presence. Despite our almost daily conversations, Ben never once had mentioned having any children, and I rather thought it unlikely. Even grown children enter into a conversation eventually. So, to be a good neighbor, I thought it best to keep them a respectful distance apart.

Thus it was, with some embarrassment tinged with annoyance, that I looked out the kitchen window to see both my children lounging on the raft, Ben beside them. Tim was being animated about something and Lily was acting her cool best to be a young lady. As I watched, they began diving into the water with great splashes and climbing back onto the rocking raft.

"Damn it." I stalked out onto the porch and, cupping my hands around my mouth, called out to them.

"What's the big deal? If he doesn't want to be bothered, he can leave." Sean came up behind me, dressed only in bathing trunks, and it was hard not to notice that the frequent client dinners were beginning to have an effect on him. "Who is he?"

"Ben Turner. " As if it explained my concern for Ben's potential annoyance, I added, "He lives alone on the island over there. I'm sure he's not pleased to be splashed by the two munchkins."

"Like I said, he can always leave."

"He only uses the raft once a day. Surely he should have some quiet."

"Too bad. The raft comes with the place." Sean grabbed a towel off the drying rack and headed to the lake.

Before Sean could get there Ben had dived off. Then, as I watched, he rolled onto his back and waved at my two appreciative children, who were applauding his skillful dive. I laughed a little at myself. I was being presumptuous of Ben's feelings. I touched my lips with my fingers, plumbing my own motives for the truth, a writer's exercise. The truth was, I had presented a nicely edited version of myself and now Ben would begin to know me through others' eyes. Crabby and tyrannical mother of two. Insurance salesman's wife.

My schedule was upended by family, so I now ran in the early morning. Before anyone woke, before breakfast on the porch, good breakfasts of orange juice and eggs, slightly burned toast, the smell of which filled the cabin until lunch, before plans and decisions, I ran. The track ran between the lake and the cabins sheltered in the hillside; great old trees, mostly birch and pine, seemed to hold the brown cabins safely on their rocky outcropping ledges. The scent of coffee and the sound of birdsong, the soft, worn, humus beneath my feet, the soft early-morning air heating up as I heated up.

These images cling to me now with a sweetness some people take from childhood memories. Running along the lake, looking down between the trees and seeing Ben Turner softly stroking through the still water in his Old Town canoe, in that memory-encapsulated moment I know what happiness is, that it is like the fog, you cannot touch it, it only moves away.

I walked back the last thirty or forty yards, cooling down, listening through my fingertips to my recovering pulse. Coming down the slope, I noticed a cardboard carton on the steps leading up to the screen porch, a big carton with a well-known cereal company name prominent. I laughed out loud recognizing the very same too-sweet breakfast cereal Ben had been sent as inspiration for a new jingle. Written in black Magic Marker: "Bon Appetite, Lily and Tim. Your friend, Ben."

Six

⟋

There was a big Cameo Lake barbecue on the Fourth of July. A yellow flyer had been stuck in the screen door, a general invitation to all the lakeside community. We all gathered at the ancient lakeside community hall, which smelled of old wood and mold. Everyone brought potluck salads, hot dogs, Jell-O, corn, watermelon, and pies. I hadn't met many of the East Side folks and none of the West Siders, if you discount Ben, who lived in the middle. It was a little hard at first, being first-time renters with no history there, but the universal leveler of children soon smoothed over awkward moments of self-introduction, and before long I was comfortable in the midst of other moms, trading stories of scheduling nightmares and soccer wounds.

Eventually a pickup baseball game evolved and we played until it got too dark to see the ball. I was reminded of church school picnics years ago, when the staid white-shirt-front and prim white-glove set pulled on madras shorts and sneakers and got loud and so out of character they were forever changed in my girlish view. Somehow, I thought, as I stood waiting for my turn at bat, somehow our children had missed that adult transformation. Their parents and friends of their parents were commonly seen running or playing tennis or roller-blading through the park. The adults in my girlhood were

47

grown-ups. In my kids' view, maybe we were just big kids without curfews. I heard Tim refer to Ben by his first name and I didn't make a move toward correcting him. I assumed Ben had introduced himself that way.

As the long July twilight faded, the lakeside gathering formed up a caravan to the site of the Cameo fireworks, a private ski area a couple of miles away on the other side of the hill. Neglecting to bring along chairs, Sean and I spread our blanket on the rough ground and lay down, Sean's head on my lap, Tim and Lily boxing us in. The display was loud, brief, and enthusiastically received by the assembled masses.

The finale over, the throng headed for their tightly packed cars. The darkness turned everyone into anonymous shapes, a single moving unit of blankets and coolers and lawn chairs. I grew disoriented and somehow got separated from Sean and the kids. I bunched the blanket around my shoulders, glad to have it in the cooling July night, trudging along with the crowd. Flakes of conversations from earlier in the day surrounded me and I exercised my ability to put names and faces together, depending a little on instinct and the limited revelations of flashlights. "Good night, Carol. Good night, Glenda, nice to meet you . . ."

I realized that I hadn't seen Ben at the picnic. It wasn't a sudden realization and I knew that, on some level, I had been waiting for him. What surprised me was my disappointment. I told myself it was because I wanted to introduce Ben and Sean properly. Walking back to the parking lot, I couldn't exactly fathom why I thought that was a good idea. Or why I thought it was important. It wasn't as if this neighborly acquaintance would be long-lived.

By the middle of their first week at the lake, charcoal-grilled hamburgers and chicken had already begun to lose their novelty and my family was keen to go get restaurant food. The day had turned oddly fall-like for early summer, and we ended by going to an afternoon movie in the next town over, and then even farther afield to a restaurant Grace and Joanie had recommended. A converted railroad depot, this place offered something for everyone, fine dining, a pub, a dance floor, and the Red Sox on TV.

After we'd been shown to our table, in what looked like the former station manager's office, I went to the ladies' room. On my way back I saw Ben at the bar, munching peanuts, sipping a beer, intent on the baseball game on the suspended TV. He had his back to me and I debated an instant before going over to him. Just at that moment a commercial came on and he lifted his beer, bringing me into his line of sight . I was rewarded with a grin.

"Hey, Mr. Turner."

"Hey yourself, Ms. Grayson." He swung around on the barstool to face me.

"Ben, thanks awfully for the cereal. Now you only have yourself to blame if my kids bug you."

"Oh, they don't, Cleo. They're great kids and it's . . . actually a nice reminder."

"Of what?"

"That life can be fun sometimes." He shook his head in self-derision. "Too much time alone. Sorry." He took another sip of his beer. For the first time I thought he might have had several before this, a flatness in his usually bright eyes. "So, what brings you out this way?"

"Tired of hamburgers. I needed a night off from cooking, and the kids needed some electronic stimulation. Sean needed a restaurant meal." I sounded like a bad hostess complaining about her guests. "How about you?"

"Yankees are playing the Red Sox and the only TV in Cameo is in Tony's Pizza and they only serve bottled beer."

"I see." The commercials were over and Nomar was up. Ben didn't look at the TV but at me. If he had had more than the pint in front of him it wasn't obvious in his speech. I pulled myself back, it shouldn't bother me if a guy liked a beer or two and a ball game alone. Ben's mild brown eyes were just slightly clouded, and in the poor lighting of the bar I could only just detect a shrinking away from me when I heard Sean's voice and felt his hand on my shoulder.

"You coming back, Cleo, or what?"

Ben didn't smile at Sean. He knew who he was and, having that advantage, Ben waited as Sean introduced himself and put out a hand, less in friendship than in territorial bounds.

"Sean McCarthy. Cleo's husband."

"Benson Turner. Cleo's neighbor."

Having, figuratively, pissed on me, they shook hands and simultaneously glanced up at the TV as Nomar fanned. I felt myself diminish as the two men postured their baseball knowledge. Finally I interrupted, "Sean, the kids are by themselves."

"Well, you're the one who disappeared," he got in, sotto voce, as we headed back to our table.

It was pleasant not eating my own cooking, eating something other than hamburg or chicken. I had a nice Yankee pot roast dinner and Sean an Italian dish of some sort. Lily and Tim opted for tacos, and the McCarthy family was happy.

The music from the lounge heated up, from easy-listening ballads to blues. At some point I realized the canned music had been replaced by live and I talked everyone into going into the dance floor area to listen to the girl singer. She was tiny, way too tiny and way too young to have the husky, smoky blues voice she had. The lights in the lounge were dimmed, dark enough now to just make out shapes in the room, couples mostly, slow dancing to the beat.

The kids discovered the arcade games in this increasingly all-purpose restaurant. Happy with four quarters apiece, they went off, and Sean and I sat at the one vacant table some distance from the band and enjoyed a last drink.

"Let's dance," I urged, "cheek to cheek."

Sean shrugged me off. It would take an act of Congress to get the man on his feet. "I'm beat. Let's go home."

"The kids still have a game to go."

Sean finished the last of his beer and waved the waitress away.

"I'll go check the kids. You pay." He tossed me his credit card and threaded his way through the crowd back toward the arcade.

The waitress had disappeared, so I picked up the card and headed to the bar to pay for our drinks. Ben was still sitting there, the game in extra innings. A car commercial came on and he pointed, "That's one of mine."

The sound was off and I couldn't bring to mind the right theme for that car. "What does it sound like?"

Ben hummed, then vocalized the notes. I instantly recognized it and sang along for a few measures. He laughed in pleasure at our little duet, then tucked his pleasure back, as if embarrassed. "Not dancing?"

"No. Sean's pulling the kids away from the games. He's tired." There was a little note of irritation I neglected to hide.

Without a word, Ben took my hand and towed me to the dance floor, where the blues singer was singing "Frozen Heart," a favorite old song from college years. We moved around the floor as if we'd practiced, a slow waltzy movement. Ben's long thin body was perfectly suited to mine, and he was easy to follow. At the last note, shimmering against the poignant words of the song, a ballad of lost love, Ben held me away and I made a spontaneous curtsy as if we had been on a ballroom floor, not the tight space of a crowded bar. I lifted my head in time to see Sean, one child on either side, coming for me.

"Game's over." Sean kept a neutral face on. "Are you ready to go home yet?"

For an instant I thought he meant Providence.

"Thanks for the dance, Cleo."

"You're welcome, Ben." I was slightly defiant in my bearing, waiting for Sean to hiss the single vituperative marital sentence it would take to condemn my fun.

There was none. At least not then. We climbed into the Volvo and pulled out of the parking lot and into a downpour. I buffered the silence with commentary about the meal, the movie, the nasty weather, the hope for good weather tomorrow, insulating the four of us with chat, keeping at voice distance the opportunity for Sean to speak of my indiscretion. I was afraid that he would see my dancing with Ben as reaction against his refusing to dance. It truly wasn't. Even as I nattered on about the delicious crème brûlée dessert, I tested my motives against his perceptions and came up clean. After all, I hadn't initiated it, it had been a spontaneous thing.

A deer darted across the road, a doe, a spotted fawn close on her tail. Sean was far enough away he didn't have to slam on the brakes and so we slowed to a halt. The doe stood her ground until she was certain the fawn was there. With a bold leap, she and the fawn cleared the brushy verge and disappeared. In the few seconds of the doe's hesitation, the four of us sucked in our breath, letting it go only as she vanished.

"Wow." We chorused.

The doe's sudden appearance shut down my distracting chatter, and I couldn't pick the rhythm up again, so I watched out the passenger window at the raindrops rolling spastically down the pane of safety glass.

When I looked back at Sean I saw that rather than being tense in that peculiar way he had when chewing on an uncomfortable topic, he wore a preoccupied look, as if his distractions were far away and he was staring hard at them in his mind's eye.

The car stayed silent the rest of the way home, the kids out cold in the back after a mild skirmish for seat room which neither of us got into.

"Come sit with me on the porch," Sean said after we muscled the two sleepy children into bed.

I boiled water for cocoa and fussed with that for a few minutes. The rain had slowed and a fine mist lowered itself over the lake until no lights were visible anywhere around. The sky above the mist must have cleared, because enough moonlight filtered through it to give the night a little pale illumination, shaping the tops of the tallest pines.

I handed Sean his mug of watery hot chocolate. He took it with a smile, a slightly self-conscious one which reminded me of our early days together, when his self-deprecating humor was charming.

"I hope you don't think I was upset that you danced with that guy."

I was glad the lights in the cabin were off so Sean couldn't see my surprise. "I guess I did a little."

"Well, I guess I can stand to have my wife waltzed by a former rock star, as long as he keeps it polite."

"A what?"

"Benson Turner, unless I'm greatly mistaken, was a member of the Interior Angles. Blues funk, late seventies, early eighties. You remember, we went to one of their concerts before we graduated. They were really big."

"I had no idea. He's never said. I just knew that he was a musician, he composes music for commercials." I felt myself grinning in the dark. Who knew. "Hey, wasn't 'Frozen Heart' one of theirs?"

"Ironic enough for you, Miss Novelist?"

"Why didn't you say something?"

"I wasn't absolutely sure until you said he was a musician. Turner sort of disappeared about ten or fifteen years ago." Sean had already lost interest in the conversation and set his mug down. He took my cup and set it beside his, then pulled me out of my seat and onto his lap. As we kissed and cuddled, the mist brought the sweet translucent strains of Ben's concerto to us from across the lake.

Seven

"I'm sorry, Cleo. I have to go." Sean brandished his cell phone like proof. He'd just come back from his daily walk and talk. His upper lip was moist although the day wasn't terribly humid, and he smelled of nervous sweat.

"What about the kids? They're not going to want to cut their vacation short." This was Wednesday. They were planning on staying until Saturday, leaving late in the day.

"I thought maybe they'd stay here with you."

"What?"

He quickly backpedaled, "I mean just for the rest of the vacation. My client is in a twist about this accident and can't wait for me to get back to work on Monday. He needs me now."

"Oh come on, Sean. Surely one of your partners can take the helm on this one?"

"This is my client. I spent a long long time and a lot of sweat cultivating him. I can't pass the baton on this one." Sean stood slightly inclined toward me on the balls of his feet, as if ready to run back home, not drive.

"When will you come back to get the kids?"

"Oh man." Sean slapped his forehead. "This really screws things up. I have to travel on Sunday, I don't see how I can drive up here, and back, and then be able to turn around and drive to New York."

I knew what he was asking without asking. The breathtaking logic behind his unspoken suggestion. He knew I'd do the right thing. He knew.

"How long is your trip?"

"Three days."

"And you've dragooned your mother into taking them?"

"They love to spend time with her."

"Why don't you come back Friday night for them? Then you can get an early start on Saturday."

"Look, Cleo, just get them packed and we can all go now."

"No. Leave them until next weekend. It makes the most sense. Besides, your mother's done enough."

Sean gave me his most boyish grin, "We'll shoot for next Friday." Registering the annoyance on my face, he hastily amended himself. "I'll be here, I promise."

Sean's parting words, "You know, Clee, the kids love it here. Believe me, I know they'll stay out of your hair."

"Rat bastard." I muttered under my breath at the departing car. He had managed to spring the trap on my suppressed maternal guilt. Rat bastard. What kind of mother lets her kids swelter in the city while she spends time on the shores of a most beautiful lake? Sean knew I couldn't, in good conscience, deprive them of the experience. He probably knew all along I'd cave in.

As Sean predicted, the kids were beside themselves with joy at the prospect of staying an extra week.

"Okay, you guys. Listen up." I sat my children down and paced before them like Patton before the troops. "Here are the rules. One: I work from morning till noon. During that time you will have to entertain yourselves out of the water. Capeesh?"

Two curly red heads nodded.

"Two: No whining."

More nodding.

"Three: You clean up your own messes and do whatever chores I give you without above-mentioned whining."

Little smirks, more nodding.

I kept my amusement tucked away. Maybe without the demands of their activity schedules and the need to spend half a day every day in the car getting them from here to there, their physical presence wouldn't be such a distraction.

"Four: No planning, no planned activities. Don't make any plans which require me to act or to drive. Okay?"

"No problemo." Tim's best Bart Simpson voice.

"Oh, one more thing," I caught them by the backs of their shirts as they bolted for the door.

A duet of moans.

"Five: Can anyone guess five?"

Simultaneous head shaking.

"Enjoy yourselves. You are about to have very little adult supervision."

"Mom." Lily, taking her position as the eldest was already becoming my sergeant major. "You don't have to worry about a thing. We'll leave you to work. We'll even make lunch every day so you don't have to."

"That would be nice, Lily."

They scurried out the screen door before I could think of anything else.

The kids were in the water two seconds after I nodded, yes. They still hadn't quite gotten the concept of not interrupting me. Even though they made their own breakfast out of the horrible sweet cereal and played outside, I was on the alert for crises. Silence was more alarming than noise. Even as they played safely on the shore, I couldn't allow myself to sink deeply into the writer's trance. Once again, I was writing in fifteen-minute increments, finding myself peering out toward the lake to make sure they weren't drowning.

Lily sneaked up on me, whispering as if that was less of an intrusion than simply bounding onto the porch. "Mom, where are the Band-Aids?"

"Who needs a Band-Aid?"

"Tim."

"What happened?" Whatever pitch-perfect sentence had been about to leave my head for my fingertips was gone and I abandoned the attempt.

The good news was that it wasn't completely horrible. In fact, it was wonderful having them there. As much as the solitude felt good, having my children there, playing in the lake or discovering the wonders of nonelectronic games, was probably worth the distraction in the long run. However, at this moment I was still angry with Sean for not giving me the option.

I saved and shut down my laptop and leaned my elbows on my little work table, chin resting on the backs of my folded hands, admiring Lily and Tim's complete love of the water. They'd be in the cold water until I made them come out. I wished I could be like that, splashing without self-consciousness, pretending to be a mermaid, or a sea monster, or a shark. Diving endlessly, playing Frisbee or catch with a tennis ball.

I could see a group of the East Side neighbors on the communal beach, which was a man-made shoreline comprised mostly of raked dirt supplemented by imported sand. Not like a seashore beach, probably only ten feet wide and twenty feet long. Our cabin's private lakefront was muddy earth dropping off to brown water. Apart from the availability of the raft from our shore, the kids preferred the beach, where they could dig and hang out with their new friends. After struggling to get my still damp suit up over my hips, I grabbed a towel and chair and headed to join them. As I went along the path to the communal beach I rehearsed the names of the women lounging on aluminum and web chaise lounges, but by the time I walked the short distance to the narrow strip of beach, all but two of the neighbors were packing up to go home for lunch.

I was greeted cordially enough, but it was clear that, as a newcomer, I was outside the group. I told myself that it would take too much effort, and would negate the purpose of my sabbatical, to try to enter into it.

With everyone else gone, the conversation between the two women hissed with gossip. The pair of beach biddies took turns sniping at every absent neighbor. Little, decidedly catty, remarks about this one's poor taste in furniture or that one's weight gain. "Isn't Margaret looking happy these days, it must be nice to be able to let yourself go." Delighting like fat bumblebees on heavy blooms, they at last alighted on Benson Turner.

"So, Cleo, you've met Ben Turner?" This from the woman whose name I thought was Glenda, or maybe Brenda.

"Yes, I have." There was something in the tone of her voice, a slight knowingness, which made me cautious. "We've bumped into each other now and then."

"We've seen you on the raft together." This remark from Carol, one notch up from accusatory.

I could see a look pass between the two women. "What'd you think of him?"

"He seems very nice. A little shy, maybe. But pleasant." I was instinctively circumspect.

"He killed his wife, you know." Glenda got the reaction she was hoping for in my utter speechlessness. "Well, not like domestic abuse, but he was responsible for her accident."

"They were arguing. Everyone knows that they were having trouble. And they say he was drinking that night." The other woman, Carol, chimed in with her lines of the story.

I closed my mouth against saying anything. I needed a moment to adjust to this new view of Benson Turner. I realized that the tone in Glenda's voice, asking me if I had met Ben, was teasing, almost derisive, and it was clear Ben was the lakeside leper. Intuitively, I knew that in order to join that group, I had to anathematize Ben with them. To join the club, I was supposed to ask them for details. I needed to get into the mud with them and evince shock and condemnation. Screw them, I thought, and opened the fat mystery I'd lugged to the beach with me.

"We only mention this because we thought you ought to know, you seem to be so chummy with him, and we didn't think he'd say anything." Imagining that they had done their job, Glenda and Carol packed up their beach things and headed up the path toward their cabins. "Nice to see you, Cleo."

"You too," I waved insincere fingers. "Good thing I don't want your company." I hissed under my breath as the two beach biddies moved out of earshot, heading home for their afternoon naps. I closed the book. They had done their job, the seeds of curiosity had been pressed into the ground of my imagination. I began to wonder what other revelations about Ben would surface before I next lay beside him on the raft. Rock star and wife killer. I could imagine the first, I could not imagine the second. But the grief in his eyes was obvious and the mourning in his music was real.

I suddenly realized that Lily and Tim were standing within earshot of this conversation. "Hey, Mom, didja bring lunch?—we're hungry." A familiar duet. I wondered if they'd been paying attention and hoped that, until I could come to terms with this fresh revelation, they hadn't.

"You know where the kitchen is."

"Okay." Lily and Tim scrambled out of the water and raced up the path to the cabin to forage.

The shallow water where I stood was warm, the July sun was comfortingly hot with very little breeze at this time of day. Later on it would pick up, the lick of the evening breeze would goose-bump the skin of the still lake, only to be licked flat again as it died. I strode out into deeper water and made for the raft.

Eight

I arrived at the raft just as Ben did. The distance from the communal beach was considerably longer than from our own shore front
and my arms ached from the additional strokes. I hauled myself up
by the ladder as Ben vaulted up without it. We landed nearly face to
face on the redwood deck. My new insights into Ben made his sudden
appearance on the raft a little startling. I hadn't yet adjusted to either
of them, and a shyness woodened my speech until I realized that
there was nothing different about Ben except my unwanted aware-
ness of his two secrets.

"Hi."

"Hi." Ben tossed me the tube of sunblock which I kept on the raft.
"So, how's my dance partner?"

"Oh, a little pissed off, but I'm making a recovery." Without
meaning to, I launched into a diatribe against broken promises and
how my work never seemed to come first. I loved my kids, but I
needed my work. I needed to finish my novel.

Ben sat and nodded enough to keep the fires stoked until I got to
my destination, Self-pityville.

I heaved a concluding sigh and smiled. "Sorry to go off on you
like that. I'm sure it wasn't the answer you were expecting."

Ben shook his head with a slight smile. "Actually, I'm relieved. I was beginning to think you were the Cleavers."

Ben had me laughing at myself and it felt good. I thought of the East Side women and their nasty suggestion. I labeled it "shrewish remarks" and shoved it aside. They didn't know him at all. I recapped the tube of sunblock and handed it back to Ben.

"Hey, Mom!" Tim's red head crested the raft's edge. "What's so funny?" He pulled himself up the ladder and greeted Ben with a modified high five, a routine they had evidently perfected when I wasn't looking.

"Your mom was just telling me you kids are a couple of nuts."

"Yep. Real nuts." Tim tapped his head. "Coco Nuts."

I thought I recognized another routine and wondered how often these two had met.

"Mom, can we have spaghetti tonight?" Lily dripped lake water all over my almost dry suit.

"Sure. Hey, you know you aren't supposed to swim right after eating."

"We didn't eat. We came out to get you 'cause we made lunch."

Instantly I was sorry for my crabbing about two such wonderful children.

"Ben, we made tuna, you want to eat too?" Tim faced Ben, his skinny legs turned out slightly at the knees like a yearling Thoroughbred, bony fists stuck in his waist, a posture more challenging rather than inviting.

"I can't today, Timmy boy. I have to go see someone." Ben stood up, his posture an echo of my son's. "Maybe another day?"

"Just like Dad."

"Tim." My warning voice.

"It's okay, Cleo. Believe me, Tim, this isn't like your dad at all." Ben seemed unoffended by Tim's charge.

"So, Ben, what about dinner?" My words preceded my thinking.

"Only if you're really having spaghetti."

"Jar sauce."

"Best kind." Ben winked at Lily.

Before diving off the raft, Ben offered to bring a salad.

"Great, but nothing complicated," I said, eyeing my children, who believed salad was simply lettuce with a tomato waved over the top.

"Done." He went over the side with a slight splash and disappeared under the amber brown water, surfacing halfway to his shore.

Ben's coming to dinner changed the entire color of my day. Instead of doing any number of things I might have, I pulled out the meager cleaning supplies and began cleaning the cabin. If nothing else, the sour-smelling towels were banished and the chipped porcelain sink and toilet were clean. I dry-mopped, conquering for the moment the usual collection of detritus and spiderwebs, endemic to lakeside living.

On the way back from the Big G, I stopped at a farm market and bought a bouquet of summer flowers for the table. I resisted candles, but made sure the kerosene lamps were full. Rain was predicted, and the fragile nature of our electricity certainly warranted such precautions.

Tim and Lily were talked into real clothes, abandoning cut-offs and stained T's for one night in favor of clean T's and real shorts. I determined that they couldn't have overheard, or understood, the vile gossip on the beach. They were too comfortable with Ben. Or maybe they simply had their own opinion. I realized that I, too, had rejected the intent and hoped that Ben himself would eventually tell me the story, set the record straight.

The table set, the spaghetti water on simmer, the brownies for dessert were cooling, and I stood, freshly showered, at the cramped three-drawer chest stuffed with my clothes. It seemed as though I'd brought nothing but shorts, T's, and jeans, one baggy sweatshirt, and my favorite cardigan, worn out at the elbows. I hadn't brought so much as a sundress, never planning on anything more dressy than the movies. Too late to do anything about it, I chose the jeans and the plain mint-green T-shirt, tucked in, adding one of Sean's flannel shirts I'd co-opted to tie around my waist like a teenager. It cooled down these rainy nights, and eventually I'd need it. I could only see my face in the tiny bedroom mirror. For someone who was supposed to be working, I certainly had a nice tan.

I held my lipstick up to my lips and then stopped. What on earth was I doing? I recapped the tube and dropped it in my dresser drawer. This wasn't a date, for God's sake.

For the first time I allowed myself to feel a nudge of guilty pleasure. I knew that it was nothing more than a neighborly dinner, but I also knew that in Sean's view, this was borderline. It certainly would be if the shoe were on the other foot. Then I thought that maybe there was some little part of me which would enjoy a little innocent revenge. Not for the old hurt, necessarily; I had long ago chosen the revenge of forgiveness for that.

I picked up the lipstick again. If Sean can go to the zoo at midday with what's-her-name, well, this casual invitation was equally innocuous. Besides, it wasn't my invitation, it was the kids' doing. No harm done. A knock at the screen door startled me and I never did put the lipstick on.

In the cabin's kitchen, Ben Turner seemed much taller, and the space suddenly much narrower. He kept moving out of my way as I went from fridge to stove, missing the beat once and making me bump up against him. We were fully dressed, yet the bump of hips somehow seemed more intimate than sitting half-naked, side by side on the raft. In slight embarrassment, I sent him to the living-room side of the little island counter to finish dressing the salad—lettuce, tomato and cucumbers. Little dishes of feta cheese, black olives, and croutons were arrayed beside the bowl.

Once the conversational staples of weather and high prices were used up, we moved easily into books and movies. We played a hilarious game of Mousetrap with the kids before I sent them off to bed. I half-expected Ben to leave then but he patiently waited, clearing away the worst of the kitchen mess while I argued the kids into bed.

"Hey, you're company, you don't have to do that." I took the dishrag from him.

"I wanted to." Ben darted past me and opened the screen door. Reaching down, he came back up with a bottle of white wine in a bucket of mostly melted ice. "Can we open this?"

I wondered for a second if I had deliberately forgotten to buy wine for the meal. If I had, it hadn't been conscious.

Ben opened the pinot grigio with a flourish, pouring two equal glasses and setting the bottle back into the bucket. Raising his glass to me, he said, "To a lovely evening, with gratitude."

I held my own glass in front of me to disguise my pleasure. I know I flushed like a schoolgirl spoken to by the football captain. I refused to let myself analyze the moment, to allow it to take on any other meaning beyond two neighbors well fed on a July evening. "We should have had this with dinner."

"Wrong color for spaghetti. Besides, it tastes better looking out over the lake."

"So, tell me, Ben, how long have you lived out on the lake?"

"All my life, in one way or another. My parents owned it, my mother's parents before that." He poured a second glass of wine into both our glasses.

"I spent my boyhood summers here. We lived in New Jersey, so the mountains of New Hampshire were our idea of heaven. About a dozen years ago I'd had some setbacks and needed to . . ." He seemed to be struggling to find the right euphemism for his action. "I needed a retreat, and Cameo Lake was what came to mind. I used the last of my money to buy the place from my parents and winterize it. I felt as though I was building a nest to get away from the world and supporting my parents at the same time. I've been here almost year-round ever since."

"You and your wife lived here?"

"Yeah. Even though we kept an apartment in New York, this was home." Ben rocked gently in the glider beside my stationary chair. He hummed a little, a light, moth-like flutter of sound. I recognized a bar or two from the piano music I would hear every evening from across the lake.

"That's your concerto?"

"Mmmm." Ben nodded in time with the rocking. "I still haven't found the flute motif. It's still all just the surrounding themes. I'm doing it backwards."

Ben began to sing the theme on "ta," and the lovely flying rhythms were colored in for me. His voice was very sweet, and moved easily from bass to tenor, where the imagined cellos and violins would take the theme from one another. His right hand described the pattern in a conductor's graceful arc. He kept singing until the notes, repeated and repeated in ascending thirds, made the skin prickle on my neck and I wasn't surprised to feel a deep emotion which might have been grief or loneliness or joy.

Suddenly I reached out for his arm, a visceral need to touch over-riding our limited acquaintance. "Ben, stop." I realized we were both weeping. I knew that he cried for the woman he'd lost but I didn't know why I was crying, except that his music seemed profoundly sad.

Though his eyes glistened in the light from the kitchen window, Ben made no move to wipe them dry. He gulped the last of the wine in his glass.

"I wish I could write words as beautifully as you write music."

Ben waved a dismissive hand. "The fact is, I'll never finish it. No one will ever hear it, and it really doesn't matter. She'll never play it."

"But someone will."

He did move to wipe his eyes then and set his glass down on the floor beside the glider. "Thanks for dinner, Cleo. I owe you." Ben left quickly, and I was left with the strange sense of having almost pierced his veneer.

Nine

❧

Early-morning rumbles turned into downpours by eleven. The garbage was rank in the bin and the kids were squabbling over who was responsible for the milk I had asked to be wiped up.

"Just wipe the damn milk and stop bickering!"

It was the second day of rain in a row and the cabin was growing smaller with each passing hour. I left Lily and Tim still fighting about fairness and stood on the porch, staring hard at the liquid sky. With the kids effectively sentenced to house arrest by the rain, I had gotten nothing of merit done on my manuscript. I stood and stared out over the gray sky, gray water, gray world, and felt a familiar twinge of resentment bloom in my stomach. Sean should have come back for the kids. He had promised me my solitude to finish my work. Why was his work always more important than mine? My midlist-sized income had provided breathing space when the business took a downturn. We had money set aside for both kids' educations; we weren't rich, but we were comfortable enough to afford a nice vacation in the winter. Didn't that count for anything?

Sometimes I felt as though I was married to an Old World patriarch. Despite the trappings and opinions of a modern man, Sean could be amazingly retro in his attitude toward our roles in the marriage. The children were my bailiwick, he was the breadwinner. Not to say he didn't take a part in their upbringing, but, like his father before him, it had devolved into that of disciplinarian and entertainer. Of course he did more car-pooling and soccer-coaching than his father had; of course he helped monitor homework, that was the way of the new man. But when push came to shove, the kids' welfare was my responsibility. And one I had shouldered with delight. Except for this week. I felt as though I'd been dealt a bait and switch, and it was hard to keep the resentment hidden from the kids.

"Mom! She hit me!"

I was ten paces down the soggy path before the screen door slammed. I wasn't really dressed for running, but I did have my old New Balance joggers on and sweatpants, so I didn't look too unusual, except that I was running in a downpour. Everyone knows dedicated runners are a little nuts. I splashed through puddles and slipped a little on the wet pine needles. I slicked back my wet hair with my fingers and kept running. The rain sizzled against the still lake surface, the only sound except my breathing. The little beach was empty, canoes tipped over, spines up. Someone's aluminum and web beach chair was a bright mark against the dull scene. I ran and forced my thoughts away from my crabby children, pulling my characters up and into my adrenaline-fired imagination. I slowed a little to give myself a fighting chance at having enough breath, that I might be able to think about my scene and not about how hungry for air I was. The rain seemed lighter in the woods, and warmer. I went past my usual halfway mark and kept going, jogging now so that I could imagine the world I was creating and forget the real one. Except that thoughts of Ben kept surfacing, little thoughts, little echoes of conversation— my curiosity about his wife and her death. That he grieved and that he loved her I thought was obvious, understandable. That he might have been responsible for her death was sad, and, at the same time, tantalizing.

I was drenched, water dripped from the ends of my hair and off the tip of my nose. My white T-shirt clung to my body as if I'd been entered into one of those tasteless contests, the pink of my skin showing through. With each step I felt the squash of saturated sneaker sole.

Three faces watched me as I walked the last fifty yards. Three expressions of varying disbelief that a woman of my intellect and sense would go running in weather like this. Lily looked embarrassed, Tim puzzled, and Ben looked amused. Self-consciously I folded my arms across my chest.

"I came to take the kids to the movies. They've got a Star Wars matinee at the mall."

"They've seen it, Ben. But thanks."

Tim and Lily clamored a duet of protest. "But Mom, but Mom! We love *The Phantom Menace*! We've only seen it once!"

"Are you sure?" This to Ben.

"Absolutely. It's self-serving, if you must know. I want to see it, and . . . well, it's more fun with the right people. Besides," and he pointed to my closed laptop, "you can use the time alone."

"God bless you, Ben Turner."

"God bless us every one. Now, scoot, you two. Find your shoes."

"You're a natural."

Ben didn't reply to this, looking away a little, and I might have felt as if I'd blundered but he was smiling.

It was decided that I would join them after the movie and we'd eat at the food court. I got there a little past the agreed-upon six o'clock. Ben was sitting on a bench outside of the games arcade, one arm casually flung across the back of the faux park bench, long legs stretched out and crossed at the ankles. I saw him before he saw me and I experienced the strangest sense of excitement, as if I hadn't seen him in a long time and we had much to catch up on. A sensation I could only attribute to seeing him outside of our normal habitat. I spoke before I reached him. "Ben, sorry I'm late."

He stood up as I approached and waved off my concern and pointed toward the game room. "I hope you don't mind that they ended up in there, but it was the only mutually agreeable place."

"You've done this before, haven't you?"

"I have nieces and nephews, so I'm not a total novice." Ben had plucked the kids away from their games with great ease. If I'd done that they'd have protested for another round. "I have two siblings and they've both provided me with terrific surrogates." Ben chatted about his family, more expansive about them than he had been about anything. Usually circumspect, he seemed to take great pleasure in the subject of his multiple nieces and nephews, and it was nice to hear his stories.

Her name slipped in then, as he was telling a story. Talia.

"Talia was your wife?"

He neither nodded nor shook his head, only made a little shrugging gesture as if reluctant to place her in the past tense. "Talia Brightman." He scratched at the back of his neck where the hair was a little long and wavy like a child's. "She was good with the kids. They liked her."

"How long were you married?" The kids had run back to the arcade for one last game, their McDonald's meals half-eaten. We were alone and the din of the food court made it seem as though we had complete privacy.

"Almost five years." Not looking at me, he added, "The accident was a year ago tonight."

I pushed aside the trays cluttering up the rectangular table we shared and placed a hand on his arm. "I'm sorry, Ben, I had no idea."

"It's all right. It's okay, Cleo. I had to spend this night somewhere, and this is far better than alone."

"Is that why you suggested the movie?"

"No. Well, maybe. Partly." Ben carefully organized the trash, keeping his eyes away from mine as if he thought I expected him to describe the accident. He stood up and walked to the trash containers. Suddenly the kids were back and he brushed his hand over Tim's buzz-cut hair. He did look at me, and then, "Cleo, I will tell you about it sometime. I just can't right now." We walked away from the food court, a child on either side of Ben. He could have meant right now in the mall, or right now in front of the children, but I knew intuitively that he meant he wasn't ready to speak of the accident to anyone just yet.

Regaining his playfulness, Ben grasped Lily and Tim's hands. "How about I buy us some ice cream?" Swinging arms like Dorothy's companions on the way to Oz, they got ahead of me.

It was later than I planned when we left the mall. I had missed my scheduled call to Sean and the phone at home rang unanswered. When the answering machine kicked in, I automatically assumed he was out with a client, or at his mother's. It really wasn't very late, maybe eight-thirty. I figured I'd just wait and call him in the morning and left that message behind with a quick apology for being late with my call.

Ten

Before I even took my run, I jumped into the SUV and headed up to where the phone would work. I think I must have woken Sean, although it was late enough this weekday morning he should have been up. His voice was thick and he seemed startled to hear my voice. "Cleo, I'm sorry I wasn't here last night."

"Late night?"

"Yeah. I think I'm getting too old for this."

"Sean, you're only just forty."

"Thanks for the *only.*"

We chatted a bit and I could hear Sean move around the house with the portable tucked up under his chin, the running of coffee water, the slam of the refrigerator door, and for a moment I was a little homesick. "You have watered my plants, haven't you?"

"Ma does, twice a week. Your violets will be fine."

"I'm making good progress."

"That's good, Cleo." I heard the rustle of newspaper and his response seemed awfully distracted.

"What time will you get here Friday?"

There was enough of a pause on the line for me to feel that first alarm of battle.

"Ummm, I'm not sure. There's a lot going on." There was no other noise on the line, he was standing still.

"You are coming this weekend?"

"Jeez, Cleo. You know, if you could just . . ."

"Just what?"

"Hang on for a little while longer."

"I can't believe you."

The day was already hot and Sean's reneging on our agreement served to build up my own heat to the boiling point. I felt the sweat burst out on my forehead and my heart beat with anger. I wanted to scream but I could not. My stilted upbringing had limited me. We did not raise our voices in my parents' home. We did not emote. I had not learned how, not even by being subjected to Sean's vociferous family; it had been too late to learn. Instead I resorted to hanging up on him. There was no satisfaction in pressing the off button. I wanted to slam a receiver down hard enough to break it. I sat in the hot car and held my head in my hands and wished that I could let go.

The car phone rang and I let it go for a couple of beeps. Then I picked it up in the hopes that Sean had quickly seen his mistake and was calling with an abject apology.

I should have known better.

"Cleo, don't do that to me again. I only mean to say that I've got a lot of traveling to do in the next two weeks and my mother isn't up to keeping the kids for that long."

He'd done it. He'd played the mother hand. I knew full well Alice McCarthy was more than up to keeping my kids, but Sean would prefer I did my duty.

"Did she say that?"

"You know she never would. Come on, Cleo. What do you think?"

"I think you're going back on your promise."

"You know it wasn't a very realistic promise. I did my best. You said you were making good progress."

"I have a deadline, Sean." Not quite true, but believable, and a word he understood.

"I appreciate that." Another pause. "All right, I'll figure something out for August, but I can't change things for now."

"Sean." I was actually shaking, sitting there in the hot car on an already stifling day, "Don't you want to see me?"

He didn't say anything for a moment, then, "May I remind you who left whom?"

"What do you mean, *left?*"

"Look, I'm sorry." Now he was backpedaling. "Of course I miss you, and want to see you. But, it may not be possible."

I was not mollified, only more deeply wounded. "I'll come home, Sean. Obviously that's what needs to happen."

"No. Don't. I'm sorry. I'll be up next weekend. I'll come next Friday and stay through Monday. A nice long weekend, okay?"

He had negotiated a truce and I accepted the terms. "Okay. Next Friday."

I was on the other side of tired where sleep is denied. I had lain for hours in the hot bedroom, spread-eagled on the three-quarter bed, chewing on Sean's words, feeling more and more angry. Giving up, I went out onto the porch and opened my laptop's lid. I got settled and opened the file which contained the sum of my three week's work, reading through a few pages, then scrolling down to where I'd left off. It seemed so bland, so trite. I could fluff it up here and there, but the fact was, the critical developments lacked verisimilitude. Simply not enough real emotion represented there. Opening up a cold Coke, I got to work.

The only light was the blue background of the laptop. The only sound the percussive thump of my right thumb on the space bar, and the occasional croak of a bullfrog. It was so quiet I allowed myself the total immersion I craved. Like being locked in a closet, I could only keep my eyes on the light of my screen, the door to my refuge.

I entered the place all writers long to go, need to go, in order to get the job done. I was in the groove, as if all senses, all thoughts and emotions were extant only in the confines of the screen and the world

I was creating. Except for having to pee and getting another Coke, I remained at work in my dark space with the heat and humidity southern in intensity, but not oppressive now. Heat which was comfort, protection, and forgotten as I directed all my conflicted thoughts into the written word.

As I drew my characters into their painful story-defining crisis, Ben's musical memorial to his wife came to mind. I stopped typing long enough to actually run it through my head, trying to capture it entirely, but only the four measures of his main theme would circle my inner hearing. I could hear the chordal progression as Ben had sung it that other evening. I didn't know the names of the chords, only that they had risen. Against the evil words of the lakeside neighbors, it was poignant and served to still their cruelty in my mind. Now, when held up against the evil befalling my protagonist, it seemed less poignant. As imagined background music for my imaginary people, it had, instead of homage, the sound of anger, pain, and misunderstanding. I felt a little corrupt in taking it.

There is a time of night which is darker than any other; a time when even the night creatures are still. Nurses will say it is the time of death.

I felt my consciousness close down. I was awake, but my impulse had slowed and I realized I'd been sitting still for some time. I reread my last paragraph and smiled at the transpositions. I fixed the obvious ones and shut down. The air was still oppressive, unmoving. Even if I lay down now, I wouldn't sleep. I stripped off my soaked boxers and T-shirt and grabbed a towel. Naked, I walked to the water's edge. By the light of Ben's porch light I could just make out the raft. Otherwise the bare night sky and the lake melded into one darkling horizon. The water was like silk against my skin. The sudden relief of the spring-fed lake water made me groan with pleasure, the only sound to be heard, and I was a little embarrassed.

In twenty strokes I was at the raft, just visible as a dark form in the dark water. Feeling for the ladder with one hand while holding the edge with the other, and praying with all my heart no spiders were within reach, I hauled myself out of the water.

"Cleo?"

Ben's voice startled me back into the water.

"God, Ben, you scared me."

"I didn't want you to land on top of me."

From below I couldn't see him in the thick night air. His disembodied voice floated above me.

"Come on up, I've moved over"

"I can't." I didn't quite want to say I was buck naked, but Ben caught on.

"Cleo, I can't see the hand in front of my face. And neither can you."

So it was that we sat, side by side, perfectly naked. We kept the distance of four boards between us. Only our voices, hushed against the amplification of the inverted air and echo of water, were visible. It was like the intimacy of the telephone. We didn't lie down, I think because that would have been for both of us a too, too vulnerable position. As it was, I was exquisitely aware of our nakedness, a feeling which began to dissipate as we talked.

As if he needed to explain himself, Ben offered, "I sleep out here when it's this hot."

"I just needed to cool my body temperature off. I've been working all night."

"I know. Every now and then you vocalize."

Had he heard me humming his tune? "I hope I haven't kept you awake."

"No. I'm restless anyway."

I heard a distant splash. A jumping fish perhaps.

"I'm pretty restless too."

"Are you all right?" Ben had detected my poorly disguised unhappiness.

"Yeah. Fine." I really couldn't go into it. I really didn't want to begin to loose the private battle between me and my husband, even to this kind stranger.

"You don't sound fine, Cleo. What's the matter?"

A man who reads nuances in music could hear the false note in my reply. "I'm just wiped."

"Kids okay?"

"Sleeping like, well, like babies."

"Sean?"

The very first threat of tears clogged my throat and my silence was eloquent.

"Hey, I'm a neutral wall. You want to talk, I'm here."

"What makes you think . . ." I couldn't finish the statement. It cost too much after a day full of emotional effort to work up the energy to pretend everything was well ordered in my world.

"He's not coming back for them, is he?"

"No. But it's all right. They shouldn't be spending the summer in the city when I'm here."

"Maternal guilt?"

"Ben, sometimes we just don't get what we think we want."

"Suggestion?"

"Shoot."

"There's a really nice day camp on the other side of the lake. Starts every Monday. They teach water safety and horseback riding. Camp Mom-Needs-Time-Alone."

I laughed a little at his joke, amazed at his perception. "I'll look into it tomorrow." I reached across the four boards to touch his bare shoulder, in the darkness a curiously intimate gesture. "Thank you, Ben."

He patted the hand that touched him, holding my fingers there. I didn't move to withdraw them. "Just being neighborly."

We were quiet then, my hand still on his shoulder. I pressed the tips of my fingers against his skin, "Ben, you do know that I can be a good listener, too."

"I know." He pressed his cheek against my fingers, I felt the day's growth of beard rough against them. "I know."

We sat quietly on the raft until a slight breeze, like a sigh after weeping, touched my skin and I realized that the hour before dawn had arrived. Darker shapes were outlined by the fading darkness. I could see Ben clearly, and if he had been less of a gentleman he could have turned his head and seen me. We slipped off the edge of the raft simultaneously, a nearly splashless landing. A cardinal's piercing note announced the new day.

Eleven

The first flashes of impotent heat lighting began just as I lay down, more pulsing sheets of light than streaks. I fell instantly asleep and dreamed of cityscapes and the voices of my children. I didn't dream of Sean. Still, my sleep was intermittent, disturbed by the light of another scorching day. By eight o'clock I was up and back at my computer. The kids slept on and I didn't chide them awake.

The humidity was layered over the lake like whipped cream over a pie. I sat in a tank top and running shorts, hunched over my laptop, rereading the last few paragraphs from the night before and trying desperately to get back into that groove where no other world but Jay and Karen's existed. Where the betrayals and disappointments were products of my controlling imagination and not about me.

Morning had not brought with it a lessening of my anger at Sean. The anger was less white hot, but no less real. It reminded me of another anger long ago. If Sean couldn't hold up his end of the bargain in this situation, why did I think he could maintain his end of a bargain now almost eight years old? He had been so contrite, so sorry, so boyish in his belief that he could be forgiven for his infidelity. So assured and yet grateful that I would be like his mother had been when Francis McCarthy cheated on her.

My parents divorced when I was sixteen. Typically, they never spoke of the cause of their separation, but I knew deep down that Mr. Ramsey was the catalyst. The separation and divorce came suddenly, without warning and without negotiation. I never saw Mr. Ramsey again. It was as if they had needed an excuse to go their separate ways, a minimum of fuss. When Alice discovered Francis cheating, she screamed bloody murder and threw a lamp at him. They stayed married and seemed content.

I looked up from my screen, still exactly as it had been an hour before, and saw Ben paddling north, up the widest part of the lake. I picked up the binoculars and focused on him as he drew the paddle through the still water. Under the scrutiny of my gaze his strokes were graceful, making the motion seem effortless, rhythmic, and strong. He switched sides and paddled on the starboard side of the Old Town, digging deeper into the lake, the motion etching fine muscle against his strong back. Thinking myself entitled to a mean thought, I compared him to Sean. My husband's physical fitness was limited to an occasional business round of golf. In spite of my chiding to be active, he remained sedentary. His natural body type saved him from being overweight, although, as I had noticed earlier in the summer, his lifestyle was beginning to catch up to him. By the time he was Ben's age, he'd pretty much look like his father. Rusty red hair faded to yellow, paunch outlined by expensive suspenders. Good suits to disguise the bandy legs.

I shook myself out of the visual punishment. It wouldn't be that bad. Sean's legs were pretty good. I lifted the binoculars again and watched my neighbor bend the trajectory of the canoe toward the pier belonging to the lakeside general store. The store had only opened for the season just before July Fourth and I found it useful only for Popsicles and the kid's bait. The price of milk was absurd and the owners carried only one kind of bread, the "squishy white bread" which my kids loved and I wouldn't let them have.

I lowered the binoculars and wondered for a moment when I had become such a nosy neighbor. I admitted to myself that I was fascinated with Ben Turner because he let so little of himself out. He was niggardly with details, letting clues drop here and there, obviously protecting himself from saying out loud that he hurt. I had meant what I said out there in the middle of the night on the middle of the raft. I could be a good listener. I hoped that he understood it wasn't really just nosiness, it was an offer to be the neutral wall he'd offered me.

Lowering my binoculars, it occurred to me that my interest had not been entirely on his story. Thinking of our midnight visit on the raft, the warm breeze on our bare skin, I recalled the sense I felt sitting there, as if we were doing something very naughty. Playing with fire.

"I know you probably have a waiting list a mile long." I stood in the dank director's cabin of Camp Winetonka.

"Well, yes. We have a repeat clientele which takes precedence over . . ."

I listened with a sinking heart to the slightly supercilious affectation of the camp director, who was also the owner, and, I believe, the cook. She was one-half of a married couple who had opened up their camp thirty-five years ago and never looked back. The place seemed very homey, if a camp can project that. Because it was a day camp, there was only the director's cabin, which was also their summer home. A teepee took center stage in the flat, dusty fire-pit area. Everything was incredibly neat and tidy, and as I waited for her to speak to a counselor, I noticed a boy scooping up a pile of horse manure.

Mrs. Beckman was a round woman, wearing knockoff Boy Scout khakis and a broad-brimmed hat, which she took off and hung on an antler as she ushered me into the office. Under the hat was a head of steel-gray hair. I had never used the description "steel-gray" for any of my characters, deeming the words way too trite. But in this case, steel-gray was the only adjective appropriate. For a minute, I thought the hard curls were a spun aluminum wig.

"Mrs. Beckman, I understand. May I explain to you my problem?"

Mrs. Beckman sat with her hands folded on top of her desk and nodded. "Of course."

"I came to the lake to write . . ." Oh God, how pretentious did *that* sound. "I'm a novelist."

"Would I have heard of you?"

"I don't know. I write as Cleo Grayson. I wrote—"

"*Cardinal Rules!*"

"Yes." I felt that little blush of pleasure which comes with some-one recognizing your work.

"And *Tillotson's Mecca.*"

"You know my books?"

At this point, Mrs. Beckman was up and around her desk and melted into a much softer person. Even her curls began to move. "Ms. Grayson, it would be an honor to have your children be our guests. We call them guests, you know."

At long last, my work was paying off.

"They start tomorrow. Full days, five days a week. Mrs. Beckman was very accommodating."

I lay on the raft, almost dry now in the intense heat. Ben had just climbed aboard. "Good. I expect that you'll get a lot done while they're learning really useful stuff like lanyard weaving and bow hunting."

"Stop it. They mostly get to do what they best love, swim and schmooze."

"Schwim and smooze, huh?"

I laughed at him, and rolled over to dry my backside. "What about you? Getting much done?" I leaned my chin on my fist.

"Enough. I have to go to New York pretty soon with it."

"New York. God, that seems a million miles away from here."

"It is when you try to get there via mass transportation."

"How are you getting there?"

"Renting a car, flying out of Boston."

"Why are you renting a car?"

"You've seen the Wagoneer? It's got over two hundred thousand miles on it and I can't ask it to do heavy work anymore."

"I'll drive you down."

Ben lay down next to me on the hot surface of the redwood raft and placed his chin on his hand. "Nonsense. You've just cleared the slate to work, I'm not going to take any of your time away from you."

"I'd love to do it . . . just give me a day's notice." My volunteering had been spontaneous and without forethought, but my disappointment as he refused my offer was genuine. "It isn't that far."

"Cleo."

I cut him off. "Look, I get very stale if I don't take a day now and then to do nothing. Or to stimulate my senses. Besides, I need to do some research." This might have been true. I could make it true. It seemed very important to me just then to have that hour and a half alone with Ben, to see him outside of the context of the lake. To see if the friendship we knew on the raft was mobile.

"Well, it would make my life easier. But that's not why you were put on this earth."

I wanted to come up with a snappy response, but his words touched something in me. Hadn't I been put on this earth to make Sean's life easier? Keeping daily distractions at a minimum while he focused on building the firm his father had left to him; asking little of him domestically except to take out the trash, a job he'd passed on to his son in recent months. Hadn't I made it incredibly easy for him to dump the kids on me? Easy for him to fool eight years ago, depending as he had been on my blind trust in him. I felt punched. Not by Ben's words, but with the sudden realization that Sean's maneuvering had triggered an alarm bell I had long thought dormant.

"Ben, sometimes I do wonder why I was put on this earth." My voice carried with it the weight of my bitterness.

Abruptly I stood up to dive off the raft, heedless of the direction I faced. Before I could launch myself, Ben grabbed me by the hand. "Jesus, Cleo, not from that side, please. The rock." The look on his face startled me with the intensity of his concern. I would almost have said that he was terrified that I would deliberately launch myself off the rock side of the raft.

"I'm sorry, I forgot." Ben still clung to my hand and I could detect a faint tremble, and I knew that I had given him a shock by my thoughtless action. I squatted down next to him. "I won't make that mistake again."

"You think I overreacted." He let go of my wrist and stood up. "It's better than not reacting at all." He dived in, swimming toward his shore with an emphatic reach. Once on shore, he didn't look back at me, just scooped his towel off the ground and went into his cabin.

I touched my wrist where he had gripped it. There would be bruising—not an effect of violence, but of caring.

Twelve

Seven-thirty. Some inner time devil made me look at the clock just as it read seven-thirty. I should be in the car making the evening phone call but I couldn't bring myself to do it. I'd go up in a few minutes. A few minutes either way wouldn't make any difference. Sean's mother had always preached, never go to bed angry, but I had. Nursing bitterness like a warm beer.

Mercifully, my train of thought was derailed by the kids pounding up the back steps and into the kitchen. They had been a little reluctant to go to camp, chafing against regimentation after these three weeks of unbridled activity. However, once Lily heard that they had horses and Tim realized he knew a boy from the East Side who attended, they were aboard on the concept and already wearing the Camp Winetonka T-shirts I'd brought back after my interview with Mrs. Beckman. In honor of the perfect solution to my work dilemma, I promised myself a work-free weekend, all play, as much for myself as for them. Tomorrow we were going blueberry picking and canoeing. I thought about asking Ben to join us, but didn't. I needed family time, and maybe Ben and I needed a little space between us.

Already it seemed as though the days were getting shorter. The long twilights of June were gone and evening settled in by eight o'clock. The heat continued oppressive, but the kids didn't seem to notice. We played a slightly moldy game of Monopoly, the fake money sticking together with the humidity. By ten, Lily and Tim were sound asleep and I was left alone with nothing to distract my thoughts.

I got in the car and drove up to the top the drive. Sean had picked up the phone on the first ring, not commenting on the lateness of my call. "I'm all set for next Friday. I'll be up around nine." He was quick to tell me this, quick to fend off unpleasantness. He was clearly relieved that I had found a palatable solution to having the kids with me. "Cleo, that's perfect. We should have done something like that from the start."

"Right."

"You have to admit that Cameo Lake is a far better place to hang out in the summer than Providence." There it was, the justification for his actions. Press on the guilt, smooth it along like peanut butter.

"Of course it is, Sean. Don't you think I felt a little selfish being here without all of you?"

"You never said that."

"No, all I said was that I needed uncomplicated time to finish my work."

"Maybe this isn't uncomplicated but it is more fair to the kids."

"And to you, Sean?"

He either missed or deliberately ignored my meaning, jumping off the subject with a bound. "I'll be up next week. Maybe we can rent a boat and sail around."

I sat on the porch and stared across to Ben's light, listening for his music, but there was none.

I woke at dawn, drenched in sleeper's sweat. I got up to pee and once up couldn't bear lying down again on those damp, sticky sheets. The night had been untempered by any breeze, the air at once still and heavy. I pulled on yesterday's shorts and tank and tied my running shoes on without socks. I took a long time stretching, listening to the variety of birdcalls. Stretching my back, hands against my waist, I looked up as a hawk launched itself from a pine tree. I thought that I should stop at the library and get a bird book so that I could begin identifying some of these creatures more exotic than the robin and jay I knew.

Putting a moderately paced tape in my Discman, I set off. No sense courting an early-morning heatstroke. I ran up through the woods along the soft path strewn with pine needles and cones. I was used to the slippery surface by now and knew how to use it. I ran quietly past the cabins with their still sleeping occupants, down to the imported-sand beach, between the rows of up-ended canoes, and on, back up through the woods, higher and higher into the deeper part of the forest. The hardest part of the run followed as I moved past a blue trail marker that served as my halfway point. Now I traveled along the ridgeline of the hills, darker and slightly cooler than any other part of the run. Here there was a little breeze and I felt it against my skin. I was tiring by now, the incline unforgiving in this weather. My pace didn't keep up with the music and the conflicting rhythms made me a little crazy. I yanked off the earphones and allowed myself to start walking. Breathless in the thick air, I bent over, a sudden stitch punching me in the side.

I leaned back against the rough surface of a pine tree, staring through a break in the tree line toward Ben's island. I touched the place on my wrist where he had held me and looked to see if I had bruised. There was no mark, but the intensity of his grip lingered in memory. He had not frightened me. On the contrary, Ben's fear for me had worked loose feelings I had not looked for in such a casual friendship. It seemed as though I was already looking to Ben for support I should have looked to my husband for. In a strange way, as much as I felt Ben was protecting himself against revealing too much, he was open to knowing me. If I had to put a word to it, he was kind. Dare I say that at this point, in such a short acquaintance, we were becoming necessary to each other, in the way certain touchstones are necessary? Was I so lonely in my life I needed Ben? Was he so lonely he needed me? I touched my wrist and told myself I was reading too much into an act of ordinary merit. Except that the look on Ben's face was extraordinary, hardened with alarm, then softening to relief. He was right, I had thought he'd overreacted, and the look on his face did nothing to explain why.

With the thought of Ben's hand on my wrist, I was thrust back into remembering why I had stood up to dive in the first place. The tiny bell tolling at a distance which spoke of danger. I listened to it as I began to walk back to the cabin. I replayed my recent conversations with Sean and I came up with nothing more sinister than his backing out of our deal, which I should have anticipated. There was nothing to speak of another infidelity except a trip to the zoo and more than one late night. Nothing except my intuitive mistrust. That was something I had learned, not something which came naturally to me. I hadn't been the least suspicious that summer in Narragansett. I was blindsided. But I had forgiven Sean, thus I was muzzled against speaking unsubstantiated doubts. We'd gone the counselor route, delved into the issues, made promises. He would behave and I would forgive. He still flirted, but I tolerated that. To the best of my knowledge, Sean had been faithful ever since.

I drove a spike into the tolling bell.

The kids were still asleep and I left them alone. I put on a pot of coffee and took a quick lukewarm shower. Selfishly, I was grateful for the gift of an hour I could work while the kids slept. I wasn't going to work at all on this Saturday, I had planned on a free weekend, but I needed to do it. I needed the power that comes of being able to manipulate and control events. Entering the world of Jay and Karen calmed me down, gave me an hour's respite from my own reality.

Thirteen

It had been a good weekend. The oppressive weather had finally broken midday on Saturday with a sudden drenching thunderstorm. We'd just finished packing the picnic basket when the sky darkened and the wind picked up. The first thunderclap startled us all and we huddled together in semi-mock terror. The booming echo off the hills seemed amplified against the bowl of the lake. Mentally I checked off all the reasons we were safe in the cabin: lower than anything else around it, no aerial, protected against the side of the hill. But when the lightening streaked blue against a deep gray sky, some primal fear made me squeeze my children closer to me.

As suddenly as it arrived, the storm moved off, leaving in its wake clear fresh air. The rain diminished, then stopped entirely, only the dripping off the pine boughs kept alive the impression that it was still raining. We went out onto the porch and I suddenly noticed my laptop, still on. "Sweet Jesus," I muttered and went to check for lost data. I trusted surge protectors only so far. No, my morning's work was intact. Too close for comfort, I shut it down and unplugged it from the power strip.

The three of us managed to drag the canoe out from under the porch and down to the lake's edge with somewhat of a struggle, leaving a deep groove in the muddy grass to mark our passage. Then came the scramble to find three life preservers. Then to find dry towels. As ever, getting there was more effort than fun. Finally, though, we were launched and paddling off for as yet unexplored reaches of the lake. A smoky darkness in the eastern sky was all that was left of the rapidly moving storm.

Ben was in his yard as we paddled across the reach between our shore and his. He waved first and we waved back with enthusiasm. Apparently caught unawares by the sudden storm, he'd hung out his week's washing. The polo shirts, khaki shorts, and blue jeans hung limp and dripping. In between the odd cotton garments, the johnnies fluttered a little, the first to dry in the new clean air. They were the kind of thing an elderly parent might wear in a nursing home and I wondered if he had mentioned that one of his parents might be in one close by. I thought he had said that they lived in New Jersey, still in his childhood home.

"I like Ben." Lily kneeling in front of the bow bench, wielded the second paddle.

"Me too." Tim was riding amidships. "He knows a lot of good jokes."

Kneeling before the stern seat of the canoe, I gripped the hardwood paddle and dug it into the slightly choppy water, angling it to set our course. "Yeah," I said, "I like him too."

I stroked the paddle against the water, glad that the fresh breeze was behind us and we were easily cutting through the lake. My plan was to circumnavigate Ben's island and picnic on the West Side of the lake, where two or three picnic tables were set up in a natural grove.

Tim leaned over the gunwale, dragging a hand through the water. Below the rise of his life jacket I could see his thin little backbone, so prominent through his tanned skin, a more precious sight than the beauty of the mountains. He, like his sister, adored Sean. At eight, Tim was more inclined to worship than Lily, at almost ten. She was more open to the suggestion that Dad could make a mistake now and then. She was becoming, as the eldest and therefore the trailblazer, adept at negotiations. Tim had no idea what freedoms he would never have to fight for. Bedtime adjustments, sleep-overs, and clothing choices were battles already won.

Sean was less a stranger to children than I had been. A singleton, I had never had the experience of group games and negotiating the peaks and valleys of family life. I'd never had anyone else to blame for the spills or the missing shoe. Sean handled the commotion with ease, firm in his rules yet happy to play catch. I never doubted his love for his family, and that was why his reluctance to join us, even for the two days he might be able to, was what kept the bell chiming in the distance.

Right shoulder aching, I swapped sides, telling Lily to switch her paddle, too, and we continued stroking without a break in the rhythm.

The lake breeze felt so good after the days of stifling heat. The air cleared now of all humidity, I barely sweated as I paddled toward the West Side shore. Tim, as navigator, pointed out floating debris, leaves mostly, blown off the trees in the storm. A branch floated close by. Tim leaned over to push it away and I yelled a caution to him, perhaps a little more harshly than required. Tim threw me a startled look and sat back down. The branch bumped the side of the canoe.

"Sorry, Tim, I was afraid I'd lose you."

"Oh, Mom." He didn't need to finish his protest. He really wasn't in any danger of falling overboard. I reminded myself of Ben and flushed a little against the idea that our reactions might be born out of similar emotions.

"Come on, Lily, let's row the boat ashore." I began to paddle faster and was rewarded with the squeals of delight from Lily struggling to keep up. Our mad paddling threw up geysers of lake water, drenching us all. We made landfall in moments and Tim leapt out to pull us ashore.

The picnic benches were still wet from the storm, the sun never quite touching them through the canopy of thick pines. It didn't matter. Nothing mattered but enjoying ourselves.

I was exhausted and fell asleep easily moments after the kids did. The ride back from the West Side was a lot harder with the breeze in our face. It took half again as long to get home as it had to get to the picnic grove. I had been asleep for only an hour when I woke suddenly. I took stock of what might have wakened me, but no sounds alerted me to either of the kids being up. Everything was still inside the cabin. The moon without its nimbus of humidity was quite bright at that hour. I got up to pull the shade and then I heard it, Ben's musical homage. I left the shade up and lay back down on my bed. The by now familiar strains were intertwined with new variations.

As he played, I thought about my characters, letting his music influence my words. Finally, I got up and went out onto the porch, where I opened my laptop. The music repeated over and over, and I could tell he was experimenting, as each repetition was slightly different. Every now and then he stopped and I imagined him writing down what he was doing, notating his work. Once more he began at the beginning of the piece, this time going through it nonstop. To me, hearing it against the backdrop of my story, it sounded like poignancy set counterpoint to mischief, developed against an underlying grief.

Suddenly the sweet piano notes became discordant and then the discordant notes became the impotent banging of the keys. Then silence. Hearing Ben's frustration only underscored my recent sense of the tenuous grasp any of us have on happiness. I sat still, letting the emotions I'd created for my characters ebb away, only to be replaced by my own. I remembered something about nature abhorring a vacuum. Not for an instant did I have an empty place without some feeling—manufactured or real—curling up in it like a worm. My anger at Sean had dissipated along with the guilt I had harbored deep down over not having the kids at the lake in the first place. What replaced that were my doubts about Sean. What stopped those from being unbearable were my distracting thoughts about Ben.

Initially our conversations on the raft were made up of general chat, then weighty discussions of things nonpersonal and outside of our lives, like politics and crime. Soon enough there came anecdotes and we swapped family stories. I spoke of my kids, he spoke of his nieces and nephews. He made only oblique references to being "on the road," such that he might have been a salesman. As yet I held back about asking him if what Sean had said was true.

I tried to speak of Sean only in ordinary ways, as he fit into those family stories. I was a little embarrassed that I had grumbled about Sean leaving the kids. In dark moments I recognized the disloyalty and the danger of making Sean out to be a villain. Yet, as much as I didn't really want to paint Sean as all bad, I knew that I was beginning to see from a distance the cracks in our marriage, the distance between us now physical, measured in miles, while the distance at home was measured in hours of silence.

Ben made very few references to his wife, keeping that part of his life closely held. But lately there had been a shift in our relationship and I knew we were at that juncture where we would begin making revelations about ourselves, about those things we kept bottled up. In the quiet I resolved to gently loosen Ben's story from him.

The silence was profound. I closed my laptop and went back to bed.

Fourteen

Monday morning I hurried the kids through breakfast and charged up the rutted drive to the main road around to the West Side and to Camp Winetonka.

"I love you, have a great time. I'll pick you up at four!" and I was back in the big car and away. I didn't look in the rearview mirror to see if they were standing forlornly abandoned or happily rushing off to meet new friends. I didn't need to know that. I just needed to get to the grocery store and back to work.

I had spent quality time with them all weekend, playing and eating and joking and falling instantly asleep. Now I was desperate to get past the midway point in my novel and on toward the end. I always likened the first half of a novel to climbing up a hill. Sometimes getting there took a long time, but once there, at the turning point, at the crisis, everything began to come tumbling down, moving under its own weight to conclusion. I was a little tired of pushing this novel up the hill, and I wanted very much to be finished with it. I had less gotten away from my daily distractions than I seemed to have multiplied them by leaving Providence.

I didn't want to take the time to drive to the next town and to the Big G, so I pulled into the parking lot of the mom-and-pop grocery store, Abair's Market. Their prices were a bit higher, but they specialized in good vegetables and fresh-baked bread. The floor was aged pine and the shelves held the staples of three generations, Postum and Wheatena, Hostess Cupcakes, and Poland Spring Water. I always felt slowed down as I walked through the four aisles which made up the whole of the store. Without Muzak to move me along, or to influence my choices, I actually stopped and thought about what I was buying. Restocked with peanut butter, wheat bread, a bag of oranges, and juice, I stood at the old-fashioned register, with its three rows of metal keys, and stared out the window at the view past the parking lot as Mrs. Abair tallied my purchases. My earlier sense of hurry had relaxed to a more contemplative mood. It was still only nine o'clock, plenty of time to devote to the novel before I needed to go get the kids.

I'd spent longer running errands than I had planned and so skipped my run and ate lunch while working. I lifted my head up from the screen only to noodle a phrase around, staring with oblivious eyes across the water toward Ben's very quiet cabin. I was barely aware of the voices coming up from the beach, children's playful shrieks, mothers' scoldings, a radio talk show host's garbled voice. It all existed outside of my screen, nothing to do with me. On this Monday, I managed to get into the dream and the outside world faded away.

When I finally pulled myself out of my trance, I was taken completely aback. I would be late picking up the kids on their very first day. "Oh shit." I fumbled to find my Birkenstocks under my chair without looking, as I hit CTRL-F and SAVE without shutting off the computer. I was at the car before the screen door slammed behind me. I peeled out of the dirt drive and onto the pavement with an embarrassing spin of wheels.

I was greeted at the gate to Camp Winetonka by two scowling children. They climbed into the car without speaking, and without arguing about who was going to ride "shotgun." I felt my heart sink at the sight of their frowns.

"So?" I finally ventured after getting the monster car turned around. "How was it?"

Their giggles had me glancing in the rearview mirror. Phony scowls gave way to laughter. "We love it . . . we had so much fun . . . we got to . . ." The grin on my face was as much relief as anything else. It was Sean's trick. Pretending to be angry or disappointed and then bursting into laughter.

"So, I should cancel the rest of your week?"

"No!" They bounced on the backseat, "We have a sleep-over on Thursday! We wanta go camping!"

"Well, you don't seem to like it very much . . ." Two could play at this game, but I let it go easily and headed for Tony's Pizza.

Tim talked me into buying two pizzas. "Let's get Ben over and we can play Trivial Pursuit."

"I don't know if he has plans, Tim."

"He never has plans."

"How am I supposed to let him know we want him to come over? What if he isn't outside?"

Lily rolled her eyes in exasperation. "Mommy, we don't have a phone, but he does."

"You'll go far in life, Lily May McCarthy."

I paid for the pizzas and asked to borrow the restaurant's phone book. I wrote Ben's number on a napkin, which made me think of a bar pickup.

We got a double cheese pizza and one with pepperoni and green peppers for more adult tastes. Even if Ben couldn't make it, the kids could take cold leftover pizza for lunch tomorrow. Lily rode shotgun and took the napkin from my hand, taking it upon herself to issue the invitation.

"Ben, this is Lily McCarthy from across the lake. We have pizza and we need you to eat the one with pepperoni. And we need you to be the brown circle for Trivial Pursuit. Okay?" She listened intently, bottom lip caught between her sharp top teeth. "Start paddling. We'll be home in—how long, Mom?"

"Ten minutes."

"Ten minutes." She listened again, "Good," and pushed the off button. She'd make a great hostess someday.

"So?"

"He's got ice cream."

It was almost five o'clock. "Hey, let's call Daddy right now." I pushed the number for Sean's office and got Eleanor. "Mr. McCarthy, please."

"Who shall I say is calling?"

I forbore to correct her with *whom* and answered with just the tiniest of proprietary flavor, "Mrs. McCarthy."

"Oh. Hi!" I was greeted with Eleanor's most saccharine rendition of long-lost friend. "He's right here, Cleo."

"Thanks." I twisted a lock of Lily's curly hair around my forefinger while I waited for Sean to get to the phone.

"Hi, honey." He sounded pleased to be called, and I felt myself giving up some of my lingering annoyance.

"We're all here, I'm going to see if I can get this thing on speaker." I pressed the right buttons, and Sean's voice came out of the phone set as if he was hidden in the glove compartment, but audible to all of us. The kids chattered about camp, overriding each other until I began to direct, giving each one the opportunity to tell a story. Sean made the appropriate remarks and then asked to be taken off speaker.

"I'm glad you called early, Clee, I'm out tonight and I knew I'd miss your call."

"Aren't you getting a little tired of dinner meetings?"

"Actually, it beats being home alone."

"I won't remind you that you weren't alone until recently. Your second-shift activities aren't new."

"It's business, Cleo."

"I don't suggest that it's not." I turned my face toward my open window. "Are you still coming on Friday?"

"Yes. But it'll be late."

"I expected that." I made no attempt to keep the sarcasm out of my voice. I wasn't above letting Sean know I was still annoyed with him, even as things were working out. "Say goodbye to the kids, I've got to get this pizza home." I pushed him back onto speaker and then, goodbyes said, off.

Fifteen

Ben brought the ice cream, chocolate chip with only one serving missing. I served the pizzas on the screened porch, citronella candles burning all around us against the mosquitoes, turning the dinner into a picnic. We polished off the two pizzas and I reconciled myself to making peanut-butter-and-jelly sandwiches in the morning. We played the junior version of Trivial Pursuit, Tim and Lily neck and neck for wedges until the last toss, when Tim pulled off his first-ever win against his sister. Ben and I had both been remarkably stupid. Lily was a little suspicious of Ben, yet perfectly happy to imagine I knew very little trivia.

After a long, hard day at camp, neither kid was unwilling to call it a night and so, with only the most pro forma of protests, they trundled off to bed with a quick good-night kiss. I was almost as nonplussed as Ben when Lily spontaneously hugged him good-night as if he had always been part of the routine.

Ben came with me to the kitchen as I pulled the unopened bottle of chardonnay out of the refrigerator. When I turned around he had the binoculars off the hook and was looking out over the lake toward his cabin.

"You get a good view from here."

I confess, a little guilty flush touched my cheeks. "Grace left them here. I like watching the birds. There are so many." It was lame, but I felt compelled to say it.

"I've got a nice amateur birder's book. I'll lend it to you." He hung the binoculars back on the hook. I handed him a glass, aware of his slightly amused smile.

We sat side by side on the iron glider, facing the water. The twilight was nearly done, only a rim of light still glowed in the West.

"Thanks for the dinner. You're very thoughtful of an old hermit."

"Not many people describe themselves that way."

"I suppose." Ben leaned back on the glider, making it move a little beneath us. He closed his eyes and breathed a settling sigh. "Mmmm, it's nice to sit here. We always meant to build a screened porch on our place, but somehow never did. We were always forced inside at night by the bugs. There were a lot of things we meant to do. Like install electricity."

There was that oblique reference, *we,* not *I.* I took the opening, as tiny as it was. "You said you and your wife lived here year-round?"

"Sort of. It was our home base, I think I told you. After my . . . ummm . . . professional setback I winterized it, and then when Talia came along I added the back bedroom. I did most of it myself, see," and he put out his hand where a scar I had noticed lay just the other side of his thumb. "Almost put paid to my career with that little mistake." Once again, Ben had skillfully moved the topic from the personal to the amusingly anecdotal, but then he reversed himself. "Actually, that was before I was married, when I was living alone out here, almost as hermit-like as I am now. Somehow nearly cutting my thumb off awakened me to how much I really wanted to stay in the music business, how much I loved to play."

"Why do you call yourself a hermit? Hermits are antisocial or religious fanatics, aren't they?"

"Or both. They are people who grapple with demons."

"Are you grappling now?" The wine had propelled me beyond ordinary polite caution.

"Yes."

"Can you speak of them?"

Ben took my free hand in both of his and lifted my knuckles to his lips. I wasn't alarmed, and although there was an element of the sexual in the act, the touch of his lips to my hand was most certainly a gesture of apology. "No. Not even to you, not yet."

"Okay." I withdrew my hand and gripped my wineglass with both.

"Cleo, when I can speak of it, I will speak to you."

"Ben, you owe me nothing in the way of explanation. Your life is yours, I'm just a nosy neighbor."

This time he simply took my hand. "I love this place. It's where I feel . . ." Ben didn't finish his sentence, so I prodded a little. "Where you feel what, Ben?"

I could see him clearly in the light coming from the kitchen, although the porch was dark, the citronella candles having guttered out long ago. Ben's face was smooth, except for the crinkles around his eyes and that natural looseness which comes with age at his jaw. There was experience described by those little ocular lines and in the grooves outlining his mouth like parentheses, which deepened as his lips compressed.

"You can tell me." Now I did press, just a little more.

"Where I feel she's still with me." His voice was so soft I almost didn't hear him.

He left soon after that. I wanted to walk with him down to the canoe, but he shook his head no. "You'll get eaten alive, Cleo. Stay put." He touched my cheek, cupping it gently in his long hand. "Thank you so much for having Lily call me. It means a lot."

His gentle touch had brought strange tears to my eyes, and I felt almost bereaved, as if there should have been more said. I shut the screen door and watched him as he pushed off, his paddle in the water the only sound now.

Sixteen

Tuesday morning I was more efficient about dropping the kids at camp and getting back to the lake before nine o'clock. I had a new pot of coffee going and my computer booted up within minutes and got to work. It didn't go as well as it had been, and I kept looking up from my screen to stare out at the lake in the July sun. I couldn't seem to block out the voices of the beachgoers, the shrieks and scoldings seemed intrusive this morning. The perpetual sound of talk radio as broadcast over a too-loud boom box annoyed the hell out of me. I turned up the volume in my Discman, but the batteries were running out and I kept getting a buzzing in my left ear which tickled my eardrum. I tore off the headphones and stood up. I'd only been at work for an hour, forty-five minutes. Hardly a day's worth. Less than a page and a half of new stuff.

I knew that it wasn't that the distractions were any worse than the day before, it was my inner agitation which kept my characters from working. An agitation born of last night's conversation with Ben. There was a lingering sense, as I seemed often to have, that I'd said too much and Ben had said too little. Caving in to frustration, I pulled on my bathing suit and grabbed a towel. Sometimes facing the distraction negates it. I headed for the beach.

I came up behind Glenda and Carol, ensconced, as usual, in low-slung beach chairs, visors and big sunglasses masking their faces, making them look vaguely E.T.-ish. Their multiple children gamboled about and I had not a prayer to figure out which children belonged to which woman. I thought I understood Carol to have the more, but I might have been mistaken. I was certain Glenda had the oldest. Suddenly in their midst without the protective coloration of my own children, I felt out of the circle. Surely this must have been what our ancestors experienced trying to join other family groups around fire pits. As expected, the verbal challenges came quickly.

"So, Cleo, not working today?"

"I am, I just needed a little break."

"How do your children like that camp?" Glenda managed to turn up her lips, the only visible moving part on her face, in a condescending smile.

"Well, they're having a wonderful time, doing very interesting things. Learning new skills." I let my own sunglass-disguised gaze linger over the tussle two of the children were having over a Gameboy. "They're learning to ride and properly manage watercraft." I'd seen two older boys in a canoe the other day, fooling around and not wearing life jackets. I had no idea if those boys belonged to these women, but I liked making the point.

"So, when's your husband coming? Friday?" Zing.

"Yes. Friday night." Zap.

"It's difficult for some husbands to make the trip every weekend, I certainly know. But I wouldn't hear of Carl not coming every weekend. After a week of kids kids kids, it's my saving grace." Carol smoothed more sun block on her stubby legs. "Of course, with the kids all day at camp, you don't have that problem."

How did these women know my business so well they could take shots at it?

"Yes, although I rather enjoy my time with my children. They're good companions."

I got up and strode into the water. The July sun had heated the shallows into bathwater, but the lake dropped off suddenly and the deep water was cold. I thought about making for the raft, but didn't.

It was too early in the day to do that. I swam back to the group, intending to towel off and go back to work.

"Have some lemonade," Glenda held up a plastic cup to me as I rejoined the group.

Maybe I'd passed muster, Glenda's condescending smile had grown genuine while I swam.

"Thanks." I took the cup from Glenda and sat on my towel. "Have you been in yet?"

Both women shook their heads. I don't think I'd actually ever seen them in the water.

I accepted the plastic cup of lemonade and sat down, happy to have some useless chat, thinking that the sniping was over. I was wrong.

"So, how is Ben Turner these days? You seem to be very friendly with him."

I dripped a little of the cold lemonade down my front, and I paused to wipe it with my fingers before responding. "Ben is fine." I wanted to ask them if they spent all their time spying on me, but I knew that the high road was better with women like these. Any protest and I'd be more interesting to them.

"Grace used to be friendly with Ben, too. Before the accident. Actually, she was a great friend of his wife's. Poor thing. You know that she was a world-famous flautist? Or is it flutist? Anyway, she once did a benefit concert for the local hospital. The lake residents sponsored it. Donated the proceeds to the hospital." Carol's voice trailed off dramatically.

I remembered clearly Grace saying she really didn't know Ben, describing Ben as a loner. Hardly the great friend of Carol's description. I had to believe that Carol was making noise out of some weird lakeside feud, trying, by my known friendship with Grace, to win me to the side on which Glenda and Carol were aligned. Intimating that if Grace was one of them, hence, by association, I should be, too. What bitches.

"They never had children. Now, of course, we can guess why."

"No, I can't guess why." I know my voice was a little sharp.

"They were having trouble." Glenda actually cupped her hands over her mouth and mouthed "trouble" as if it had been the word "cancer" in my grandmother's mouth. Or "Negro." Or any of those words not spoken aloud in polite company.

"What kind of trouble?" I demanded quite loudly.

"Well, I heard they were having difficulty with her traveling so much. You know, her concerts took her all over the world. She was in great demand and he wouldn't go with her."

"I was told by someone who knew, that there were drugs involved." Again Glenda mouthed the words "drugs involved." I assumed because of the kids being within earshot.

"What did happen?" I had to ask. I had wanted Ben to tell me, but I couldn't pass up the opportunity to know for myself.

"Well, no one really knows what the circumstances were. Just that she hit her head and never regained consciousness. And that they'd been seen to argue in the parking lot of a restaurant. So . . ." she flipped a hand palm up in the classic attitude of foregone conclusion.

Glenda snapped her head around to yell at her kids, interrupting the flow of the story, effectively ending it. "Any rate, she's been gone a year now and he's still walking the earth, unrepentant."

"Oh, no. You can't say that." But Glenda wasn't interested in any challenge to public opinion about Ben Turner. She lurched up and to the water's edge to shout at the kids. Carol screwed the cap to the sun block back on and made no comment.

I thanked them for the lemonade and walked home.

I sat in my wet bathing suit and pounded out sentences, putting words in my characters' mouths, smoothing out the disturbance in my heart by feeding it to them. And all the time I was typing, I kept thinking about Ben, about how I could not imagine him in domestic violence.

I heard a sound like a music box, one hand playing the piano. A gentle theme, uncluttered, pure. Joined then by a bass chord, consolidating the motif, giving it force and structure. I hadn't heard this before. It was new, daylight born. Sweeter, happier, than what Ben had composed before.

Seventeen

Grace and Joanie had sent not one but four postcards from Tuscany, which I picked up at the Cameo Lake post office's general-delivery window. The three were to be read in order, and duly numbered. Like a comic book narrative, the cards spelled out Grace and Joanie's adventures.

"Eat" said the first. "Drink," said the second. "Making lots of Merry," said the third. A fourth, real message, joined the trio: "Having a wonderful time, glad you are where you are. We will regale you with lots of stories when we get back. In the meantime, we are thinking of you on your sabbatical and expecting to read something brilliant when we get back. Okay? Still enjoying your solitude? Love and kisses from the girls."

Solitude. I could only imagine what Grace's reaction would be when she found out exactly what had become of my solitude. I climbed back into the car and pointed it toward the camp.

I hadn't gone out to the raft at noon. I told myself I was finally in the groove, but the truth was, I wasn't sure I could face Ben today. I was trying not to be troubled by the harsh criticisms of my morning's companions, but it wasn't easy. It was clear that at least some residents of the lakeside community held Ben responsible for his wife's accident. The overtone of domestic violence was hard to miss. But I knew that whatever had happened, it could not have been deliberate. I just knew that. It occurred to me that maybe he'd rejected their sympathy in some way and that was what made them so bitter. No one likes their compassion turned away and Ben was so private, it might be construed as hostility.

I saw Ben climb aboard the raft. I was still in my suit, thoroughly dry by now. I sighed and bent back over my keyboard. When I looked back up, he was gone.

I wouldn't let the kids talk me into pizza for a second night. I'd bought pork chops and had a craving for a normal Tuesday-night dinner. Chops and rice and green beans. The Big G had a sale on frozen pies, so I bought a blueberry one.

"Can we invite Ben?"

"Lily, we can't do that every night. It's a little too much. Besides, I only bought three chops."

"But we like him and he likes us."

"Sweetie, just because you like someone doesn't mean you have to invite them to dinner every night. Too much of a good thing spoils it."

"Tomorrow?"

"We'll see."

"We need to bring our sleeping bags on Thursday." Tim was very excited about the prospect of a camp-out. We'd done some camping as a family, and he'd slept out in the backyard any number of times, so this wasn't his first experience of sleeping outdoors. But it was the first time he'd do it without the option of climbing into Mom and Dad's double bag when the noises got loud or the air too cold.

Lily was more ho-hum about the idea. She'd made several girl-friends and viewed the camp-out as more of an outdoor sleep-over. I saw her slip several bottles of half-used nail polish in her backpack Wednesday morning, afraid of forgetting to bring them on Thursday, I supposed.

I was oddly uncomfortable with the idea of being alone in the cabin. I was quite used to their being there with me at night now. We were in an established and happy routine. I toyed with the idea of inviting Ben over and then backed away from it. It seemed just a little too inappropriate without the chaperonage of the kids. It was possible that it might even be construed as more than a simple dinner invitation. It would be hard to be alone with Ben in a different context than the raft, the borders would somehow be widened and less clear. If we were in different circumstances, if we were equally unattached, it would be a natural outgrowth of what we had begun in neighborly acquaintance: a hike, a ride, a shared family meal. But I wasn't unattached, and neither was Ben.

By Wednesday morning the discomfort of Glenda and Carol's comments had dissipated, leaving only a slightly bad taste in my mouth. I got the kids off to camp and headed back without stopping anywhere. I had already taken my run in the half-hour before the kids had to be up. The early morning was my time alone on the lake, uncluttered by catty women and plastic beach toys.

This morning the only other person awake at six was Ben Turner, bent from the waist and tossing bread crumbs to the ducks. He was intermittently visible through the screen of undergrowth outlining the trail as I jogged along. Ben saw me as I broke through the brush and sprinted along the last twenty yards of lakefront. He stretched upright and waved. I waved back, slowed to my cooling out walk, and waved again as he continued to watch.

"Hey, Grayson, nice form!" Ben cupped his hands over his mouth.

"Thanks, Turner. Alert the Olympics for me!" I couldn't help but grin at the mischievous flattery.

"You look gold-medal-qualifying to me!" Ben waved again and headed indoors.

I continued walking; my shoes off, I put my feet in the cool morning water. I was still grinning. A little flirting felt kind of nice right now. Beyond that, I was glad to have the equilibrium between Ben and me restored, even if the off-balance was only in my own head.

*   *   *

It had gotten hot again. More overheated than hungry at lunchtime, I changed into my suit and headed to the lakefront without stopping for lunch. My usual black maillot was smelling pretty nasty from repeated dunkings in the lake and being left to dry over the back of a chair. I found my other suit, the dark blue one I had bought when Sean and I went to Barbados a couple of years back. It was more abbreviated that my other one, thin strings held up the plunging front and the back scooped down to just above my derriere. I remembered Sean's wolf whistle at the first sight of it. I remembered him untying the strings. I had a moment of carnal anticipation of Sean's Friday-night arrival.

Ben made it to the raft at the same time I did. A cascade of lake water surged from his lanky body as he lifted himself up, bending back down to offer me a courtier's hand up. As he did, I was aware of the view he had down my suit front. I looked up to catch him, but his eyes were averted politely from stealing a peak. A rogue disappointment licked at me. I could use a little validation of my attractiveness right about now.

We flopped down on the raft deck, both on our backs, our arms folded beneath our heads. We were perpendicular, me east-west, Ben north-south. A passing airplane or bird would have seen us T-shaped, my head at Ben's waist.

"Had lunch yet?"

"No, I was too hot to eat." I rolled over, cheek on arms.

Ben rolled over, "Do you like tuna?"

"Are you offering?"

"Yes. As long as you don't mind a messy environment."

"Well, we can always eat outside."

"Ha ha."

We lay a few more minutes on the raft, just quietly enjoying the soft motion of it, lulling us both until Ben slapped the deck and proclaimed it lunchtime.

My body was superheated by the baking sun and the water as I

plunged into it was shockingly cold. We both charged for the opposite shore, not exactly racing, but it looked like a race nonetheless.
Ben's height was the determiner over speed, though, and he climbed
out ahead of me.

"If you want to rinse off, the outdoor shower's over there." He
pointed toward the left side of the cottage. "I'll get you a clean towel."

A pull chain controlled the flow of the cold-water shower. A bottle of Pert shampoo, slightly gooey with spiderwebs and the detritus
of trees, sat on the wooden shelf. It didn't seem like a man's shampoo,
and I realized it must be left over from Talia. I squirted a little in my
hand and washed my hair, forgetting for a moment I would get it wet
again when I went back.

Ben had given me a huge pink bathsheet, which I wrapped
around my hips Polynesian style. It actually looked nice with the hal-
ter top of the bathing suit. Quite suitable for lunch with a friend. I
combed my hair with my fingertips, crunching the waves into shape.

I followed a little path of bluestone flags to the back door. The
screen door stuck a little and I banged it with my hand. Ben stood at
the sink, looking at me with a faint smile on his face. "Whole wheat
okay?"

"Fine."

Through the archway I could see the main room of the small cottage. At its center a piano, a baby grand. I couldn't imagine how they
had gotten it out here. Barge? Piled on the closed cover of the black
instrument were tapes, a tape player, headphones, notebooks, a half-
empty coffee mug, two kerosene lamps, and a cat.

"Don't go in there without a hard hat."

I laughed and went in anyway. The piano faced the French doors
which overlooked the lake, and, as I could see, Grace's house. Ben had
the same view of me as I had of him.

Ben's winterized cottage was quite different from the other cabins. Sheetrocked walls and polished wood floors, fitted screens and
the tschotkes of permanent living. An upholstered chair where
another cat lounged stood in front of a cold fireplace.

"I always wanted a cat. My husband is allergic." I squatted down to scratch the orange tabby's chin. On a side table was a collection of framed photos. An elderly couple, she in blue, he in a dark suit, a formal portrait, perhaps a fiftieth wedding anniversary photo.

"Those are my parents. Last year. No. The year before." Ben corrected himself as if it mattered.

A second five-by-seven photo was of a band, circa the late sixties. They all wore long hair, one in wire-rim glasses, all in faded T-shirts and tattered jeans.

"Is this you?" I pointed to a thin boy, his rich brown hair falling in waves around his face. A sweet face, but razor sharp.

"Yeah. We were going to be the next Rolling Stones. My first garage band. The Ultimate Indignities. I played with them in high school, all Grateful Dead and Creedence Clearwater Revival, but we broke up after graduation. We all went our separate ways, different schools. Different interests."

"Where did you go?"

"To the New England Conservatory of Music."

"What happened to the others?"

"Well, Cliff, the guy with the granny glasses, is a banker. John, the one with the guitar, is a pediatrician in Boston. Stewie, our bassist, died of lung cancer three years ago. Pretty much the national average for garage bands after high school." Ben had picked up the slightly dusty photo to point out who was who. He dusted it off with his T-shirt and set it down.

"Sean says that you were a member of Interior Angles." It seemed at last the right moment to ask. "Is he right?"

Ben nodded, a little shy smile lifting one corner of his mouth. "Yeah."

"The only rock concert I ever went to was one of yours."

"I wish I'd known. I'd have tossed you a piece of clothing." He alluded to the band's signature behavior, peeling bits of clothing off and throwing them to the screaming fans.

"I'd still have it if you did. I loved your music. I still do."

"We weren't bad. I think that if things had turned out differently, we might have evolved with the times and still been around. Like

Santana or Steely Dan. But, you know, the truth is I just wasn't cut
out for it. I hated that whole lifestyle."

"Sex, drugs, and rock-and-roll?"

"Something like that." Ben shrugged. "More that I really disliked
the constant travel. I'm too much of a homebody to get off on the
relentless night after night, city after city. And, honestly, I hated the
whole fame thing. I couldn't visit my parents or my brothers without
some asshole photographer following me. Anything normal I did
became distorted by the press. And I was out of the studio too much. I
like writing music. That's what's fun. Not prancing in front of an
audience."

To forestall my asking, he picked up the third framed photo.
"This is Talia."

The candid picture was taken close up, her face in one-quarter
profile, her eyes, even in the shading of the photo were clear light
blue, artfully lined above and below so that they stood out as the fea-
ture one's own eyes were drawn to, and away from a small, thin-
lipped mouth which was not smiling. Her fair hair was pulled back,
and I thought she looked like someone who was a product of private
schools and privilege.

"She was very lovely, Ben."

"Yes. She was beautiful." He cleared his throat a little, as if
uncomfortable with the conversation, then, "That picture's from her
debut album. I cut it down to fit the frame." Ben set the picture back
down on the side table. I noticed that it hadn't needed any dusting.

When he leaned past me to replace the photo, there was a fraction
of pause in his movement, an infinitesimal hesitation in him. A slight
smile on his lips, as if of recognition, as he caught the scent of the
shampoo in my still damp hair. Then he straightened up and gestured
toward the French doors. "Let's eat outside, the porch is cool." Maybe
I imagined the pause.

I needed the bathroom just then and Ben pointed to the hallway
off the living room. "First door on your left." More photos adorned
the short hallway of the addition, mostly of Ben and Talia, and groups
of teens I could only assume were the nieces and nephews. I could see

into a small bedroom, unmade bed and folded laundry piled on a chest of drawers. Next to it, the closed door of what must be the second, added-on, room. Hunting for a fresh roll of toilet paper, I discovered a half-used box of tampons under the sink and I thought, How sad. How long did one keep little reminders of daily life on the shelf after a death? Would I throw out Sean's toiletries or keep them in their accustomed place forever?

It would have been so easy to abandon further work to the hot, sultry afternoon, stay where I was on Ben's cool porch. We talked of movies and books, politics and places. Then, already emboldened by having asked him about being in the band, I asked him to tell me more about his life as a rock star.

He was a little reluctant, and I might have felt bad asking him about it, but finally he nodded. "All right. What do you want to know?"

"Why the name Interior Angles?

"Rolling Stones was taken."

"No, you know what I mean."

"Finger in a dictionary." He took a bite of sandwich and passed me the potato chips. "What else do you want to know, Ms. Writer?"

"The whole experience, how did it start and why did it end?" Having asked the question, I suddenly had a vague memory of the Interior Angles' breakup. Some tickling in my memory about a bad end. I almost withdrew my question, but Ben started talking.

"Okay. Here's the short version. Interior Angles enjoyed a meteoric rise to fame after ten years of hard work. We'd managed to become a sought-after opening act for the really big groups, even once the Grateful Dead. I'm sure you can relate to instant fame."

"Yeah, after a dozen years of struggle, it always looks instant."

"Exactly. Well, Artie Sheldon came into our lives and we felt like Jason and the Golden Fleece. What we didn't see was that we were the fleece. Anyway, we hit the right promoter, the right label, and the right song. You might remember it, 'Frozen Heart'?"

The melancholy tune immediately came to mind. I nodded, but didn't interrupt.

"Anyway 'Frozen Heart' made us a household name. We got tons of airplay, good venues, lots of money. The album sold well and we hit it big. Instant acclaim, a Grammy, public recognition, paparazzi, the whole nine yards. All based on one song on an otherwise mediocre album.

"And, of course, the record execs wanted a clone. So I acted the whore and for almost as long as it took for Interior Angles to strike it big, we stayed there as I pumped out mediocre hooks on hummable tunes. Stan Allen, you probably remember him by his stage name, Stash, kept telling me to shut up and enjoy the perks. For him it was women, for Todd, the bassist, it was drugs. Kevin, my writing partner and our drummer, well, he kept his passions pretty close to the chest. He didn't want the world to know he was gay. Thought that it was counter to the image Interior Angles projected of womanizing rock stars." Ben chewed his bottom lip a little, "Truth is, he was fundamentally and musically more suited for Andrew Lloyd Webber than the Angles. But it was his decision to protect himself." Ben offered me another glass of iced tea. I shook my head to decline.

"Anyway, we played the part well. Kevin and I churned out the songs, only occasionally introducing real music. We traveled so much that none of us had homes. We were rootless troubadours, the recording studio seemed the only constant in our lives.

"It came to an end rather abruptly." Ben leaned over to pour himself more tea. The way he held the glass I imagined he wished it was something stronger. He no longer engaged my glance in his narrative, but stared out toward the raft, scenes playing in his memory which he then selected to share with me.

"We were in Buffalo. It was the millionth night of a two-million-city tour. Or at least it felt that way. We'd been on the tour for almost a year. As we almost always did, we hung out in Kevin's suite. Artie used to complain that we all requested separate rooms but then stayed in one. We were due at the venue at nine-thirty, so we had a couple of hours to kill. Todd and Stash were doing lines of coke. We had reached that point in our careers where coke was like, well, Coke. Inevitable and available. Kevin was in the bathroom taking a shower. I remember thinking that he was taking an awfully long time, even for Kevin, who was notoriously vain. I was watching the national news in a desperate attempt to catch up with world events. This was about at the time of the Iran-Contra scandal.

"Suddenly there was an unholy crash from the bathroom. Assuming that Kevin had slipped, I went to the bathroom door and knocked, 'Hey, Kev, you okay?' Nothing except the sound of the shower. I looked back at Todd and Stash, but they were mid-snort. I banged on the door once more and when Kevin didn't answer, I pushed the unlocked door open. I was hit in the face with built up steam. Something was blocking the door and I assumed it was towels. I pushed hard, and squeezed through. Only it wasn't towels blocking the door, it was Kevin. He had hanged himself on the shower rod and it had collapsed under his weight. The crashing I'd heard was him falling.

"Most of what happened next is still a blur. I know I screamed for the others to call nine-one-one. I remember trying to get the rope, his bathrobe belt, from around his neck. I remember telling him over and over he couldn't do this to me, he couldn't die. But what stays with me most are two things: Stash and Todd scrambling to hide the drugs before they called for help, and Artie's reaction."

Ben set his glass back down on the picnic table and ran his hands through his recently trimmed dark hair. His movement made me notice a tracery of gray along his temple. "Artie never once expressed grief or surprise or outrage. He paced and lamented the idea of canceling the concert. He talked us into going on anyway." Ben affected a stentorian voice. " 'The show must go on, it's what Kevin would want.' We were so stunned, it made sense. We watched the paramedics take Kevin out of the suite in a body bag. We gave our statements to the police, and then we went to our limo and made it to the concert only an hour late. We could hear the fans screaming over the opening band: Angles! Angles! We were deafened by the cheering as we paraded onto the stage. One, two, three of us. I pulled aside the drummer from the opening act and asked him to sit in.

"I was okay for about five minutes. Halfway through the first song I stopped playing. The crowd was so noisy, I don't think they noticed, but Stash did. He shot me a look of confusion, like he didn't get why I might be upset. I started playing again. About twenty minutes into the set I did the unforgivable. I walked off the stage.

"Do you know what was most bizarre? None of us had asked the question: Why had Kevin committed suicide?" Ben squinted toward the raft and then looked at me. "I walked off the stage and out of my career. Artie and the record company sued and got most of my money as well as all my Interior Angles music, and I was back to working as a sessions musician."

"And that's when you came here?"

"Yes. I needed time to regroup. To face one of those demons I told you about the other evening. In the sixties we would have said I needed to find myself, but the fact is, I was depressed and I needed time to decide how I wanted to go on. I tried a little alcoholism, but I never took to it. So I came here and got to work winterizing the house. Nearly lost my thumb and that made me realize that I wanted to stay in music, but not as a performer. At least, not that kind of performer." Ben picked up an Oreo and twisted it apart, then looked at me watching him and put it back together with a sheepish smile.

It was getting on and we both had work to return to. But there was one more question my probing curiosity wouldn't let lie. "Ben?"

"What?"

"Did you ever find out why Kevin did it? Was it AIDS?"

Ben shrugged and sighed. "No. Actually, it wasn't. The truth is, I really don't know exactly why he did it. I've tested a lot of theories, but they all seem to reflect how *I* was feeling then. How *I* was feeling, not Kevin."

"How was that?"

"Trapped, enslaved by the very thing we'd wanted."

Eventually I got up to go. I had taken up too much of his time as it was, and I apologized for it.

"Let's call it even, I've kept you from your work. Shirkers unite."

"Sounds like a name for your next rock group."

"Not in this lifetime."

In life, one almost never makes true eye contact. Too much is required. There were whole days I know my husband never looked directly at me. He didn't have to. He knew me so well. Ben looked into my eyes as I handed him the pink bathsheet. I looked back and we smiled, some connection suddenly made. When I write such scenes in my novels, there is always a deep significance to the looks. In real life, I was unclear exactly what our eyes had said to each other. All I knew, as I stepped into the cold lake water, was that I had no intention of ever sitting on the beach with those women again. My allegiance was with Ben Turner.

I was back at work quickly, a glance at the clock had told me there was no time to lose. I had less than two hours before I had to go get the kids. My days seemed so brief, especially if I let myself lollygag over lunch. And now I was dallying, thinking about what had just happened, pleased to have pierced something of Benson Turner's armor.

The image kept coming back to me, an impression rather than an observation, of Ben leaning over me, pausing as he catches the scent of his wife in my hair. There had been no reaction, nothing recordable, but the movement, or cessation of movement, as one would do if star- tled. I rolled the imagery around and thought about using it in my work-in-progress, but there wasn't yet a way to fit it in. There would be, though. Maybe not in this book, but in some as yet unimagined work. My observer self had taken notes while my physical self had very much liked the nearness of Ben's reach as he replaced the photo.

Eighteen

"You're an asshole!"

"*You* are!"

Boys' voices shattered my focus. I looked up to see two canoes, side by side, each bearing two boys, paddles raised in some contest. As I watched, it was clear they were each trying to capsize the boat of the other. None of the boys was wearing a life jacket. I pulled Grace's binoculars off the hook and took a better look. I guessed them to be in early adolescence, maybe thirteen or so. I thought I could pick out two of them as the sons of my erstwhile beach companions. I mentally shuddered to think of my own son behaving like that. Foul language, playful as it was, echoed against the buffer of hillside and came right at me. I scanned the beachfront to see if I could pick out any one who might be their parents, but the beach, at noon, was clear.

I watched as the canoes rocked violently, one boy in each standing, legs spread to keep the boat steady, paddles athwart like Robin Hood and Little John on the bridge. I couldn't tell from their language whether it was really play or if there was some antagonistic action happening in the middle of the lake.

"Stupid idiots." I said aloud, lowering the binoculars and averting my eyes from what was easily a tragedy in the making.

"Knock it off, you kids!"

Ben's voice, angry and authoritative at the same time, startled me into looking up again. I picked up the binoculars and watched the drama as Ben, in his Old Town, speed-stroked to where the boys were.

"Are you complete idiots? Where are your life jackets? And where the hell are your parents?" Through the powerful lens, I could see Ben's shoulders working furiously as he approached the two canoes. The voices were oddly delayed, I could see their lips move, then the yelling reached my ears.

"Back off, mister." One of the more aggressive boys raised his paddle. "You can't tell us what to do."

"You want to drown, do it on the other side of the lake. Get away from here." Ben had backstroked to a halt, close to but out of reach of the pair.

"Fuck off, wife-killer." With that last volley, the standing boys sat down and, with eloquent disdain, paddled away.

Ben remained where he was, paddle across his knees. I lowered the binoculars, not wanting to see his face.

Ben didn't meet me on the raft that afternoon. I stayed only a little while, not wanting to look like I was waiting for him. The kids were at their overnight camp-out and I had what seemed like acres of unrestricted time to work. I planned to use the half an hour I lay on the raft to imagine the next scene, to run bits of dialogue through my head as the late-July sun dried my old black suit.

Half-expecting Ben, I had a hard time bringing my concentration to the level I needed, but it was the other thing diverting my thoughts which I had the hardest time shoving aside, Sean's sudden elusiveness.

I'd called the office yesterday afternoon after picking up the kids and the receptionist had said Sean was gone for the day. I'd called home, no answer. I called Alice and she professed no insider knowledge of Sean's plans. I hadn't thought much more about it, except that he wasn't home by seven-thirty, and I might have shrugged the call off except the answering machine wasn't on. I went back to the car and drove to the top of the road at ten-thirty and he still wasn't home.

I almost called Alice again, but it was too late. None of this would have been more than annoying except that he wasn't home when I called at six-thirty in the morning. Abandoning any thoughts of the novel, I examined the various red flags to see if I was in any way justified in my fears.

Ben's sudden shout shook me out of my reverie, "Hey, Cleo!" Ben was fully dressed and standing on the shore.

"Hey yourself." I lay on my stomach, head to the north.

"Is this the kids' camp-out day?"

"Yes."

"I won't keep you, then, but can I take you to dinner tonight?"

I didn't answer right away, using the action of sitting up and turning toward him to give me time to prepare my reaction. In that second I chose to accept. "Sure, I'd love to, Ben. What time?" With the band-shell acoustics of the lake, I was certain my voice was as audible as the boys' voices had been. Take that, East Side biddies.

Shouting over the distance, we agreed on seven o'clock. As I dived off the raft, I couldn't help but notice Glenda and Carol on the sandy beach, sun hats distinctly turned my way.

I wasn't quite sure what to make of this invitation, only that I was pleased to have it. More and more, Ben struck me as a lonely widower, one who enjoyed the company of a fellow "artist," one who needed companionship of a neutral, unjudgmental, kind. And, of course, I wouldn't let him pay for me, that would make it a date, and I was a married woman. I allowed myself to believe that I was looking forward to this dinner exactly as if it was with Grace or any chum. That's what I told myself. Nothing to it. Everything aboveboard. I discounted my earlier reluctance to invite him over for dinner on this evening of being alone for fear of the suggestion of impropriety. This was different. Public. I could rationalize it very well. Besides, Sean knew Ben. Not that I would ever be able to share this moment with Sean. He wouldn't understand, he'd see it as all very innocent at the outset. Out of control in the next instant.

"Cleo, you're making more of this than there is." I spoke to the face in the mirror. I could have meant Ben's invitation or Sean's absence.

With Ben's car in the shop, for what he claimed was the eighty-second time that year, I would drive. I sat on the grassy slope just above the muddy rim of shore as Ben glided towards me across the lake, standing up as he jumped to shore and pulled his Old Town up on the grass beside me.

"You look fabulous."

"Thanks. It's just an old sundress." I don't know why I said that, I'd bought it that night we went to the mall.

"Red is nice on you. It suits your coloring."

I felt a little blush of pleasure. "You have a way of making a girl feel like a girl."

Ben politely chuckled at my stupid remark and pulled on his seat-belt. "That sounds like that silly line from *Notting Hill*. You know, where the Julia Roberts character says something like,"—and here his voice mimicked a high-pitched girlie sound—"I'm just a girl who is asking a boy to love her."

"Hey, I *like* romantic drivel. I write it." I gave him a playful punch.

"Yeah, and I went to see that movie alone, that's how bad I am."

We decided to go back to the same place where I'd introduced him to Sean as it was the nearest to a fine dining restaurant around. We chatted comfortably about this and that, Ben bringing me up to date on the news of the world, encouraging me to give him amusing anecdotes about the kids' first week at Camp Winetonka.

We were about halfway there when the phone chirruped. I felt a little mis-beat in my heart. I knew it had to be Sean. "Excuse me." I lifted the handset, "Sean?"

Ben kept looking out the passenger window in a noble attempt to give me privacy. "Why don't you pull over and I'll get out?" he mouthed.

I did and he got out of the car.

"Sean, where have you been?"

"What do you mean?"

I rehearsed for him my several useless phone calls.

"I know, I screwed up the answering-machine tape, but I was home after eleven. I had a client dinner."

"So where were you this morning?"

There was static on the line and I could barely hear him. For the first time it occurred to me that he was also on a car phone. "When?"

"Six-thirty this morning."

"Oh, golf. I had an early tee time with the client."

It made perfect sense and I felt the doubts recede. Then I wondered why he'd called me half an hour earlier than our set time. "How come you're calling me now?"

"Taking a chance I'd get you. I've got yet another client dinner and I didn't want to miss you again."

"Boy, Sean, I sure hope all of these dinners turn into paying customers."

"Me, too." The connection suddenly improved. "Clee, would you hate me very much if I came up on Saturday morning?"

I felt the ice water in my veins. "Yes."

"It's really important or I wouldn't . . ."

"Sean, you do what you have to do. I, too, have a dinner date and I'm going to have to sign off." I jabbed at the end button, missing it the first two times I aimed. I wish I could say that I was surprised that Sean wanted to delay his arrival. I wish I could say that it was legitimate. I wish I could say that his behavior didn't send the alarms sounding, but it did.

As I sipped my first glass of wine of the evening, I thought of the last time I had been here, and naturally it was the dance that Ben had given me that came soonest to mind. Thinking of Sean's unexpectedly bland reaction to my having done so, it suddenly hit me why he might have been so indifferent, and I gasped, inhaling a little of the wine. I choked and tears spontaneously welled in my eyes. I was uncertain if they were from coughing or from a new interpretation of Sean's uncharacteristic unconcern. Of course he was unconcerned, he could hardly make a big deal of my dancing with a man when he was . . . What? What proof did I have, except an eight-year-old memory, that my husband was repeating history? Why couldn't I believe that he was really having a run of new clients, all needing special attention? A monster thought climbed out of the cave of my head and licked its claws: I was never going to trust Sean. I didn't trust him.

Ben was on his feet and pounding my back until I raised my hands to signify uncle. "I'm okay," I managed to splutter out. Ben's thumping became gentle rubbing across my shoulders. I was aware of its warmth on the cool bare skin of my shoulders. "Thanks, Ben."

He leaned over me and whispered in my ear, "Remember, always chew your food."

I laughed and tried again. The wine soothed the muscles of my throat but not the burning behind my eyes.

"Cleo, is something the matter?"

I shook my head, forced a smile and determined to enjoy this serendipitous companionship.

We considered the menu for a few minutes, then I ordered baked haddock and Ben ordered steak. We were seated at a table for two, off to the side of the dining room. It looked more intimate, more romantic, than two recent friends of opposite genders should be seen to be. For a few minutes we sat quietly, not having to talk, sure enough in our acquaintance that the quiet moment was nice.

When I first met Ben, I thought he had a nice face. Over the past few weeks, becoming familiar with his expressions and charm, I'd come to think him quite good-looking, maybe even handsome in a gentle sort of way. I liked the way he ran a hand through his hair when he told a story, and the way his fingers worked an invisible keyboard even as he lay on the raft. Once one of Sean's sisters remarked about some stranger, admiring his build. I was still a newlywed and so was she and I made some comment about a wandering eye so soon. Siobhan laughed and said, "I may be married but I ain't dead." I sat there quietly with Ben and knew that I had come to see him as a man, and I was a little frightened by how powerfully that attraction lay hold of me. I was afraid of it. Unconsciously, I fingered my wedding band, twisting the wide ring around my finger as if it were suddenly too tight. I looked up to see Ben looking at me.

Somehow the grief that I had detected in his deep brown eyes had diminished since knowing him. I often saw amusement there, even pleasure as we chatted on board the raft or bumped into each other at the grocery store. Or as he played Trivial Pursuit with my children.

"You were right to yell at those kids today."

Ben's smile melted away. I hadn't meant to remind him of the horrible name the boy had called him, only to praise him for being a caring neighbor. But in an instant I knew that there was not one without other. He dropped his glance back to the tabletop, fingering his silverware into perfect parallel lines and said nothing.

"They were stupid boys, wannabe gangstas. Their parents ought to be shot for giving them so much freedom."

Ben kept his eyes on the table, and I knew I was never going to pull grace from this faux pas. "Ben . . ."

"Cleo, I didn't kill my wife." He looked directly at me, daring me to look away.

Words, my life and living, failed me. Instead I reached out across the table and grasped his wrists. "I know you didn't."

He took a long breath, "No, you don't."

I struggled to come up with words to convince him I did understand that he wasn't responsible. But I didn't yet know the circumstances and so hesitated a little too long. "Ben, I don't know what happened. Until you tell me, I can't judge for myself. But I know, knowing you, that whatever did happen was . . ."

"What happened was a terrible accident." His liquid brown eyes froze over and I kept my grip on his wrists. He didn't try to pull away. I had never seen such a gaping wound. "I shouldn't let them get to me."

"They aren't worth it."

"You have no idea how much . . ." He did pull away then, some self-editing reflex preventing him from saying what he so obviously needed to say.

"How much what, Ben? Tell me."

"How much it hurts to be rejected because of something you had no control over. There, I've said it. Now you know that I'm all façade, that I just pretend to be aloof from the snide remarks."

"We all have façades. We build them as self-defense against the indefensible."

"What have you got to build a wall against?" He lifted his glass to his lips. His eyes challenged me at first, then softened into an invitation.

I didn't say anything for a minute. I had never spoken of Sean's affair to anyone since it happened. I'd kept the story so locked up that I hadn't even used it in my work. "Don't pick at that scab." My mother's directive. "You'll scar." She was dead before Sean and I got married. She'd called his family lace-curtain Irish and refused to meet them. She and Father, in an unexplained moment of togetherness after their divorce, died in a car crash of their own inebriated fault. I once said I thought it had been mutual suicide. Anything to prevent their daughter from "marrying beneath her." Alice McCarthy had enfolded me into her family, and the most legitimate way to stay was to marry Sean.

"When I was pregnant with Tim, Sean had an affair with a neighbor."

Ben stayed quiet, his silence opening a path for me, allowing me to tell the story without bends or twists in the journey.

"Every summer in July all of the McCarthys go to Narragansett and rent a couple of cottages. Sean's is a big family and where they used to be able to fit in one, now, with all the husbands and kids, they have to rent two. This was eight years ago, and Francis, Sean's dad, was still alive. The women went to the beach for the month and the men, Francis and Sean and Margaret's husband, Jack, all stayed in Providence and came down on weekends. The traffic from all those husbands and fathers traveling south was awful and they'd all try to come down midday on Friday to avoid it.

"Lily was fifteen months old, just beginning to toddle. I was seven months along and feeling like Shamu. Everything was swollen, belly, breasts, ankles, wrists, you would never have recognized me. Lily and

I stayed with my in-laws. Sean's youngest siblings were there, too, so it was a house of women, happily going to the beach all day and eating hot dogs every night. We only cooked when the men came home.

"Every Friday, Sean and Francis and Jack arrived, sweaty and city-dressed. Ties loosened around their necks, they arrived looking tired and saggy. On that first Friday they arrived, Sean, who hadn't seen me in a week, made some flip remark about my size. It wasn't especially meant to be hurtful or demeaning, but, being hormonally challenged, I burst into tears and his mother took him to task. 'You made her this way, be proud of it.'

"Sean apologized but there was something in the way he kissed me that made me think he found me slightly repulsive. As if he had to make himself touch me. We had always been very physical with each other and I craved him. By the next Friday, we had somehow given up physical love. He kissed me hello and goodbye and held my hand as we walked along the beach, but we didn't make love. I know that some men find their wives more attractive when pregnant, but Sean was quite clearly not of that number."

I took another swallow of the first glass of wine and smiled at the server setting my haddock in front of me. Ben poured a second glass from the bottle he'd ordered and let me go on.

"I had a doctor's appointment in the city on a Thursday. Alice was going to drive me up and then I would spend the night at home and come back to the beach with Sean and Francis on the Friday. Lily was going to stay with the family. This was to be my first night away from Lily, and I was in anguish about it. Tuesday morning I got a call asking if I could change my appointment to that afternoon. If I hadn't been so on the fence about leaving Lily overnight, I might have said no, I couldn't change my plans. Instead, I saw the change of appointment as a sign from God that I should just go up and back the same day and not be away from my baby. Given Sean's sudden reluctance to touch me, I figured it wouldn't really matter to him whether he saw me just for lunch or slept beside me in our bed at home.

" 'Can you drive yourself? Do you want me to go with you?' Alice asked, but I assured her the forty-five-minute drive up and back wouldn't tax me at all. I took orders from everyone around for various missing things to bring back from Alice's house, things like the extra set of car keys, the pair of sandals Siobhan had forgotten under her bed, last month's *Good Housekeeping* with the recipe in it for fruit barbecue sauce. The stuff of living ordinary lives. I kissed my baby and off I went to change my life forever.

"I didn't call Sean to tell him I was coming. I had some silly idea that I'd surprise him at work and make him take me out to lunch. I had time, so I went to Alice's house first and collected the desired items. My house is only a street over from hers, so it seemed the most natural thing to go there next. I knew that Sean was neglecting my plants, and I had a couple of things I wanted to take back with me as well."

By this point in my narrative I could feel my heart pound as if I were reexperiencing the event from eight years ago. I stopped long enough to slow its rhythm. I allowed myself a mental deep breath by commenting on the food we were slowly eating. Ben encouraged me to keep telling my story with a gentle nod and a soft gesture of his fingertips.

"The house was as much of a mess as I had expected. Dishes, towels strewn, papers piled in every chair. I knew he'd get it tidied up before I got home, but also that I'd spend the last month of my pregnancy cleaning the house. He'd call it nesting, I'd call it house reclamation.

"I went into the bedroom to get the maternity jeans I'd left behind. The bed was like a storm-tossed island, or a battlefield. Pillows punched, blanket on the floor, and sheets twisted tornado-shaped. 'At least they aren't the same sheets I put on when I left'—I actually said it out loud. These were the newer, monogrammed ones, an elegant white on white, an anniversary present from his parents. I grasped the top sheet and pulled, then lifted the corners of the contour bottom sheet. A tiny square of foil bounced on the floor as I yanked. Even as I bent over to retrieve it, I knew what it was. In novels, such an act is the catalyst, the thing which sets into motion the story. The conflict. The mystery.

"In my life that action—picking up the condom wrapper from

my bedroom floor—was more like an abrupt ending. At first I sat on the edge of the bed and looked at the empty package. Then I carefully placed it on the nightstand on his side of the bed. Then I took it back and crumpled it up and flushed it down the toilet. The heat of that July day was suddenly unbearable. I needed the soothing breeze off the bay. I saw myself in the long mirror on the back of the bedroom door and I began to cry. It seemed to me then that I was at fault. I had let myself grow huge with this baby, safe in the knowledge that I had sprung back to normal within days after Lily. I had left Sean by himself. I had left Francis McCarthy's only son alone. We all knew that Francis had what they so quaintly called the 'roving eye.' We all knew, at least those of us older ones, that he'd cheated on Alice. Now Sean had cheated on me. I finished stripping the bed. I bundled my brand-new sheets under my arm and went out to the trash, where I stuffed them into a half-full pail."

Seated in that intimate corner of the restaurant, the soft and sexy eyes of a different kind of man focused on me, I felt myself pull away from my story and back into the present and I was very glad to be there.

"Did Sean ever know you'd found out?"

"Oh yes. He did. I remade the bed. I went to my appointment and got a lecture on blood pressure. Then I drove back to Narragansett and found Alice. She'd lived through this and I needed her to tell me what to do."

"Let me guess—she recommended you stay with him?"

I nodded and finished the last of my haddock. The fish had grown cold and I only ate to give myself time to construct my narrative more effectively. "Alice held me and rocked me and whispered, 'There there,' over my head. 'They all do it, Cleo, it doesn't mean anything. You're his wife and the mother of his children and it's to you he will always come home.'

"I was too tired and too demoralized to stand up and debate her Old World point of view. 'Things have to be different, Alice. I can't live like this.' She agreed I must confront him, I must know who the woman was and I must exact punishment. 'How did you punish

Francis?' 'I hit him, square across the face, and then I told him the next time I would leave him.' 'And he remained true?' 'I never caught him again.' " Telling this story whole, speaking it out loud for the first time to anyone outside the family, I suddenly realized that all this time I had missed the nuance behind those words, "I never caught him again."

Ben's conducting fingers brought me to speak the conclusion.

"Alice called Sean and told him to come to Narragansett that night. At first he thought the baby was coming and he got very excited. 'No, Sean. You need to tend to your wife about something else,' and she hung up on him. Thus alerted, Sean arrived contrite. We needed a privacy the crowded cottage couldn't provide so we walked to the closest beach and sat in the sand. It was sunset and any other night this would have been a romantic scene, shimmering Narragansett Bay, red streaks in the West, golden bands shooting through the strips of clouds on the horizon.

" 'Who is she?' I asked. Not, 'How could you do this to me,' or 'Why?' or 'What were you thinking?' What I most wanted to know was *with whom*. It seemed almost more important to me to find out it was someone who might look like me, like I usually did, rather than someone random. Does that make sense?

"He named a woman who lived a couple of houses up, a slightly older woman, a divorcee with three kids and not a lick of sense in her head. 'She came over to make sure I was eating properly. She brought lasagna. We never meant . . . ' She was attractive, I suppose, in an overdone, kind of former-beauty-queen way. But what fascinated me most was her preying on my husband. You see, that's how I saw it. She was older, lonely, horny. Sean was classic weak male, thinking with his other head, as we put it when the sisters and I discussed the matter. It was a family matter, this mistake of Sean's.

"I told him I should leave him, that he deserved nothing less. He begged my forgiveness." I set my utensils down side by side on the plate and folded my hands into my lap. I stared at my clenched fists, stared at the wide wedding band on my left hand. Then I looked up at Ben. "And I did. I gave him my forgiveness. And, you know, I've never told that story to anyone because, in making my peace with Sean, I made an implied promise to keep the incident buried."

The busboy came and removed our plates, leaving dessert menus behind.

"The thing is"—I didn't look up at Ben—"I think that he may be doing it again." I hadn't expected to say that.

Ben simply reached across the table and took my hand. "Why?"

It seemed, as I told Ben about the little things which alarmed me, that maybe I *was* jumping to conclusions. They sounded so minor. I sounded so suspicious.

"I can't tell you you're right or wrong, I can only say that once trust is broken, it's almost impossible to fix it properly."

I was feeling as if I had monopolized the evening with a dull bit of ancient history. I was tired of it and moved to change the subject. "Ben, it's an old story and one which comes nowhere close to the loss you've endured."

"Unhappiness is unhappiness, Cleo. I think that maybe infidelity is pretty much the same as an accident. Sometimes it takes a while to assess the extent of the damage done."

We let ourselves be quiet for a few minutes. Then Ben reached across the table and took my free hand. "Cleo, maybe the most important thing about your story is that you took a second chance. And I don't think that you've regretted it. But I never got a second chance. Talia never gave me one."

"Why did you need one?"

"I let our lives grow apart."

We danced. A slow dance to a bluesy song. Ben stood up and held out his hand to me. At first I shook my head, but he winked and smiled and wouldn't take no for an answer. "I wrote this tune. It's from Interior Angles' second album, so humor me."

He placed a gentle hand on my waist, and held his other hand flat against mine. Again I was struck by what a good dancer he was. I had been so concerned with Sean's reaction the last time Ben asked me to dance, I couldn't give myself over to the pure enjoyment of it, of being skillfully moved around the tiny dance space. I felt how close our hips were as Ben leaned a little, how warm his hand was against my waist, how my fingers curled into his. When the dance ended I felt as though I had been kissed.

"We should go." I said

"Yes. We should." He answered.

Nineteen

It was after ten-thirty when we left the restaurant. After the air conditioning inside, the night heat was breathless. I drove slowly, not inebriated, but knowing that I'd had two glasses of good wine. We were very quiet in the big car.

We got to the cabin and it seemed natural that I should get out of the car and walk with him to the overturned canoe. I felt a strange reluctance to let Ben go, to let him paddle away across the dark lake. "Will you have a nightcap with me?"

Ben had already gotten to the canoe and flipped it over. "I should go."

"Ben, can I ask you a question?"

"Sure."

"Why did you ask me out tonight?"

Ben walked back up the path. I could just about make him out in the faint yellow of the porch light above us. "Why did you accept?" We stood very still in a moment of exquisite hesitation. He reached both hands to touch my face, then kissed me. It wasn't a quick, chaste kiss between friends. Now I took his face in my hands and kissed him. We let our tongues play experimentally. I felt a long-dulled desire flourish.

"I shouldn't have done that." Ben brushed a lock of hair away from my cheek.

"I'm glad you did." I touched the hand which touched my face.

"To get back at your husband for old sins?"

"No." I might have said, "For new sins," but the truth was, Ben's kiss was exactly what I needed. It had been so long since I had been kissed with more than marital affection. So long since my last first kiss, I'd forgotten how incredibly sweet and unexpected it could be. I didn't want him to think that I regarded such a sweet moment as anything else.

Ben's hand still touched my face. The porch light glittered in his brown eyes, and I could see that neither one of us would regret the moment.

"I should go," he said again and gently pulled away.

"Thanks." Our hands touched, fingertip to fingertip.

"Thanks?"

"For reminding me what it's like to live a little dangerously."

He shoved the canoe into the water and climbed aboard. I watched until the darkness swallowed him.

I lay a long time awake, thinking about that kiss, about the fire it had ignited in a banked bed of embers. Oh, I was on dangerous ground. That's what I'd meant. I was playing an emotionally very risky game with a man who deserved to have someone come to him unencumbered. Nothing could come of teasing ourselves. Then I thought, Ben hasn't asked anything more of me and I don't believe he will. Satisfied with that, I told myself that we understood our boundaries and that we would not cross them. A kiss good-night was not so serious. Even such a one as we had just shared. True, he should not have kissed me and I should not have kissed him back. But I lay alone in my bed and gave myself the freedom to not regret it.

I woke at dawn wondering how we should greet one another when we met, as we surely would, on the raft.

I ran and then heated coffee to get my creative juices flowing. Jay and Karen were looking very dull to me and suddenly I was struck by the absolute certainty that Jay would cheat on Karen. It had to happen. For so long I'd been avoiding the adulterous plot in my novels, afraid that I would spill some truth out onto the page. Now, in telling Benson Turner my story, I had somehow broken the seal on the envelope and the contents were public record. I bent to the task and the morning flew by. Nothing about their story resembled mine. As always, the genetic material was shuffled and made wholly new.

Twenty

I had two loads' worth of laundry and was blessed to be only one of two people using the small laundromat this beautiful afternoon. I'd put in almost six hours of writing by one o'clock, choosing to stay put rather than go out to the raft. I didn't see Ben out there, either, and I imagined that he, too, was a little uncertain how we would greet each other this morning.

The heat in the rectangular yellow building was intense and I went outside to sit on one of the available picnic tables. The Dairy Bar was situated close by and I went over to buy a hot dog for lunch. Bees followed me from the Dairy Bar window right back to my picnic table. They seemed to like the smell of the relish I'd layered on my hot dog and I had to watch every bite I took not to eat one of them. Ben joined me almost as soon as I'd sat down.

"Hi."

"Hi," I answered over a bite of hot dog. "Laundry day for you, too?"

"I came in to pick up my car." Ben gestured toward the Cameo Lake Garage. "Timing belt this time. I think it may be time to put this one down."

"My timing belt went just before I got here. That's why Grace lent me her SUV." It was a little hard to believe that we could be having such a mundane conversation, as if the past evening had been something I'd committed to paper, not memory.

"Grace hasn't been one of my fans now for over a year."

"She has been misled."

"At least she speaks to me when I see her."

"Has she been blunt with you? I mean, Grace generally speaks her mind."

"A little."

"Poor Ben. I know how scathing Grace can be."

"Oh, she wasn't exactly scathing. But she was blunt when she accused me of leaving the community out of the mourning process when I didn't have a funeral service."

"Surely she knew that was your decision. It might have become a media event had you not."

"Apparently, according to Grace, I robbed this community of something when I . . ." Ben turned his face away in an effort to chose his words. "When I didn't."

"Do you think that's why they've been so unforgiving?"

"Part of it. That, and the part where they think I . . ."

"Ben, please don't say it."

He didn't look at me for a moment. "It's the impression they were left with. To tell you the truth, it's one that I've encouraged in them."

I wanted to reach over and brush the hair from his forehead, as I would had he been my child. But I settled for brushing the hair from my own forehead in sympathy. "Why, Ben?"

He didn't answer me, only shrugged away the question. I stood up to go collect my dried laundry. Ben caught at my arm as I crossed in front of him. "Can you give me an hour?"

I looked at my watch, I had some time before I had to go get the kids and I said as much to him. Then asked him why.

"I need to show you . . . I need you to see something."

I threw my dried clothes into my basket without folding them. Ben took the basket and set it in my car and then we got into his aged Wagoneer. Within a few minutes we were on an unfamiliar road and moving away from the lake in a more or less westerly direction. Ben gave me nothing by way of preamble. No clue at all as to where we were going, except that it wasn't far, maybe only twenty minutes away. There was something in the set of his jaw which prevented me from demanding anything more. My only comments concerned the scenery, which was comprised mainly of trees and roadside shrubbery waving in the backwash as we sped past.

The two-lane road became the Main Street of another small New Hampshire town. To my left the ample firehouse, to my right a library and municipal building. Ben downshifted before he put his signal on and we turned onto a side street, then half a block down, into a driveway which took us around the back of a small, squat brick building. Ben slid into a parking space and turned the car off. He didn't move for a minute, both hands still on the steering wheel. An odd pressure in my chest felt a little like fear or maybe more like nerves.

"Ben?" I wanted him to tell me now why we were here, at this nursing home. I thought I knew, but I wanted him to tell me before we went in. I needed some clue to what I was to see. I needed to rehearse my reaction.

"Come on." He was out of the car, almost not waiting for me, clearly anxious about doing this, as if it had been impulse to bring me and he was on the edge of wishing he hadn't.

We went around to the front of the building, which I could see had been designed to mimic some aspects of New England architecture, with the ornate lintel over the heavy fire door and the fake shutters on the flanking windows. Inside, the carpeting gave over to creamy tile almost instantly.

"Hi, Ben. How are you today?" A man dressed in the blue clothes of a maintenance worker greeted Ben.

"Pretty good, Erv. No complaints."

"Wouldn't do you no good, anyways."

We walked past the empty nurse's station, although two women in perky floral smocks greeted Ben in the corridor with almost coworker-like casualness, as if his presence there was expected and routine. As it certainly was.

"Benson, how ya doin' mon?" Another very young man with a Jamaican lilt high-fived Ben. "Ya going to play for us today, mon?"

"No, maybe tomorrow, Clyde."

I watched Ben transform from tense and guarded, to relaxed and comfortable in the presence of these various caregivers. Obviously here he was safe because here his secret lived.

"Cleo, this is Talia."

We stood in the doorway of a single room. I stepped slightly in front of Ben and then I could feel his hands on my shoulders, encouraging me to go in. I didn't know if I should speak. If she could hear me. What would I say?

Talia lay flat, various plastic tubing emerging not so discreetly from under the light blanket. A ventilator protruded from the base of her throat. A monitor blipped—measured respirations, I supposed, monitored heartbeat. Her blue eyes were open, unfocused as a newborn's, staring blankly at the ceiling, where someone had pinned a Matisse poster. At the corner of her still mouth, a tiny bubble of moisture glistened, the sunlight through the open window illuminating it into prominence.

"Hello, my love." Ben leaned over and kissed her, making the tiny droplet disappear. "I've brought a friend to meet you."

I felt myself want to cry, not just for Talia, but from the sadness of Ben's resolute cheerfulness.

Ben pulled two chairs up to the bed, taking the one closest, allowing me the one at the foot of it. He took Talia's hand and began massaging it. Her arm was like that of an old woman, the loose skin over the atrophied muscle soft and fluid as he gently worked it. "I met Talia when I was forty. I was just climbing out of the trough of my rock career and finding good work as a sessions musician in New York. She was twenty-three, nearly half my age. It's unfair to ask a beautiful woman if she's ever noticed a beautiful woman, but if you'd known her then, you would have been as taken with her as everyone else whose path crossed hers. She had a luminescence, like an internal pilot light kept her ready to glow at all times. As if she held the secret to happiness. She played that way, reviewers called her sparkling.

One reviewer in particular said she sounded like champagne, effervescent and rare." Ben set Talia's right hand down and moved to the other side of the bed, where he picked up her left hand, and his thoughts.

"Is it too trite to say I fell head over heels? That's exactly what it felt like to me. Suddenly I was infected with this same happiness. It was as if all the weight of my self-destructed career, my grief and perplexity with Kevin's death, my demons, were blasted away by Talia Brightman's smile. I remember going to my sublet apartment after our second recording session and looking at myself in the mirror. I literally looked myself in the eye in the bathroom mirror and told myself to go slow. She seemed so ethereal that I was afraid the force of my love would make her disappear, like she had made my demons go.

"This was about the point in her career when she was desperate to move away from classical repertoire and into jazz. It was a chancy thing, only Winton Marsalis has made a dual career of it. In Talia's mind, she wanted to abandon what she'd been so successful at, what her lifelong training had focused on, and get into a form she was fascinated with, but untrained in. I became her co-conspirator. I knew people. I'd been in the industry since college in one form or another. I'd jammed with some terrific jazz musicians all around the country, going into these smoky, stinky nightclubs in Chicago and God knows where—heading out after Angles concerts, enjoying the relative anonymity of playing for people who had no clue who Interior Angles were. So, I introduced her and she practiced and somehow along the way I talked her into marrying me." Ben was finished with the left hand and came back around to me.

"We should go."

I won't say I wasn't relieved. I remained on the vinyl and metal chair, sitting forward, uncomfortable in a way I was embarrassed about, hoping that my discomfort wasn't obvious to Ben. "We don't have to go yet." I turned away from my childish dislike for being in a hospital room. "I can go outside if you want some time alone."

"I won't be long." Ben squeezed my shoulder gently.

*   *   *

I went straight out, seeking to let the warm breeze take the nursing home odor out of my nostrils. I walked down the short block, turned, and walked back, sitting down on a bench a little way from the front door. I knew that Ben's bringing me here to see Talia was because I had shared my own secret last night with him. To show me that we all have things we keep from others. Except that Ben's sharing had not explained anything to me, only created more questions.

An old man sat on the bench opposite to mine and in the time it took for Ben to come out, smoked two cigarettes. He smoked them slowly, considering each inhalation. By the scruffy slippers on his feet, I assumed he was a resident, given outdoor smoking privileges. He carefully dabbed each of the two cigarettes out on a scarred spot on the iron framework of the green bench and then got up and went inside. As he passed through the wide wooden door, Ben came through. Seeing me sitting there, he smiled and put his baseball cap back on. "Thanks for being patient."

"Ben, I'd feel bad if you hurried for my sake."

We walked quickly back to the parked car. The passenger-side door creaked in loud protest as Ben opened it for me. "Is it very expensive to have her there?"

"About like having a child in a little ivy college." Ben adjusted the rearview mirror. "This is a good place, despite being out here in the middle of nowhere. Her parents were very upset with me keeping her here in New Hampshire when they had found a place in New York that specializes in cases like Talia's. But this place is very caring and she gets the same therapies as she would in a big-city place, maybe even better. We have a guy named Jeremy who is her private nurse and he gives her the best care possible. He's teaching me some things, you know, basic nursing care, so that when she becomes . . . end-stage, I can bring her home."

Benson Turner had been grieving for the dying, not the dead.

"Can I ask you something, Ben?"

He kept his eyes on the road in front of us, but nodded. I'm sure he must have known that I would ask.

"Why do you let everyone think Talia is dead?"

"Is that what they think?"

"Ben, you know that they do, you told me yourself they resented you because you didn't have a funeral service. Why have you let this evil misapprehension go on, let those women treat you with disdain?"

"Cleo, I don't know those women. Despite what I said last night, I really don't care about them. They only knew Talia slightly. Since I've lived on the lake they've always treated me with disdain, because I was different from them, didn't fit into their worldview. But, believe it or not, it was the greater world I wanted to keep out of our business. You have to understand that as a popular recording artist, Talia was a public figure. Having dealt with being a public figure myself, I knew exactly what kind of hay the press would make of this tragedy. We—her parents and I—decided it was wiser to simply let them believe she'd died that night, and then we'd never find photographers sneaking into her hospital room. They don't even know who she is at the nursing home. There she's Talia Judith Turner, resident of room one-oh-four."

"They know who *you* are, though?"

"Some do. But it's been long enough, not many care or are impressed."

"Clyde asked you to play for them."

"Sometimes I flex my classical training and play a little Mozart or Rachmaninoff for the residents. Sometimes just play-it-by-ear show tunes. Depends on my mood."

"You come every day?"

"No. I used to, in the beginning, when there was . . ." He cut himself off. "I come about every other day. Jeremy convinced me that I didn't need to come every day. Or spend whole days sitting by her side. He's been pretty blunt with me on occasion."

"How?"

"By not letting me delude myself into hope."

We were almost back to Cameo, another three minutes and we'd be in the parking lot of the laundromat. If I were writing this scene I knew that this was the last opportunity for the important dialogue to be said. Pressed by time I reached out and touched the hand which rested on the stick shift. "Ben, you have to know that I'll say nothing about this to anyone."

"I wouldn't have brought you if I couldn't trust you."

"Why *did* you bring me?" There it was, the important question.

He turned into the dirt lot and put the car in neutral, letting it idle as he thought about his answer. He sucked in a breath and let it out. "I guess because you are the first person to come into my life in a long time with whom I feel safe."

Over the awkward barrier of the gear shift we hugged, then kissed each other's cheek as good friends will. Then I got out of the car and waved goodbye, wondering if now Ben would tell me the story of how the accident had happened, enabled now by this event to ask him.

Twenty-one

T he kids were indistinguishable from the twenty others all
dressed in shorts and Camp Winetonka T-shirts. Everyone was
uniformly dirty and overtired. Only Mrs. Beckman seemed rested
and perky in the wake of the overnight. Lily looked a veritable
Medusa: her curly hair, caught erratically into a knotty ponytail, was
threaded through with bits of leaf mulch and some unidentifiable
substance which might have been juice or sap. Tim struggled to get
his unrolled sleeping bag stuffed into the car while attempting to
climb in on top of it. I had to sort him out, separating little boy from
sleeping bag, and get both into the car.

"So, was it any fun?"

"Yeah. It was fun." Exhausted, thus listless, my two were asleep
even before we achieved the main road.

"Fun is such hard work. I wonder why any of us do it," I said to
the sleeping forms in the backseat.

The bumpy road leading to the cabin shook the kids awake.
Rejuvenated by even a twenty-minute nap, they were the first to catch
sight of a car parked just under the cedar trees. Sean's.

"Daddy's here! Daddy's here!" Almost before I could bring the
monster car to a complete halt, they were unbelted and out of the
car.

"Yikes. Who would have imagined this." I threw the car into park and unsnapped my own seatbelt. "Well, what a surprise."

Sean was wearing his aviator-style sunglasses. His mint-green polo shirt was fashionably untucked from his khaki shorts. He wore the old topsiders he'd had since we were first married. Coming up the path, I couldn't help but notice how worn they were, the leather laces dangling in ancient square knots, the stitching shot along the toes. When I hugged him, he smelled freshly showered, and his hair was still damp.

"How long have you been here?"

"You'll be proud of me, I left the office before noon."

"I'm sorry I wasn't here." By way of explanation, I pointed out the laundry basket filled with unfolded clothes and sheets. I would have been here if I hadn't gone with Ben.

Sean scampered off with the kids, who were anxious to show him newly discovered treasures of the lake. I lugged the heavy laundry basket into the cabin and wondered at this new Sean. Had I finally pierced through to his conscience? Or maybe it was my ill-considered remark about a dinner date. Either way, I was glad he was there and I set about making dinner.

It was natural that soon after the kids went to bed we would tumble into bed ourselves. Sean wanted the light off, although the bedroom faced only deep woods. Aware of the thin walls, we were very quiet, two invisible bodies touching and tasting and moving. We danced the intimate dance, and yet the moves seemed unfamiliar to me, robbed of sight on that moonless night, as if danced with a stranger. Sean was vigorous and I was ready quickly, but it was the accidental thought of Ben's kiss which triggered me.

A sudden cold front kept us from swimming, and thus, from the raft. Twice over the weekend, I saw Ben stroking his canoe toward the town landing, then, a couple of hours later, homeward. We kept indoors as the cold front produced drizzle. If Ben played at all, I never heard his music that weekend. I didn't run, got my period, and used the menstrual energy to clean the cabin top to bottom and make a real winter dinner for my family two nights running. On Sunday morning Sean decided to stay until Monday morning, a decision that necessitated his driving to the top of the hill to call Eleanor to let her know his plans. "You can't call her in the morning? Why bother her at home on a Sunday?"

"Eleanor hates surprises."

"What possible difference can it make to her to know today or tomorrow morning at eight that you're staying longer?" I was annoyed, both at this controlling secretary and at my husband for letting her be that way. "Who's the boss?"

"Hey, just let me call her, no big deal." He grabbed the car keys from the island counter and stomped out, clearly annoyed himself. At me.

I put a kettle of water on for tea when Sean left. It had boiled and reboiled three times by the time he got back.

"Did you get her?" I asked as he dashed back into the cabin, trailing bits of pine mulch on his wet topsiders.

"Yeah. I found her."

"You should have told her you're taking the whole day off." I poured water into his mug, "You could, you know. We could go hiking while the kids are at camp."

"Oh, Cleo, I'd love to. And I will, but not this week. I've got to head to Pittsburgh on Tuesday."

"But you will come back next weekend?"

"Definitely. Can't keep me away. I have to admit, this place is growing on me. I miss Narragansett, but this place has one superior quality."

"What's that?"

"My family isn't here."

"Are they at the beach now?"

"Everybody who was going went last weekend. They send their love to you. Oh, and I forgot to tell you, they want to know if you want to go down and join them for a little while."

"Your mother went?"

"Of course, she's the matriarch of Watch Hill."

An unaccountable foreboding wafted through me, I tipped a little tea out of my mug. I dashed to the sink to grab a cloth, when I turned back around Sean was wiping the drips up with a paper napkin. I leaned back against the sink. "Are you all right at home by yourself?"

Sean looked up at me from under bushy eyebrows. "I'm fine."

Sean happily drove the kids to camp on Monday morning on his way home, leaving me to get a run in and started on my work before eight-thirty. Our goodbye kiss was perfunctory, a couple's kiss, signaling solidarity and a certain superstition that, should anything happen in the meantime, we had at least kissed goodbye.

I stretched with deliberate slowness on the little patch of grass at the lakefront, using the picnic table as a barre. The cold front had moved off and the day was pure dry warmth. At that early hour, there was little noise emanating from the other cabins as I ran by, nearly silent except for my footsteps against the nicely moistened leaf mulch. I had used up the last of my batteries, so I ran without accompaniment, keeping my rhythm with remembered strains from Ben's music. And then I was hearing Ben's music. I matched my stride to the allegro section of the piece, the playful lighthearted theme. I began to run so fast, my breath and my footsteps obscured the actual music, but by now I had heard it enough, I could fill in the missing phrases until I caught the sound of it again. I realized that Ben had committed the notes to paper, that what he had been working on for weeks had codified into actual music and that what I was hearing, as it went on and on without the usual stop and start, was something no longer first-draft but almost complete. Complete except for the solo part.

The allegro segued gently, easily into the adagio, just as I began to slow down. Then the music stopped, leaving me to walk through my cool down alone.

I wrote for a couple of hours, but my work was slow and mainly disjointed. The impulse which had given me my conflict had leveled out and now I had the technical work to do, the weaving of foreshadowing and believable character reaction. It was a little hard getting back to work on Monday morning, just like a real job. I was fidgety and eventually I abandoned the attempt and climbed into my suit. The water was charged by the breeze still cool from the weekend's weather. Little choppy waves kept splashing me in the face as I swam to the raft. It wasn't yet noon. I climbed aboard the raft, puddling it with the drips from my suit, slipping a little against the slick surface. I lay down to get out of the cooling breeze, and as I did I heard Ben's screen door. I think I held my breath as I waited for him.

He climbed onto the raft quietly, as if he thought I was asleep up there. I felt him lie down next to me, my eyes closed against seeing him. I opened them at his touch, the slight grazing of his fingertips against my bare arm. "Cleo."

"Ben." Unaccountably, tears threatened. I hoped he thought the moisture lake water and not from the tenderness I felt at the sight of him. Tenderness he had no right to, tenderness I had no right to feel. I sat up quickly, deliberately giving the moment short shrift. "You've finished the allegro movement?"

Now it was his turn to look not at me but stare with pleased eyes at the view beyond. "Yes. It's the last bit before I really have to get down to work and write the flute melody. But . . . how did you like it?"

"It was wonderful." I touched him then, saying without thinking, "Talia would be so pleased."

"I hope so. I think that it just needed a little happiness to move it from garbage to music."

I knew that he meant he'd needed a little happiness. That in some way I'd given him a little by sharing his secret with him. The weight of this emotional responsibility kept me from looking at him.

I was perfectly aware that somehow Ben had slipped into my erotic world, the physical presence of him reminded me of that. But it was more than that which made me glad he was opening up to me, and yet equally afraid of his candor, afraid of the entanglements such revelations bring.

We had so much more to say to one another, but Ben clamped down on the moment with a complete change of subject. "Hey, do you still want to give me a ride to Boston on Wednesday? Promise me that you'll do it only if it's convenient. Otherwise I'm going to rent a car. Really. Not a problem."

"Ben, I want to go. The camp-out is Wednesday this week and I'll have all the time in the world. Besides, like I said, I need a day in the city. Recharge my batteries. Buy new batteries. Go to Tower Records and get some new running music. "

"Okay. But if you change your mind—"

"Just shut up, Turner. I keep my promises."

"Cleo?" Ben was on his feet.

"What?"

"I really am glad you came with me Friday." He stood on the coaming of the raft, not looking back at me. "I'll see you later." His splash threw a fine spray of water over me and I shivered.

Twenty-two

"Mom, is Daddy coming back on Friday?" Lily paused with her cereal spoon in mid-flight.

"He hopes so. Why?"

"Do you think he could bring me my Barbies?"

I kept my smile under control. Lily was in that peculiar limbo of almost too old for dolls, yet occasionally falling back under their spell. She had been very deliberate in not bringing them with her. I cleared my throat and promised to call Sean and ask him about the Barbies.

I tried our home number first, it being just before eight and I knew that often Sean liked to stay home and do paperwork before going to the office, where the phone could be a nonstop interruption. The phone rang and the erratic answering machine kicked in, but the outgoing message was missing and I knew that it wouldn't record. "We've got to get a new answering machine one of these days." I pulled out onto the main road. No sense trying him at the office until after eight-thirty. Providence traffic was horrible and I knew there was no chance Sean would be in just yet.

"I really want them, Mom." Lily was just a thread shy of whiny. "Clarissa and I want to play with them this weekend. She's got a bunch of clothes her grandmother just sent." Clarissa being her new best friend from camp. Clarissa lived nearby on the East Side of the lake.

"Okay, you push the number for Daddy's work."

Tongue tucked into the corner of her mouth, Lily pressed the digits for McCarthy and Lenihan Insurance Group.

The familiar voice of Audrey, the firm's longtime receptionist, came over the reedy speakerphone. "Hey, Aud, it's Cleo McCarthy. Sean in yet?"

"No, he's traveling, Cleo. Pittsburgh, I think."

"Shoot, I forgot. Apparently I'm losing my grasp on time up here. Tell you what, transfer me to Eleanor. She can give him a message when he calls in."

"Eleanor's out sick. I'll be relaying messages today."

"It's real important."

Audrey chuckled when I gave her the message about the Barbies. "Got it. I'll make sure it's the first one in the pile."

"Thanks. Give my best to the family."

Lily punched the off button and sat back in the big seat. Her little mouth was moued like a disappointed movie star.

"Hey, Audrey's good. She'll make sure he gets the message."

"Yeah, but he won't remember by Friday."

"We'll try later in the week. It's only Tuesday."

Kids deposited, I headed back. Halfway back, the car phone bleated. Assuming Audrey was as good as her word, I picked it up, expecting Sean calling from the road. But it was Ben.

"I thought I might catch you in the car at this hour."

"Ben, hello. Yeah, just dropped the kids off."

"I wanted to let you know what time tomorrow. Is it okay if we leave right after you drop the kids off? I have an eleven-thirty flight, so I thought I might go with you to the camp."

"Fine. Perfect."

"I'll see you tomorrow, then."

"No raft today?"

"Probably not."

"Visiting a friend?" We were both aware of the insecurity of cell-phone transmissions.

"Exactly."

"Give her my best." I don't know why I said that, but it seemed exactly right.

The next morning, Ben helped the kids lug their sleeping bags out of the back of the big car and then tousled their hair in affectionate farewell. He climbed back in and we headed back to the main highway.

"You're too nice to my kids."

"They're good kids. "

"Yeah, they pretty much are." I wanted to ask him why he didn't have kids of his own, fumbled around for a phrase which wouldn't be intrusive or cruel or more than just idle curiosity. "Did you . . . had you . . . ?"

"Wanted kids? Oh, yes, I certainly did. We talked about it once or twice before it became clear that Talia's career was our child." Ben kept his eyes on the road ahead of us as if he were driving. "That sounds bitter. I'm not. So, the short answer is, no, we never had kids."

I reached out to him, just a little consoling touch on the arm.

He did look at me then, a quick charming smile. "Stop at Dunkin' Donuts. I'll buy you breakfast."

We didn't have scads of time so we hit the drive-thru. Ben formulated my coffee to the exact specifications I like and then sugared his own. We spoke of neutral things, favorite doughnut flavors and whether Dunkin' Donuts or Bess Eaton doughnuts are better. Pulled up personal memories of when things tasted better, of our first MacDonald's fries or clam cakes at Rocky Point (me), first pretzel with mustard on it (Ben). We kept our conversation light until we got almost to the border between New Hampshire and Massachusetts. By then I needed to stop.

There seemed to be an inordinate number of women waiting to

use the facilities at the State Liquor rest stop. I glanced at my watch
and hoped that Ben wasn't glancing at his and thinking he was in
danger of missing his plane. We still had two hours, but who knew
how the traffic might be further south. If it had been Sean waiting for
me in the car he would have been huffing by now.

When I did finally get back to it, Ben was casually leaning against
the car, drinking bottled water and thumbing through some tourist
pamphlets he'd picked up in the information area. "Hey, we ought to
bag New York and head over to the Flume Gorge Park. It sounds
wonderful. Cascading water and all that."

"Ben. We've all been to the Flume. And the Old Man in the
Mountain, and all the rest of it. You have to go to the city. You have
work to do."

"Spoilsport."

"Slacker."

We were pretty close to Boston yet the traffic, by this time, was thin,
even in the Callahan Tunnel, and I reached Logan easily, with half an
hour to spare. Ben's flight was on USAir, and it was relatively easy to
find the terminal. I followed the signs into the cool, shadowed under-
building of the drop-off area, pulling alongside the curb behind several other cars dropping off passengers. I waited in line, just like dropping the kids off at school, then pulled ahead after a car pulled away
from the curb, leaving me space behind a silver Toyota with Rhode
Island plates. As people do, I noted the plate framed by the logo of the
dealership in Cranston where we'd bought one of our cars years ago. It
was a vanity plate, ELNR 2 and I sounded it out phonetically.

Ben had just turned to thank me for the ride when the passenger
got out of ELNR 2. Almost simultaneously, the trunk lid popped open
and a young woman climbed out of the driver's side. She reached into
the trunk to grasp a garment bag, a distinctive cranberry color with a
broad blue paint stain across the shoulder, the result of a careless
moment when I was painting the woodwork in the kitchen and Sean
came through the door.

"Cleo?" Ben's voice carried the exact timbre one uses to settle an angry animal. "Cleo, what is it?"

We both stared out the windshield at the scene before us. The young woman, short and sort of plump bordering on voluptuous, handed my husband his bag. That was all right. I could leap out of this borrowed car and call to them. "Hi! what a coincidence . . ." But then, and I was aware of Ben's hand on my shoulder, gripping it, then this big-haired girl, this ELNR, wrapped her arms around Sean's neck and kissed him with the unmistakable passion of a lover.

Oblivious to the tan SUV with Rhode Island plates parked right behind them, unobservant as ever, Sean broke away from her only long enough to catch his breath and then dipped his head for more. His hand playfully cupped her rather round bottom crammed into stretch-fabric hip-huggers. I could hear their voices through Ben's half-open window.

"I'll call you tonight."

"I'll be lying there."

I felt physically sick, completely incapable of moving. My hands were still gripping the steering wheel and every emotion I had experienced eight years ago in finding the condom wrapper increased exponentially by this visual confirmation of my husband's great lies. I heard the passenger door of Grace's car open and shut. I kept staring at the spot they had occupied, even after Sean disappeared into the building and the silver Toyota pulled away from the curb with a jaunty acceleration.

"Cleo, move over." Ben pushed me gently into the passenger's seat. I did what he said, fumbling a little with the button on the seat belt until he reached across and opened it for me. I was fighting the same kind of nausea you get when you hit some vulnerable place, half sick, half faint.

Ben climbed in and drove away from the terminal. Coming out from under the building, the sunlight hurt my eyes, making them water. I fumbled for my sunglasses while Ben paid the toll at the tunnel, then took them off and held them in my lap. Ben had us back onto the interstate, heading north.

"Ben, what are you doing?" I finally seemed to wake up to the realization that he was not only driving, but going back to the lake. "You should be on a plane."

"No. I can go another time. No big deal. I'm not going to leave you now." He gestured toward the phone and I nodded. He punched in a number and smiled at me. "Harry? Ben. Look, something's come up and I'll have to postpone till next week. No. I'm fine. Really. No, Harry, that's not it. Not this time. Trust me, I'll be there on Monday. Absolutely."

He pressed the off button and signaled to pass a truck.

The sick feeling had subsided, but I could feel a kind of internal vibration as if I was shaking on the inside. I looked at my hands, but they were steady. "I feel as though I'm in a familiar place, unpleasant but familiar, like I've been here before."

"You have been, Cleo. You never forget even if you do forgive."

We were almost back to the state line. "Ben, I can't let you put your life on hold for me. You need to get to New York. Please, let's rebook your flight."

I reached for the phone but Ben simply shook his head and covered the keypad with his hand. "Look, Cleo, I know I've presented a pretty whitewashed view of my life with Talia, but I can tell you that I've been in this cruel place too."

"What do you mean? Talia cheated on you?"

"Yes."

We were holding hands, gripping each other as if trying to save our own lives.

Twenty-three

❧

"I suppose they spent the night in Boston." I broke the quiet in the car by voicing the skirling thoughts in my head. I was trying to make sense of Sean being at Logan, when he was supposed to be in Pittsburgh. I was trying to make sense of being in a borrowed car behind him at the exact moment he is kissing his lover. "If I hadn't been so long in the ladies room, we wouldn't have been there to see it. I wouldn't know anything. I would still be in my lovely deluded world."

"Cleo, don't do this to yourself," Ben warned gently, then signaled to get off the highway and into a rest area. He pulled into a parking space and shut the car off. Unbuckling his seatbelt and then mine, he pulled me over to him and just held me. I didn't struggle against his comfort, only let the first volley of weeping commence until I was embarrassed that I'd wet his shirt with tears.

We stayed like that for a few minutes, then I pulled away and buckled myself in. "I'm okay. Thank you."

"Anytime." He started the car. "Would it be insensitive of me to suggest getting some lunch?"

We found a little diner along an old New Hampshire state road. I ordered something I knew I wouldn't eat, and then did. Ben didn't try to distract me with small talk, just kept sliding things from his own plate onto mine, his pickles and his chips. All the time we spent in silence, my thoughts tumbled over themselves with roisterous uncontrol. I was afraid to let them out, to give voice to the rage I was dealing out to myself, one moment convinced I had been a party to Sean's duplicity. I'd not only given him the opportunity, I'd not paid attention to the dim and distant alarm when I should have. Because of my selfish need to be alone to write, I'd turned my back on a charging bull. At the same instant I wanted Sean to be responsible for his own weakness.

We got back on the road, keeping off the highway and on the long secondary route toward Cameo Lake. We passed silently through small towns and past farms and Pick-Ur-Own-Blueberries (or -Corn or -Apples) stands along the way. It was almost as if we were out for an old-fashioned Sunday drive. I saw the brown state park sign indicating the Flume at the same time Ben signaled for the turn into the parking lot.

"I think we need to go back to our original plan."

"Our what?"

"Instead of going to New York, let's go see the Flume." Ben had the car parked and was half out of the car before I could say no.

For some reason, it seemed exactly the right thing to be doing. I was too jangled to go home and wait for tomorrow afternoon, when I could pick up my kids from camp. I was too angry to sit still, and it was once again too hot to run for as long as it would take to outrun this familiar trauma. Ben had sacrificed his work to keep me from being alone. Besides, he seemed really keen on doing it.

I went to the ladies room while Ben bought tickets. The large room was empty except for a dainty older woman dabbing a wet handkerchief on a stain on her blouse. Her eyes met mine in the mirror as I fingered the waves of my brown hair into some semblance of neatness. "Have you been up yet?" she asked.

"No. We're just about to go."

"You and your husband?"

"No. I don't have a husband."

Oblivious of my lie, she gathered her handbag and pushed open the door of the ladies room.

I felt a little remorseful, having said that to this innocent old lady, but at the moment, it seemed pretty true. I certainly didn't have the husband I thought I'd had.

Ben was waiting by the photo display of the hanging rock, now no longer hanging. "All set?"

"Yeah. Let's go."

As we walked by her, side by side but not hand in hand, the old lady chanced to look at me and winked. I was so taken aback, I pretended not to notice. It was as if she had unaccountably given me the thumbs-up.

A whole mass of Japanese businessmen were ahead of us, waiting for the jitney, so we hung back until they had boarded it and waited for the next. They looked uniformly out of context for the breathy, deep New Hampshire woods, in their black suits and conservative ties.

The next jitney came along without too much delay, and this one was ours alone. I began to feel a sense of the surreal as we climbed up the mountain road. I was so very far away from where I imagined myself on this morning. I had meant to be shopping. I had meant to look up some geographic details at the BPL. I had meant to treat myself to a big book store, to surreptitiously check to see if my titles were still in stock. Instead, here I was, a tourist on a noisy bus, beside a man I new both intimately and not at all. My interior shaking began again, chilled from the inside. I must have shivered in the drier, cooler air because Ben slipped an arm around my shoulders.

The Japanese businessmen massed at the trailhead, listening with solemn concentration to the young Japanese woman describing the natural phenomena of the gorge. We slipped ahead of them easily and began the ascent up the wooden stairs to the platform promontory which overlooks the cascading water. The voice of the guide faded behind us and the only sounds were the natural rushing of the water and the insistent birdsong around us. At some point Ben had taken my hand and now he pulled me along and up the steps to a cavelike outcropping where the water pooled. We found a fairly comfortable rock in the shade and sat down.

The Japanese tourists passed us by, nodding a little in our direction and then the place was ours alone.

Ben gathered my left hand between his. "I think the most important thing you should know is that this is not your fault. It wasn't your fault the first time and it isn't your fault now. What I mean to say is, Sean's affair most likely has nothing to do with you, with your worth or even with how much he loves you. Sometimes things happen that are beyond our control, or the control of those people hurting us."

"I don't understand." I meant I didn't understand how he knew so precisely what I was feeling.

Because he hadn't spoken of this to anyone, he stumbled at first, then warmed up and began to tell the story, picking up rhythm as he went along. "I was all wrong for Talia. I was too old, too goy, too former rock musician. I was everything her parents feared for her, so I was, in her eyes, perfect. For a while that was enough. For a while our mutual interest in getting her jazz career launched was enough. But the truth is that we were opposites, the only thing we had in common was music. We only saw eye to eye in that. She craved fame, I'd had it. She liked being the wife of a former rock star, I wanted only to create a quiet home. In the end, she wanted freedom and I represented constraint."

Ben pulled himself into the present. "Sorry, I don't mean to digress, but you should know the background so that you understand the ending."

"Tell me the story any way you want. We have all the time in the world."

His voice had become soothing, melodic in a way I hadn't noticed before. I leaned into his story, happy to devote my concentration to it instead of to my own. I understood the power of the bedtime story. Even though the ending would prove to be scary, the telling of it would be cathartic for both of us.

He took a moment and then continued. "I believe we had what might be termed a tumultuous marriage. Sometimes the only thing I was certain about was that we loved each other. I was certain we did because the music we played together was proof of it. It was like our child, newly created each time. We could begin the day screaming at each other about her traveling too much or my wanting to be here instead of at some New York publicity event, but when we got to the studio, my God, it was all forgotten as her notes shadowed by mine described a love affair with sound."

I realized that as he spoke, Ben had drifted into that lonesome abyss where memory becomes acute, where it becomes present time. It was what he was seeing, it was what he was reexperiencing, and I was only audience to his private soliloquy. I waited for him to tell me why I should accept no fault for the mess my marriage was in. Waited for him to pick up the story of his own shattered life.

"Sometimes I think that I fell in love with the music, not the woman. The first time I heard her play it was if she was an enchantress. She used her whole body, swaying and dipping with the sound of her own creation. Her eyes were closed and she was as mesmerizing to watch as to hear. How could I not have fallen in love?"

I stroked his forearm, let him know I was there and listening. It seemed as though we were alone in a vast wood. It was growing late and no more groups of Japanese tourists wandered by as we continued to sit on the flat rock near the outcropping. The incessant rush of water lay as background music to Ben's story. I thought to myself— what a cutting thing it is to love someone.

"Eventually we grew apart. The distance between us was physical. Talia was on the road more and more, and she was resolute in not letting me do more than join her for a weekend if the tour took her close by. She said that she respected my distaste for touring, she didn't want to interfere with my composing, she loved me but it was better that she go it alone.

"I allowed for her age, her natural desire to be young among youth, not dragging an old man around with her, who might disapprove of some of the choices she made. Choices endemic to such a lifestyle."

I thought I knew what he meant by choices. Although he didn't come right out and say it, I assumed that he meant he had turned a blind eye to the drugs. As we sat in the shadows of the woods and the sun began to lower, cooling the air around us into a comforting breeze, Ben talked.

"By last year, Talia had pretty much stopped coming home. She'd only come twice to the cabin on Cameo Lake in the previous six months. So it was a complete surprise when I heard the taxi horn blowing and there was Talia, standing at the boat ramp, waving this big straw hat she only wore here.

"She was so radiant, even from that distance, I could see the luminescence in her smile. Even knowing that she graced everyone with that smile didn't diminish its impact on me each time I saw it."

I thought of Sean's practiced insurance-man smile and knew exactly what Ben meant.

Barefoot, Ben had jumped out of the canoe before it crunched onto the pebbly surface of the beach and taken Talia up into a big swooping greeting in his arms, grateful for her returning embrace. "Why didn't you call and tell me you were coming?"

"I wanted to surprise you."

He wanted to ask how long she would be there but was reluctant to burst the bubble of happiness. Inevitably it would be too short and he would try to convince her to stay longer. Save the argument for later, he told himself.

Sitting in the bow of the Old Town, Talia trailed her fingers through the still water of the July lake. She didn't talk but seemed content to let him paddle her home in silence. Ben stroked slowly, unwilling to let the moment pass too quickly.

Talia seemed very tired, almost lethargic and went to bed immediately for a nap. Subsuming an overpowering desire with concern, he tucked her into their bed and went back to review the music he'd been working on. The handwritten notes on the staff made no sense to him as he could think only of Talia sleeping in their bed and his need to touch her. As quietly as he could, Ben slid in beside the sleeping form of his wife. In the lingering July sunset, he could see that she seemed faded, paler than usual, and the dark circles beneath her closed eyes made him wonder if she was eating properly—or had she replaced food with something more satisfying? While she slept, Ben ran his fingertips down the inside of her left arm, and then her right. He knew he was looking for signs of needle marks and was immensely relieved not to see any, and then ashamed he had even considered such a thing. There was something about the way she had come home unannounced, her pensive silence, and the quick retreat to bed which alarmed him. He had the fleeting thought that she'd come home to tell him something, and then changed her mind.

At that moment Talia wakened and looked up at him looking down on her. She raised the arm he had so recently been examining for marks and brought his head down to hers.

Afterward they went out to dinner. Talia was quiet in the car, watching the familiar scenery pass by, offering measured responses to his attempts at conversation. She was a little livelier in the restaurant but faded back as they ate. Until he mentioned a piece he was working on for her.

"Tell me about it."

For twenty minutes they forgot everything which lay between them and focused on a new composition Ben had planned to surprise her with on their anniversary. As he hummed the tune, described his vision of the harmonies and where the voice of the flute would soar over the accompanying piano, Talia looked at Ben with the only kind of love she seemed capable of expressing to him.

"I can't wait to hear it."

"Let's go home and I'll play it for you."

An odd thing happened then, Ben told me. They rose to leave and were stopped at the cash register by a disheveled-looking man. Stringy hair hung down over the frayed collar of his work shirt. He had the sallow skin and deep under-eye pouches of a hard drinker, and when he smiled at Ben, his grin was snaggletoothed and gapped. "Hey, aren't you Benson Turner?"

Ben shifted a little away from the guy, then put out his hand, "Yeah. I am."

The man grasped Ben's hand in a painfully enthusiastic crunch. "God, I followed you across this country three times in 1983. I . . ."

"Come on Ben, let's go." Talia pulled him toward the door.

"Hey, I gotta tell you, I love you, man!" The guy stumbled back against the counter. "You were the best."

Ben felt Talia's tug and called back, "Thanks. Thanks a lot."

"Jesus, Ben, you can't be letting people like that get in your face." Talia's voice was loud in the quiet street.

"Hey, it's been a long time since anyone did that. It feels pretty good." Ben's own voice was a little louder than he intended and he was a little embarrassed as people they knew from the lake walked by.

"Well, if you hadn't squandered your talent, it might happen more often."

For some reason, the whole incident soured the moment. They climbed into the car, Ben behind the wheel. He tried to leaven the moment with a joke—"I just realized, we only went across the country once in 1983."

Talia shrugged. "At least my fans are clean."

"Hey, he's just a local burnout case. I'm sure not all of my fans turned out like that. Some of them might even have grown up into investment bankers."

"Still. He was pretty disgusting."

"Talia, come on." Ben was losing patience with her. Losing patience altogether, and suddenly his restraint was gone. "So, how long can I expect you to be around?" He hadn't meant for it to come out with so much hostility, but her attitude had gotten to him.

"I'm leaving tomorrow."

"You can't be serious. You just got here."

"I assure you, I am serious. I have a concert in a couple of days."

They drove home in silence and Ben wondered when their relationship had become so fragile.

"There was something there, something which had brought her to the lake, something which she was holding back from me. I knew it and I was so afraid of it that I couldn't ask her what was bothering her. Maybe if I had, things would have turned out differently."

"Ben, it does no good to think that way. Like you said, some things are simply not our doing. Not our fault." I wanted him to go on, to tell me exactly what had happened that night, but instead he stood up and pulled me to my feet. "Look, it's getting late and the park will be closing."

"Ben, don't stop now."

"Cleo, I can't. I will, I promise, but right now I need to stop." He walked ahead of me and I scrambled to keep up.

Twenty-four

Ben opened the screen door of the porch for me. "I'll stay if you don't want to be alone. Right here," he gestured toward the porch glider cluttered with the detritus of my first printed draft, crumpled papers flung in exasperation at the inconsistent printing of my old Epson.

"You don't have to, Ben. I'm all right. This is a familiar place, after all. I've been in this position once before. Eventually the hurt dulls and I go on."

"Okay, but only if you're sure." There was something in those gentle brown eyes. Telling even this truncated story to me had left him bleeding a little, the scab picked. He had hurt himself by trying to comfort me. I knew that new healing could now take place for Ben, but he hadn't yet recognized that fact for himself.

"Unless you want the company . . ."

He didn't respond.

"Stay with me. I've got an open bottle of wine."

"Thank you, Cleo." Ben reached out a little, as if he was going to touch me but didn't and instead slid his fingers into his pocket.

We sat on the glider and stared out over the calm lake. It had still been a little light out when we got home and I hadn't put on any lights. We sat, shadowed from one another in the growing dark. The moon was just rising and still low in the East, giving only meager light to the reflecting pool before us. We were quiet, content for the moment in our silence, lost in our own thoughts. The wine was crisp and cool and went down very easily and was gone too soon. Grace had left a bottle of whiskey under the sink and I fetched it .

Ben poured out a little for himself but I refused it. After a few minutes he sighed, a profoundly unhappy sound. "May I put my arm around you?"

"Yes." Our voices were very soft.

"I need to tell you the rest of it. The rest of my story."

"I'd like to hear it."

That night they had arrived home safely, leaving the Wagoneer at the boat ramp and taking the canoe across the lake. "It was as still as it is tonight. The moon was low in the West, but I could see my shoreline easily. Talia sat in front of me, still silent, still brooding. The white of her dress literally glowed as we glided by the raft, and if we had been in better moods I would have called her my moonbeam."

It wasn't terribly late when they got home and Ben thought that maybe they could retrieve part of the evening by looking over the composition he'd started. "Would you like to hear the piece?" he asked her. All Talia's earlier enthusiasm for the piece was gone, leaving in its place a kind of weary good sportsmanship.

"Okay."

Ben retrieved the composition paper from a pile on the piano. "It's still really raw, but I think you'll like it." He began playing, aware of Talia standing behind him, reading along as he played, softly whistling as she added her own interpretation to his notes. "That's good, Talia, that's a nice counterpoint."

He ran out of notes and he stopped. Talia placed her hands on his shoulders and leaned her cheek against his head, filling him with despair because he knew before she said it that she was leaving him.

"Why, Talia? Haven't I given you enough freedom?"

"I'm in love with someone else."

"As if she couldn't stand the cruelty of her own words she left the room. As if the only way to stop them was to run. I couldn't move.

My fingers still rested on the keyboard but I couldn't feel the keys beneath my fingers. I could still feel her breath on my ear. 'I am in love with someone else.'

"I heard the French doors open and then slam shut. I knew where she was going. She wasn't a good swimmer. The moon was gone by now and it was fully dark. The raft was a stretch for her and she seldom got that far, but she did that night. Last summer was very hot and dry. The level of the lake was down and the rock even closer to the surface than usual. But she hadn't been to the lake all summer, she didn't know that. How could she have known? I should have warned her. Reminded her about it. But I stayed at the piano, slowly tearing the music into a thousand pieces like ashes. She would never play it. No one would ever hear it." Abruptly Ben put his face in his hands, his story over.

No, I knew that his story wasn't quite done, there remained a missing detail. But I knew that I wouldn't hear it tonight. Maybe I would never hear exactly how Talia came to go off that raft. I forced back my natural curiosity and stroked the back of his hand still covering his eyes. Then I rubbed his back, conscious of the muscle which lay below his cambric shirt, aware of his scent, made pungent by his emotion. I lay my cheek against him, inhaling his scent, suddenly understanding the power of pheromones as my craving for his touch grew. We were the wounded, the wronged. But I refused to give ground to the thought. It would be too easy to take advantage of each other. I stood up and Ben got to his feet, going to the screen door. Understanding me exactly.

The humid oppression of the heat coupled with the humid desire Ben had inadvertently triggered made sleep impossible. I lay naked on my bed, windows wide against a breathless night.

Doglike, it circled me, a sudden comprehension of Sean's temptation. I understood at this moment what it was like to feel the power of new desire. I beat it, the empathy, back. No, I chastised it, it wasn't the same at all. The empathy panted, teeth bared—oh, yes it is. No, I said, this is his fault, Sean's. And Talia's. Ben and I were but two sad souls meeting over our lovers' betrayals.

I heard a splash. It was like a call to me and I left my bed to walk along the path to the water's edge. The risen moon illuminated my way. The water shimmered in its beam, laying a cosmic road to the raft. I swam in the cold silky lake water, slow even strokes, counting them like beats in a measure as I swam toward Ben. The water eddied around me as I reached the ladder. I took Ben's hand and climbed up, the water on my body shining in the moonlight.

Later I would analyze my actions. Later I would examine my motives. Later I would feel sinful. Now I simply reveled in being physically loved by a man who didn't know every contour of my body, who spent forever exploring it, reveled in touching a man whose skin was new territory, whose taste was a new flavor. We moved together on the hard raft like we had moved together on the dance floor, our hips aligning perfectly, his fingertips startling me with boldness. He was rougher than I would have supposed, given his gentle nature, and I found I liked the hard grip of his hand pulling against my hair. Excited by the daring of our act, I allowed Ben exploration I had never allowed Sean.

Sean was my first. Until now, my only. I couldn't honestly say that I would have done this thing had Sean not betrayed me. But once done, I kept it for myself. Ben, in loving me so well, celebrated the part of me which had foundered. It was no longer about Sean, it was about me. Both Ben and I needed the reassurance of physical love, proof that we were still worthy of it. By Ben's loving, I was taken completely out of this world and lifted to that place where nothing but touch exists, where no thoughts except of release, can form. I cried out against Ben's hand across my mouth. A second later I covered his against being heard. First we cried, little salty tears of grief and joy, and then we laughed and held each other. Then we lay still, as nature untangled us. The breeze across our sweaty bodies was gentle, stroking us cool.

"If you were writing this, writing a story about a woman who discovers her husband is philandering, how would you portray her?"

"Well, its a pretty typical plot. Generally what happens is that the woman, the protagonist, finds she's stronger without him. That her long-sublimated inner strength carries her out of the situation until the philandering husband seeks to return to the fold and she finds she has the strength now to reject him. After great unhappiness—mind you, she's usually totally unaware of his straying ways until one chance encounter—she realizes she's happier without the bastard." I started to giggle. "And, of course, she finds her true love in the next-door neighbor."

Ben stroked my side, gently tracing the curve to my waist, and then to my hips. "Is the neighbor usually a pensive loner?"

"Sometimes, but not always." I wondered for a moment if he would misunderstand this. "Ben, you have to know that I am not using you to somehow get back at Sean."

"Use me, if you need to." Ben kissed the tip of my chin. His arm was beneath my head and we lay facing each other on the hard surface of the raft, still rocking gently against our recent rhythms.

"I have to deal with Sean in my own way, and I haven't yet figured that out. But I don't want you to ever think I would use you to somehow get back at him."

"I know that. This is simply a moment between you and me. No one else."

"Ever." I knew what he was saying and was relieved by it. Neither one of us would go away with expectations. I knew we were both in emotionally vulnerable states; I didn't want to fall into the temptation of thinking it meant a future. Not now.

The moon began to share the sky with the edge of the sun. Birdsong warned us of day and we dived off the raft and made for our separate shores.

Twenty-five

At noon, unplanned, we met on the raft. Half a day's sleep and we had both regained our equilibrium. "How are you?" I asked and he said, "Fine, how are you?" and I said, "Fine." We lay on the raft and dozed for a few minutes, just glad to have the sunshine on us, our fingertips discreetly touching.

My laptop remained closed this morning. I hadn't been able to do more than drink coffee and sit on the glider, trying to make sense of my life. Now my stomach burned and the only thing clear to me was that I had to leave the lake and go home.

"Grace is coming tonight." Ben's voice startled me out of my half-sleep.

"What? When did you hear that?"

"She left a message on my machine—reluctantly, no doubt. She couldn't raise you on your, her, car phone, so she assumed I'd be willing to give you the message. Of course, I wasn't home last night, so you've got very short notice."

"How like Grace. She sends me up here to get away from distractions and then joins me." I might have laughed at the irony, but I was too soulsick.

"Maybe the lesson here is that there's no such thing as getting away from your distractions."

"Or developing new ones." I linked my fingers with his and let the magnitude of what we had done roll through me. It wasn't as if I'd been seduced, or as if I had chosen to break my vows out of mischief or immorality. Ben and I had comforted each other, and if I stayed on the lake that comfort would take center stage against the anguish of my marriage. The ultimate distraction.

Ben rolled from his back to his stomach and tweaked a lock of my wet hair, "She wants to know if you have anything done."

"Oh, really."

"So, do you?"

"Yes. It's nearly done."

"What's it about? Do you mind my asking?"

I shrugged. It's always hard for me to synopsize the unfinished. "It's a story about strangers coming together against great odds, becoming friends, and then losing each other . . ."

"And then?"

"I don't know. I haven't finished it." I took my hand away from his and sat up. "I have to go home, you know."

"I know. What will you do?" Ben sat beside me on the edge of the raft facing north.

"I don' t know. It's not a very simple question. I've been sitting on the porch, wondering why I don't just give Sean the boot. But it's not just Sean."

"No, of course not, there are the kids. These things are so hard on them."

"Not only the kids, Ben. Sean's family is the closest thing I've ever had to a real family." I felt the pressure in my chest build as I articulated this truth for the first time even to myself. "I love them like my own, and they've always treated me like one of theirs. How can I ever walk away from them?" I was embarrassed at the flood of tears leaking from my squinting eyes. I wiped them away, angry at them.

"Cleo, if they love you, they'll find a way for you to stay part of the family. You'll always have the kids in common."

"It's complicated, but thanks, that helps." I didn't add that the other complication was that I wasn't sure I didn't still love Sean. Would I let his weakness force our life apart? Or my weakness?

As I slipped into the water, Ben remained on the raft. "Hey, Cleo, about your characters . . ."

"What?"

"I hope they find each other again."

"Me, too."

As soon as I reached the top of the drive I called Sean's office. Once again I got Audrey, who reassured me before asking that she had given Sean the message about the Barbies.

"Oh, right, the Barbies. Well, actually I need you to give him another message."

"Do you want me to pass you along to Eleanor?"

"No." Surely Audrey had heard the sharp intake of breath. "I want you to give him this message. Not anyone else."

I told Audrey to tell Sean I did not want him coming up tomorrow. I would be going home Saturday morning. Then I wondered at the wisdom of giving him warning. Of giving him an extra night. It couldn't be helped. The last thing I wanted was to upset the kids by hauling them out of camp a day early. There was going to be enough upset in their future.

Lily and Tim were as tired and cranky as after the last camp-out and they clambered into the car with very little comment to me. "It was okay, yeah, can we have pizza?" Tim's usual greeting.

"Grace is coming tonight." I watched their faces in the rearview mirror. The cranky exhaustion dissipated briefly as my children got excited about the arrival of their pseudo-aunt.

"When, what time, where will she sleep?"

"Those are exactly my questions," I said and pulled into the parking lot of the Big G.

The whole time I was cleaning up and driving and picking up groceries, my stomach kept churning against the moment when Grace, my dearest, most perceptive friend, would divine my situation.

I played a mental tennis game between the opposing racquets of telling her about Sean's affair and not telling her about my friendship with Ben. It wasn't that I didn't want her to know either of these things, it was more how she would react to them. I expected her to be angry at Sean, I expected she'd be annoyed at me for forming a friendship with the lake pariah. Screw it, I thought. If Grace has chosen to dislike Ben because of some lakeside gossip, it was her loss. I wouldn't betray Ben's secret, I had promised.

An unfamiliar car was parked in the driveway when we got back. As soon as we pulled in beside it, Grace came bounding, as only Grace could, to sweep us up in her arms. "Hello, hello, hello, hello!" She kissed the children and told them to go into her room and find their presents. Then she stood, holding me at arms' length, studying me for a second before squeezing me tight. "Sweetheart, you look fabulous. Tired, overworked, but fabulous."

"Grace, you do, too. Tell me everything."

"First things first. We came home early because Joanie's mother fell and broke her hip. Of course I wouldn't let Joanie come home alone, and as she's with her mother in Boston and our student tenants still have a week of summer school left, well, there's no place left for me but here. Between you and me, I could use the stillness. We did nothing but tour and eat and walk the whole time in Italy. It was fabulous." Clearly *fabulous* was Grace's word of the day. I let her take me by the hand and bring me into the house. "What have you got done?"

On the island counter, neatly piled, were three hundred and fifteen pages of an almost complete manuscript. "I've been busy."

"See, I told you this was the best thing in the world for you." Grace gave me another of her bear hugs and then whispered in my ear, "But how come the kids are here?"

"Long story."

"After they go to bed?"

"Yup. Should be early tonight. They were at overnight camp last night and they never sleep when they're there."

True enough, and almost as soon as dinner was over, they trundled off to bed with hardly a protest. I grabbed the half-empty bottle of chardonnay and our glasses and went out onto the porch. Grace settled herself on the glider. She was wearing one of her trademark flowing dresses and with visible additional avoirdupois she'd earned while in Italy, she looked wonderfully Rubenesque. With a dramatic fling of her unruly gray-streaked black hair, Grace patted the seat next to her.

"I have to pace this one out." I poured a little wine into her nearly empty glass and more into my empty one. In novels, the hook at the very beginning, the very first words the writer speaks to the reader, are the most critical. It is the hardest sentence to write. I perched a little on the writing table and drew words together which would be my first sentence of a sorry tale. Direct, as always with Grace, seemed best. "Sean is having an affair."

I let my words sink in. To her credit, Grace didn't flinch. Nor did she rush me with rebuttal or confirmation of suspicion. She pursed her lips and said, "Go on."

I tried to give the story a framework, a chronology, but as I told it, I realized that I had no framework, no timeline. It had happened, I had seen it. Grace kept my glass full and her eyes on me and her comments to herself. The only twitch I saw in her eye came as I explained why I was at Logan when I was. Finally, sated with telling, I sat beside her and she enfolded me in her big arms.

"Cleo, will you leave him?"

I shrugged, voiceless now, raw with talking.

"*I* would if I were you. He might tell you it's the only time he's done something like this, yada yada . . ."

"It's not."

I felt Grace's interest in the swift shifting of her weight away from me. "What?"

Tired, a little drunk, I gave her an abbreviated version of the eight-year-ago fling.

"Sweet Mary, that man ought to be castrated."

"Grace, please don't." I was feeling pretty dizzy by this time and Grace's presence seemed to be growing bigger and bigger as I sat there beside her. I love Grace, but she can overwhelm me about the smallest things, never mind something of this magnitude. I always said it was the director in her. "Grace, I have to go to bed. I didn't get much sleep last night."

"I'll sleep out here."

"No. I changed the bed for you, I want you to take it. I actually like sleeping out here. And you won't hear me when I get up to run in the wee hours."

"Okay. You don't have to twist my arm. I'm too big to be comfortable on this old thing, anyway." Grace got to her feet, a little inebriated as well, and less graceful than usual. "Tell me something, though, before I leave you."

"What?"

"What does Ben know about this? He was there when you saw Sean kissing his tart, did he realize what was going on?"

I hadn't told Grace about Ben's taking me home, about our day-long journey back and the hours at the Flume. I'd glossed it over, saying only that I was dropping Ben off. "He knows everything. He was a great comfort to me that day."

"Hmm." Grace could impose a tremendous weight on that little hmm. I'd heard her do it to Joanie when her partner did something Grace didn't like; I'd heard her do it to students when they presented airtight defenses for late work. I'd been the recipient on more than one occasion. Imbued in that little hmm was deep disapproval and disappointment. "Well, give me a kiss good-night. Sleep well."

A night bird called, seeking its mate. Then I heard Ben's piano, softly playing the now familiar motif of his homage to Talia.

Twenty-six

I awoke to the sound of frying meat and banging pots. Grace was up, the kids were up, and I had slept miraculously late.

"Good morning, sleepyhead!" Grace flourished a spatula. "Go pee, then sit and eat. Coffee's ready, your mug is on the table set so beautifully by these two incredibly cute children."

Lily and Tim, still in pajamas, giggled. I didn't let Grace or the children see the tears in my eyes as an unforeseen sense of well-being, of being taken care of, washed over me. My world may be cracked in the middle, but Auntie Grace is cooking. Everything's gonna be all right.

After breakfast and while the kids got dressed for camp, Grace and I walked out and down to the water's edge, our third cups of coffee in hand.

"I'm always delightfully surprised at how beautiful this place really is. I was so right to send you here."

"Yes, in the main. Yes, you were." I might have made some wry comment about how being here had opened up new challenges for me, but I held my tongue. Instead, I looked across the shimmering lake at Ben's cabin and smiled to catch sight of him heading our way in his canoe, his bike athwart the bow. "Looks like we're about to have company." I gave Grace a "be nice" look and waved to Ben.

"You do know Benson Turner, don't you." My voice was just a shade on the challenging side, daring my oldest best friend to diss my newest.

Jumping out of the grounded canoe, Ben hauled it up onto the waterfront grass and walked over to Grace with a slow boyishness. "Hello, Grace."

"Hello, Ben." There was a moment's hesitation as they sized each other up and then they kissed, cheek to cheek. Suddenly Grace reached out and wrapped her arms around Ben. "It's good to see you."

Ben smiled into Grace's shoulder and then looked up at me. "And to see you, Grace. I've missed you out here this summer."

"Well, enough mush." Grace pushed away from Ben but hung on to his hand. I knew that Grace was clearly reconsidering sides in the ongoing lakeside controversy.

"I came to beg a favor. Can I hitch a ride to town?"

"Are you still driving that beat-up old buckboard?"

"Only when it runs, Grace. Which apparently this morning it has chosen not to do."

Ben muscled the bike into the back of the SUV and climbed in, teasing the kids about something, making them laugh. We let the kids be a buffer between us as we headed toward camp.

After dropping the kids, we drove along in silence to Cameo, where I would drop him and his bike, listening like true New Englanders to the local weather report on the car radio. A brief cool front moving over the mountains, more heat later.

"Are you leaving today?" Ben's question was sharp and unexpected.

"Tomorrow. I'm going to Narragansett."

"Why?"

I gave a little shrug. "I need to be with Alice, my mother-in-law. I can't be alone with Sean right now, but I need to be home."

"Cleo, will you ever come back?"

"Ben." We were quiet again. The news broadcast over, we kept listening to the oldies rock station, and when the DJ introduced "Frozen Heart" I had to keep Ben from shutting it off. It was the longer, live version recorded at one of their concerts. I'd forgotten what a great song it was, forgotten how powerful and evocative good rock music could be. It had the power to remind me of what passion and loss can sound like. Stash's voice crying out the words to the chorus:—*You will never, no never, be lost to my mind. Frozen forever in my heart*—seemed suddenly too personal and Ben snapped the radio off.

"Ben, you may say you sold your soul to the whore of success, but your music was really quite brilliant."

"It was all right."

"And your homage to Talia is brilliant, too."

I had grown so used to some of Ben's mannerisms that it didn't surprise me when he ran a hand through his hair and rubbed his face. "Cleo, remember when I told you that I'd been writing a new piece for Talia, the one I wanted her to hear that night?"

"Yes."

"The one I destroyed?"

I nodded.

"It's become my concerto, my homage."

When I got back to the cabin, Grace was already at the beach, schmoozing with the beach biddies. I had a moment's anxiety that she would be discussing what I had confided in her and then chastised myself. However voluble Grace might be, she was not a breaker of confidences. I stripped to take a shower, then changed my mind. I grabbed the last dry towel in the cabin.

It seemed only natural that I swim to the raft. I couldn't face the women on the beach, even with Grace there. On board, the air was cooler than my wet skin, and I was a little chilled. The sun was behind new clouds, too muted to bake me dry, so I lay down only to get away from the breeze. The breeze was picking up, already it had changed the surface of the lake from the glassine of dawn to rough fish-scale shapes, prelude to wavelets. I caught myself making up similes to describe the water and knew that perhaps my next book would take place near a lake.

The gentle movement of the raft was enough to put me to sleep. With no one to distract me I slept until I heard the spooning of the paddle into the lake. I sat up and watched as Ben left the beach in front of the cabin and stroked towards his own. Neither one of us called out or gestured. I simply sat and watched as Ben took long powerful strokes against the force of the increasing breeze. As he passed the raft, he slowed the forward motion of the canoe down, J-stroking to a near halt, but standing off, about ten feet away.

I know you don't fall in love with someone in the course of a month, but what I felt for Ben seemed like it might, under the right circumstances, have become love. We had let each other see more of ourselves than near strangers ought, and in that moment, as I watched from the raft and he kept the canoe still with his paddle, it was impossible for a simple greeting to pass between us. So we said nothing, only smiled. And even that seemed overweighted.

I could see the orange cat sitting on the short wooden pier, standing up as Ben came alongside and arching its back in a luxurious stretch. I lingered for a moment to watch Ben climb out of his canoe and hoist the lashed bicycle off the bow. Then I stood up, ready to go home. As I moved to the edge of the raft I could see Sean standing on the porch steps, just watching me. What I felt for Ben was equally offset by my anger at Sean. Two extremes of my emotional repertoire.

Twenty-seven

In some dreams we struggle to make headway through a crowd or through sand or through water. I struggled to make headway against the rising breeze, the wavelets grown into erratic chop, splashing me in the face and choking me. I lacked the strength to make it to that shore and for one brief, completely selfish instant thought I'd simply let myself go under.

My feet touched the bottom, the ooze threading up between my toes as I walked out of the water and onto the muddy embankment. I was instantly chilled in the breeze. Sean stayed on the porch, watching me as I wrapped the floral bath towel around me. "I take it you didn't get my message."

"No. I did. I checked in when I landed this morning and when I got the message you were coming home tomorrow, I just headed up. I was halfway here anyway."

"What did you do, rent a car?"

"Yeah, why?"

"Because I know you didn't take ours to Logan."

"How could you know that?"

Grace hallooed from the path, letting us know before we saw her that she was coming. Leaving her beach chair and bag full of reading materials and sun block on the grass, Grace came up the stairs and took my shoulders, moving me a little aside, almost but not quite planting herself between Sean and me. "How about I pick up the kids from camp and head back to the city?"

I kept my eyes on Sean, now standing back a little, a willful pout on his lips. He took a step backward. "What's going on?"

"I'll throw a few things in a bag for them and write you a note with permission to take them. But Grace, can you take them to Narragansett, to Alice's?"

"Of course."

Then I remembered her student tenants. "Where will you go?"

Grace kissed my cheek. "Joanie's mom's. Not to worry."

I broke away from Grace's grip and went into the cabin.

"Cleo, what's going on?" Sean called after me, but made no move to follow.

"Sean, you and your wife need some time alone." Grace had pulled herself up to her full height, meeting Sean eye to eye and daring him to ask anything else. She left him on the porch and came in to collect the things I had stuffed into a knapsack.

I grabbed the top page of my manuscript and tore it in half, scrawling permission for Grace Chichetti to pick Lily and Tim McCarthy up today. I added that this would be their last day and thanked Mrs. Beckman for everything. Folding it over, I read the typescript of the novel's first sentence, and immediately thought of a better one. Karen and Jay had become quite different people than those they had started out as. I kissed Grace on the cheek and went back out to the porch, where Sean still stood, arms folded over his chest, on his face a reflection of his father's scowl.

"Awfully sensitive of Grace to take the kids and give us some alone time." His dark look belied the words.

"We need to talk."

Abruptly Sean's scowl vanished and he pushed past me to the kitchen. "Is there anything to eat in here? I only got pretzels and coffee on the plane." He started opening and shutting the cupboard doors, not finding anything to his liking. "I rushed up here so quickly, I didn't stop to eat lunch."

"Why did you rush up here?"

"I told you, I thought I'd help you pack."

"You are such a fucking liar."

I seldom use that word. It stopped Sean in his tracks.

Twenty-eight

"Okay, Cleo. What's going on?" Sean was still confident enough in himself, he said this casually, as if he knew he could talk me out of any annoyance I had with him over something inconsequential. He opened the door to the refrigerator.

"Just tell me something, Sean McCarthy. Was she worth it? I hope you think she was, because she's cost you the game."

Sean very carefully shut the door, sat on the barstool opposite mine and sighed. I could see the whirling indecision on his face. His Irish coloration gave away his thoughts. I could fairly narrate the dialogue going on in his head by the flush and fade of the color in his face. *Should I tell her the whole truth, or some variation?*

"Let me help you. I saw you at Logan on Wednesday. A day after the day you said you were going to Pittsburgh. I saw Eleanor and you together. I saw you kissing goodbye in a decidedly noncollegial way."

"Why were you at Logan?"

"Don't, Sean. This isn't my story, it's yours. I'm going to give you the punch line, but first I want to hear the story from your lips."

"I don't know what you think saw, but it was just a friendly kiss between colleagues."

"Like the condom wrapper was just a condom wrapper left by some friendly neighbor?"

Sean stood up, his enormous sigh told me that he knew the game was up. I expected him to say what he had said the first time. "She doesn't mean anything to me. I love you." But he didn't. He didn't say anything, only took an apple out of the bowl on the island counter and went out to the porch.

By nature, I wanted civility. I wanted this to be over, and I didn't want any yelling or lying or any more accusations. I wanted to be done with it. My parents managed to separate and divorce without raising their voices. They managed to be married for twenty years without ever raising their voices. But by the sheer magnitude of Sean's silence, I found myself on the verge of screaming. Aware of the acoustics of the woods and the lake, I lowered my voice to a hiss. "What have you done?"

Sean lifted his head to look at me and in between bites of apple told me his version of the truth. "About a year ago I hired Eleanor as my administrative assistant. She was so capable and so interested in moving up that it was easy to adopt a kind of mentoring role with her. She asked questions and made suggestions and before I knew it, was really indispensable to me. Then, slowly, I realized that there was some magnetism between us. I began to think of her when I shouldn't be.

"I thought that if I told you about her, it would neutralize the attraction, make her harmless. So, I told you that I brought her back a T-shirt from New Orleans. No big deal. Nothing compromising there. You never even remarked on it. But she was so thrilled, Eleanor was so excited to think I'd thought of her that the whole idea of trying to avoid what was happening so naturally was stupid. You see, no one in recent years had thought I was, well, worth a crush."

"I've never refused you."

"It wasn't sex. Not really. Not at first. It was puppy love. Hers for me. It is golden to be in a place where everything you do or say is brilliant and amusing."

"So you were flattered by her crush."

"Completely. Stupidly."

"But you're a grown man. You know how fragile that is, and how to put on the brakes."

"Cleo, at some point I realized I didn't want to make it go away."

"And what did she think? What have you told her? What promises have you made or implied? That you'd leave me for her?"

"I swear to you I've told her nothing, promised her nothing. It hasn't been like that. She knows we're Catholic."

"So, you're telling me this kid is in it just for the sex or is this some kind of sexual harassment?"

"Cleo, stop it. No."

"Have you promoted her?"

He looked down at the apple core. A little more flush tinged his ears, and I noticed for the first time how faded his once brilliant hair was, nearly creamy yellow, only a vestige of the red remaining. Sitting down, his belly was more pronounced and I realized that his summer of dining out had taken its toll. His light of love might roll over someday and wonder what the heck she was thinking the day she pursued an older man. Older man, Sean would only be forty-one next spring.

"How old is Eleanor?"

"Twenty-six."

"Classic"

"It sounds pretty trite, but she is very mature."

"How long has this been going on?" In my mind I thought that if he named some brief period, maybe only since I'd been gone, I could handle it. The damage would be great but not mortal. It would mean it was my fault for leaving him, that once again he simply couldn't be trusted but that it was not beyond fixing.

"Maybe ten months."

I had been sitting down, and now I slipped back against my chair, my hands unaccountably shaking. I pressed them against the arms of the chair. "Do you love her?"

"I think I might."

It was as if he'd hit me. I struggled to get up and walked down off the porch. Halfway along the grassy slope I stopped and was taken with violent purging, literally vomiting up all the pain this man had just fed me. I wiped my mouth with the corner of the floral towel still wrapped around me.

"Cleo." Sean hurried off the porch and tried to touch me but I ran away, so afraid his touch would destroy me. I ran into the woods, still wiping the bile from my lips, my bare footsteps erratic and painful against the twigs and detritus of the forest floor.

The truth was, I understood Sean better than I had expected. I, too, had known that sweet forbidden attraction to someone who hasn't lived with you, who hasn't borne the contentions and disagreements. But what Ben and I had done was not born out of flirtation and adolescent crushes, but out of a bittersweet need. It was not the same. As my feet pounded the path, I knew that my own weakness had compounded the error Sean had made. It was not a question of whether I should forgive Sean again, but whether I held our marriage dear enough to save. At what point had we let go of each other so carelessly that others could take our place?

Twenty-nine

I needed the cool water to clear my head, I needed the baptism of immersion to cleanse my aching heart. I dived under the surface of the golden brown lake and kicked toward the raft. It seemed farther away than usual. My lungs, air-deprived, hurt and I surfaced only a quarter of the way there. I struck out, heedless of form, the water splashing my face and going into my mouth. I was panting with the effort as I climbed the ladder.

Ben was there. He sat there, warm and golden himself in the late-afternoon light. His soft brown eyes met mine as he held out a hand to pull me aboard. "Are you all right?"

"No." My legs seemed suddenly very weak and I gracelessly sat down. I realized that I was shaking as if I had just run sprints, with the same kind of breathless burn in my chest. I drew my knees up close to my chest and wrapped my arms around them, then rested my cheek against my knees.

"Can I put my arm around you?" Ben stood on the opposite corner of the raft, distancing himself.

"No. It wouldn't be a good thing to do"—I looked up at him—"as much as it would be the most wonderful feeling in the world right now."

"Pretend I am." Ben wandered to the other corner of the raft, the corner facing Grace's cabin. "Should I leave you?"

"No. Please. I feel better having you at least this close."

"Shall I speak of inconsequentials?"

"That would be lovely." The burning had stopped and I had control of my breathing. I knew I could only sit out here on the raft with Ben for a few minutes before I would have to go back and reopen the discussion with Sean. I wanted to give us both time to regroup.

"I've started it. The flute part."

"Oh, Ben. That's not inconsequential."

I couldn't see his face as he kept his back to me.

"Tell me something—why didn't you write a jazz piece in her honor? She was a jazz musician, after all."

"I might have done that except that the beauty of Talia's jazz was her improvisation. No matter how I might write it, whoever played the piece would never sound like Talia. It would never be her piece as it would have been had . . . had things turned out differently that night. You see, I can imitate her style but I could never replicate it. What I've done is create a symphonic poem which, I hope, acknowledges her spirit more than anything else."

"What happens when it's done?"

"For a while, nothing. The truth is, I don't think I could bear hearing it."

"Maybe you will. Someday." I suppose I meant after Talia, after he is able to stop mourning.

He had come nearer, standing over me as I continued to hunch with my arms around my knees. Ben let the tips of his fingers brush my neck, the light touch sending a frisson down my spine, not of desire, but of an unspoken connection. Then he placed one hand lightly on the top of my head, a gentle blessing of fingertips.

A splash in the distance startled us out of our momentary intimacy. Sean had dived into the lake and was swimming toward the raft. Watching him eke his way closer to us, we remained as we were; Ben's hand on my head, my arms wrapped around my knees. When Sean reached the ladder, Ben moved to the edge to jump off. Then he stepped back and away from the edge. "Hello, Sean."

"Oh, Turner." Sean extended his hand in professional greeting and then looked down at me. "Could I ask you to . . ." he waved in the direction of Ben's cabin.

Ben didn't move right away. He looked from Sean to me and waited until I nodded. Ben strode to the edge of the raft and executed a perfect dive off the north side of the raft, breaking to the surface twenty feet away before striking back toward his western shore.

I realized that Sean had swum out here not to reconcile, but to agitate. He was now on the offensive. "You seem pretty chummy with that has-been rock star."

"Stop it, Sean. This is about you."

"Is it?"

I could see that he was grasping at straws, hopeful that he could somehow turn the onus over onto me. He could hardly imagine that I already wore the weight of confused guilt. Twice over I blamed myself for his wandering, held myself accountable for his predilection. He was like an addict suddenly off the wagon and somehow, by being his wife, I pushed him. The more frightening to me was that he gleaned my deeper guilt; more terrifying in that I could no longer hold myself as purely wronged.

Sean was deeply angry, that I could see by the florid color of his face. He began pacing from one side of the raft to the other, making it rock with an erratic tilt, making it hard to stand in one place. "Maybe I should go have a talk with Mr. Rock Star."

"Sean. Don't. Don't be stupid. This has nothing to do with him."

He stopped pacing and came up to me. Instinctively I took a step back. "No, I don't suppose you have ever known temptation." His voice was a low growl, a warning. There was a challenge in it, defying me to prove him wrong, challenging me to defend myself on a different field than the one he'd put us on.

"Why do you want to bring other people into our problem?"

"That's right, let's not expose ourselves to the scrutiny of others. Let's keep our voices down and ourselves under control." His voice had begun to rise in defiance of any embarrassment his behavior might bring.

"Sean, stop it." I moved away from him and went to stand at the west edge of the raft. I didn't want his voice to carry across to the east side, mortified that the beach biddies would make gossip out of my husband's performance. Ben was playing and I hoped that he couldn't hear us over the sound of his own music.

I needed to bring the conflict back to its origins. "Don't try to make me out the villain here, Sean McCarthy. You're the one who's jeopardized our marriage with your cheating. What makes you think that I can go through this again? What makes you think that I'll just roll over and forgive you again?"

"I haven't asked you to."

I felt the nausea rise and leaned over, my hands on my thighs. "Get out of here, Sean. Get away from me before I kill you." They were only meant as metaphor, but my words were sincere. Sean was killing me with his lack of contrition, with his evident reluctance to make an effort to save our marriage. I had found out about this affair while it was still important to him.

"I'm going home." Sean stepped to the western edge of the raft, about to dive off.

"Sean. Don't." Instinctively I put a restraining hand on his arm.

In an instant I saw that he took my touch as forgiveness.

"It's not safe to dive off this side."

The mad rocking of the platform had diminished to a gentle sway. He spoke softly now and I was vaguely aware that Ben's music had stopped. "Cleo, for a long time now you haven't needed me. I know I'm pretty dull stuff, not glamorous like your rock-star friend." He held up a hand against my protest, "But in the last year, Eleanor has made me feel as though I still have it. She thinks that I'm exciting, thinks I have something to offer. You know, Cleo, you haven't gotten the best of me, I still have plenty to offer."

"What nonsense." I wanted to rebut him, wanted to prove him wrong with just the right comeback. But I couldn't come up with the words. He might have been right. "You've been pulling away from me. You've been the one to look elsewhere."

"We've pulled ourselves apart, Cleo. It's no one's fault." He suddenly seemed so reasonable, so determined. Or was it resignation?

"Sean, if I hadn't found out about your affair, when would you have told me?"

He didn't say anything, perhaps a little nonplussed.

"I mean, if Eleanor has been such a boon to your ego, surely you mean to make something permanent of it."

"Until today, I didn't feel as though I had come to that point."

"Until now."

"Yes."

"Get out of here now, Sean McCarthy. Leave me alone." I folded my arms tight across my midriff, pressing against it to feel something besides nausea.

Sean dived off the raft with a graceless splash and headed to shore. I crumpled to the deck and now I sat there to wait until Sean's rental car left the yard. I grew chilled as the air cooled off and the breeze picked up. I wrapped my arms around my legs and tried not to shiver. Sean was taking his time. I saw the outdoor shower door open and heard the sprinkle of shower water.

Finally he appeared, standing on the porch steps, shielding his eyes against the glare of the setting sun. He seemed to be waiting for me. Waiting for me to change my mind, to come take the argument to some more reasonable level. To say, *It's okay, honey, you certainly deserve a girl on the side*. I didn't move.

At last Sean turned and walked up the leaf-strewn path to the driveway. I heard with relief the sound of his car starting. I dived off the raft, instantly warmed by the water. My muscles relaxed as I swam, but the cool air touching my wet skin as I climbed out of the water started me shivering again. I ran into the cabin and grabbed a damp towel.

Sean had used the last of the hot water from the tiny water heater. Half rinsed and no warmer, I bundled into jeans and my sweatshirt and heated water for tea. Mug secured between my hands, I stared out through the big picture window at the growing darkness and ground my teeth against the gristle of my thoughts. This young woman, this secretary, had seen something in my husband I was blind to. But I must have seen it once. Had our lives become so separated that even the memory of the spark which had ignited us into a couple was so diminished I couldn't, twenty years later, recall it to mind? What had Sean displayed to this girl, that she would fall for a middle-aged, slightly overweight insurance salesman? What had I missed? Or thrown away?

I didn't want this to be about other people. About Eleanor or about Ben. I needed to keep my mind on what was happening between Sean and me, and how, somewhere along the way, we'd stopped being important to each other.

Thirty

I don't know how long I sat there. Long enough that my tea grew cold and the room dark. It was very quiet, quieter it seemed than any other night on the lake. Even the bullfrogs and the night birds kept still. I was listening and it seemed as though the isolating dark had stranded me from everyone. The cabin lacked even a noisy clock to remind me that I wasn't alone. My children were gone, their sudden departure without farewell leaving me with a disturbing sense of permanence. What if something happened? My straitlaced upbringing had not allowed for fanciful superstition, but my twenty years with the McCarthy family had exposed me to plenty of crossed fingers and knocks on wood. Never go to bed angry, always leave by the door you entered. It seemed to me that there was some aphorism about always say goodbye. I'd said goodbye to neither my children nor my husband. In this soul dark moment I could believe that I would never see any of them again. I imagined losing Lily and Tim to this corruption in their father's life. If anyone knew that I, too, had been corrupted, I might truly lose them.

I tried to stand and shake off the enervation. I needed to pack, to gather our belongings spread from one corner to the other of the cabin, load the big car, and go home. Yet I sat there, letting the dark cultivate my fears within its protective shield, a petri dish for my

emotions and my fears. Within the dark I imagined a broken umbili-
cal, like the lifeline to an astronaut. I saw myself floating away, reaching back, just grazing the fingertips of someone. I pinwheeled away
and then suddenly noticed that the other astronaut was moving away
from me. I must have dozed, the imagery so unchosen.

A light and fluid sound came to me then, I might almost have
imagined it, so delicate and faint. Music. Sweet and hesitant, then
stronger. A flute.

I stood and went to the porch, looking across the lake toward
Ben's darkened cabin, the only light there his porch light, my Gatsby
beacon. The flute music stopped and I heard the screen door screek
open and bang closed.

I was cold again and suddenly desperately afraid of being alone,
of letting my random thoughts control and frighten me. I took my
fleece jacket off the peg and walked out of the cabin to the lakeside.
Grace's canoe rested half in and half out of the water, the painter tied
to the picnic bench to prevent it drifting away. I groped for the knot
and untied it. The paddles were in the canoe and I used one to shove
off.

I struck out for Ben's porch light, which glowed as it had every
night since that first night in June when I sat on my porch, wondering
if coming to Cameo Lake was a stupid idea, a selfish move, or if it was
exactly what I needed to do. I stroked gently, soundlessly, across the
expanse between our shores.

As I drew closer, I could see the tiny flicker of a citronella candle.
The hyperacoustics of the lake brought the sharp sound of bottle
against glass.

"You shouldn't be on the water without lights." Ben's voice was a
whisper, yet clearly audible.

"I know."

"Is this a good idea?"

"Probably not." I felt the bow of the canoe strike sand. I could just
make him out, a dark shape coming toward me.

He bent down and hauled my canoe up onto the beach without
my getting out. "Let's go inside."

We walked side by side. I was acutely aware of the enfolding dark and Ben's hand around mine. As we crossed the porch, he picked up the bottle and glass beside his chair.

Inside, Ben lit a kerosene lamp on the piano and then took a second jelly glass out of the breakfront. Without asking, Ben filled my glass with scotch and dropped an ice cube in. "Sometimes drunk isn't a bad place to be."

"Are you an alcoholic?"

"Occasionally I turn to drink. I did when Kevin died, I did when Talia . . ." He paused, unused to having someone know about Talia. "After her accident."

"Ben." I wanted him to stop this.

"Hey, I'm an ex–rock star, I'm not pure. Never pretended to be. Just because I maintain this quiet, controlled image . . ." He sat heavily into a chair and I realized that he was pretty well gone.

"Ben, what set you off tonight?"

"How can you ask that of me?" In the soft light of the lamp, his eyes were shadowed, impossibly deep in his face. Involuntarily, I thought of Heathcliff. "Haven't I already told you my secrets?"

"Not all of them, Ben. Not all your secrets. Not really." I did sit next to him then, afraid of my own candor.

He was quiet. Whatever rage he had allowed me to see the tip of, was shoved back down into submission by the next gulp of scotch.

"Ben, please don't do this to yourself." I rested my hand on the hand which held the glass. "Or at least tell me why."

"Cleo." He shook his head. "It would be the epitome of unfairness to burden you further."

The first swallow of scotch had burned tears into my eyes. The second felt better, and I drained my jelly glass to feel warm and unstructured. It was a different calm than drinking wine.

"Are you going to divorce him?"

I fought the urge to lay my head down on Ben's lap. "I think it's what Sean wants." *Do you love her? I think I might.* Abruptly I stood up, needing to quell the urge to seek the comfort I imagined Ben's hand stroking my hair would give. It seemed safer to be moving around the dim room, keeping some physical distance. The yellowish light from the kerosene lamp glittered off Talia's flute, lying on top of the closed lid of the baby grand, and I walked up to it. The gold mouthpiece reflected the light more warmly than the silver body of the instrument. Beside it, the photo I'd noticed before.

A little shrine, I thought. A Talia shrine. I must have said it out loud because Ben's voice, clear in the darkness, agreed with me. "I suppose it is. Occasionally I take it out and put my lips where hers spent so much time. It always tastes like metal. Like she often tasted. Unyielding."

"Gold is soft."

"Talia was cast iron."

I pulled a rocking chair to face Ben, still sitting on the cluttered couch. He poured more scotch into my glass and then into his own.

I should have left then, before my judgment was any more clouded by the exhaustion of my spirit and the scotch. But I couldn't. He seemed so sad, like me, caught between anger and despair.

"What happened, Ben? Why do this to yourself tonight?"

He didn't say anything for a time and then laughed a short, mirthless laugh. "Your husband."

"I don't understand."

"You love him."

"Why do you say that?"

"You stopped him from going off the west side of the raft."

"And why does that bother you?"

"I didn't stop Talia from diving off." Abruptly Ben stood up and began circling the small illuminated space in front of the piano. "I was on the raft when she went off. It was as dark as it is tonight, the moon gone down, and the motion of the raft under our feet was disorienting."

I stayed in my chair, watching him appear and disappear through the ovoid pool of kerosene light.

"She wouldn't let me touch her. I thought that maybe she was afraid she'd lose her resolve to leave me if I touched her. She kept backing away."

Ben suddenly came to a standstill and grasped the back of the rocking chair I was sitting in. I felt his shaking through the narrow spindles of the seat back.

"The odd thing was that, beneath all the anger, I believed that we would survive the moment, and that it would even maybe make us stronger. That this was the moment for us to begin to try harder. That there would be a second chance."

Ben let go of the chair and I put a foot out to stop its rocking.

"She was just within reach. I could feel her breath on my arm and in the dark I could have reached out and held her. I could have reached my arms around her and held her against me and against any struggle. She realized it and said the last words she would ever say to me. 'Don't touch me.'" Ben's voice was a soft hissing mimic of how Talia's must have sounded that night. "Then she turned and dived off the raft."

Now I was on my feet, frantic to put my arms around him, to hold him safe against this haunting with my own need to be touched, to be held safe against the cruelty of love. He kept moving, as if propelled by the immensity of his story, unable to stop the headlong rush of words, as Talia was unable to halt the impetus of her dive against the rock.

"So, you see, the lake community is quite justified in shunning me. I did cause the accident. Only it wasn't that I physically pushed her, it was that I didn't put out a hand to stop her." He stopped then and let me put my arms around him. "It was my fault." His voice was cracked and hoarse as if he'd been screaming, but he wasn't weeping. I was.

"Ben, you can't say that. You know that's not true."

"I knew what was going to happen. I knew the direction she was facing. Yet in that split second when I might have called out a warning or put out a hand, I didn't."

"Ben, you were hurt and angry."

"And in that moment, silent." He pulled away from me and picked up his glass, taking a mouthful, closing his eyes against the burn. "And that's the difference between you and me."

* * *

We were silent for some time, standing apart, on either side of a rag rug on the floor. The colors of the rug in the kerosene light were questionable gray or blue, white or yellow. I stared at them, trying to remember. Ben picked up the flute and took it apart, wiping each one of the three joints carefully with a cloth before setting it into its case.

"Maybe you will be able to write the flute part when she's gone."

Ben kept rubbing the gold mouthpiece and said nothing. I hadn't meant to be cruel or outspoken, only truthful. Scotch truthful. For a moment I wondered why my parents were so inhibited if this is what scotch did for me. "I mean that maybe you haven't given up hope that she'll come back."

He snapped the case shut and walked away from the piano. He went to the wood stove and put a match to an already laid pile of newspaper and kindling. Still quiet, he added two logs and then stood up, rubbing his long hands against his jeans.

"Do you want me to go?"

"I want you to stay." He might have meant forever.

The dry wood popped and the kindling crackled. The sudden warmth in the chilly room felt good. We came together in front of the stove, reaching out to one another in a natural way, compassionate friends. Needing the affirmation we lent each other, needing the physical release from our overwhelming pain, we held on. They were separate pains, yet similar enough to be numbed by the simple act of touch. And comforting touch became loving touch and we gave in. The rag rug served as our oasis, the kerosene lamp flickered and failed as we sank to the floor. In the dark every sensation was heightened by its unexpectedness. I was aware of the rough surface of the rug, but absorbed into the feel of Ben's hands on my skin. For however long it was that we lay together, and I could not say how long, we built an impenetrable wall around ourselves, keeping our troubles outside and only our passion within.

As soon as we lay quiet, feeling the vibrations grow still and our pulses slow, the walls were breached and it all came back. Our separate guilts would now and forever be blended by our common sin.

"If we ever do this again, may I suggest we use a bed?"

I chuckled, amazed that either of us could make a joke. Amazed and certain that there would be no third time.

Thirty-one

It was harder than I could have imagined to leave. In a few short weeks, Cameo Lake felt as familiar and beloved to me as my own neighborhood. As I bundled up clean and dirty clothes and searched under beds for missing sandals, it felt like a safe harbor from the anticipated turmoil of my return to Providence. As much as I would associate Cameo Lake and this cabin with the anguish of Sean's betrayal, it would equally be the place where I had found some comfort.

I pressed thoughts of last night out of my head with fingertips. The scotch had left me queasy, the memory of last night made me dizzy with the vertiginous dance of guilt and joy. One minute I could blame Sean for driving me into another man's arms and the next be grateful to him. In lockstep with those conflicted thoughts was the steady tramp of knowing I might have done it anyway. At once I dropped onto the glider and burst into tears. I wanted to be with Ben yet I didn't trust my feelings, so certain that they were born of Sean's betrayal. I wanted to heal my marriage, but at the same time I didn't want to because it would mean losing Ben. The weeping ceased and I went into the bathroom to be sick.

* * *

The last thing I loaded into the SUV was my laptop. I had packed it into its protective case, inadvertently reminding myself of Ben putting the flute back so carefully. Treasured items. We had agreed, in the first gray light of day, that we would say our goodbyes then. We would not prolong something which neither of us could reliably say wouldn't be the last time we would see each other. In the hours when we had held on to each other, we had not talked about a future together, only our futures apart. "What will you do?" we had asked each other, and agreed that our central problems needed to be resolved before we dare trust this new thing between us. We didn't say it, but it was implied. Ben was waiting for Talia to die. Until then, he was entailed, voluntarily, willingly. As for me, I needed to decide, with Sean, if our marriage was worth holding on to. If Ben stayed a part of the equation, I could never decide fairly.

"Go home, Cleo, figure it out and whatever course you choose I'll abide by. And be happy for you."

How had we come to understand each other in such a short time?

I intended to head straight down to Narragansett but didn't. Grace had taken the kids down there, so I knew that my house in Providence would be empty. Empty except for Sean, of course. I needed to talk to Alice, but I needed more, in that moment, to see my home. To sniff the air of my territory and lay claim to it. I'd head down late, join the family at suppertime, and after the dishes were done and the children put to bed, talk to Alice, divine from her the path to take. She had guided me through the difficult ordeal of making funeral arrangements for my parents. "A child shouldn't have to do this," she said, although I was twenty-one and had never felt like a child. She agreed that we shouldn't delay the wedding, scheduled for less than two months later, stood up against those who raised an eyebrow: "This child needs stability and joy." Even while my mother was still alive, Alice had mothered me. It hurt very much now to imagine life without her advocacy. If Sean and I split, how would she divide her love? He was blood, I was not.

*　*　*

After the muted colors of the cabin, the brightness of my kitchen seemed glaring. Everything seemed smaller than memory and it took me a few minutes to adjust my perceptions. The house was neat, a little dusty but not horrible. I dragged the overstuffed bags into the laundry room and loaded the machine. That done, I wandered back through the kitchen to the living room. On the floor, in front of the CD player, was a CD jewel box. We'd been replacing LPs with CDs for years and I vaguely remembered Sean buying the Interior Angles' first album, the one with "Frozen Heart." The box on the floor, lying there like a dueling glove cast down in challenge, was that CD box. Defiantly I put the CD into the player and let Ben's music loose in my empty house. I walked upstairs to the bedrooms and pulled open Sean's bureau drawers. They, too, were empty. Without any discussion, Sean seemed to have decided that I planned to throw him out. Or had decided he wanted to go. *You will never, no never, be lost to my mind. Frozen forever in my heart.*

Leaving the washing machine agitating through the first cycle, I climbed into my own minivan and backed out of the driveway. I needed to see my children and I needed to see Alice.

The traffic wasn't too bad at this time of day on a Saturday. The beach traffic was all heading home and the traffic heading for the beach was thin. I felt the strain of all the driving I'd done this day in the back of my neck, and I hoped that Siobhan would be there and give me one of her back rubs. When I turned down the short street where the cottages were, I could see that only Alice's Oldsmobile was in the drive. Everyone must have gone to the beach and suddenly I was afraid that I would be locked out. The back door, though, was open and Alice was in the kitchen. She was making a pot of tea, almost as if she'd been expecting me. "Hello, Cleo." I fought back tears as Alice unselfishly gathered me to her in a big hug.

We spoke of the children, of course, waiting until the water was boiled and steeping in the Brown Betty before getting down to brass tacks, as Alice always called the facts of any situation.

I looked at her as she sat facing the backyard. I thought she looked pale, too pale for someone two weeks at the beach. The lines so deeply embedded in the face of a woman who had raised six children to adulthood and lost three more in infancy were like the telling lines in the cross section of a tree. Did I imagine new ones creasing deeper into troubled cheeks? Aware of my scrutiny, she turned to look at me.

"Your hair wants cutting." Second-generation Irish-American, Alice's inflections had a shadow lilt to them. Her life, built in an immigrant community bounded by Church and neighborhood, hadn't allowed for much development. Now her neighborhood had changed complexion and the Irish were no longer deprecated new-comers. Others had taken their place on the low rung of the New England caste system. In Alice's life beyond her family, only the Church had remained a constant. We had moved her a few years ago into a two-family house a street from ours when her neighborhood had been all but abandoned and become unsafe. She owned the house and rented the top floor to an African-American family, the Carlsons. They were young and I worried that they would soon be moving into their own house and we'd be looking for new tenants before long.

"I know, I'll get it done next week."

"You've got to take Sean back."

I was surprised at that, at the swiftness of her coming to the point. It hurt that Alice was so obviously misunderstanding the real issue.

"Alice, this is his choice. He's the one who left. He's the one who—"

"As did his father before him."

"So you think that makes it all right?"

"It's the way of a man."

"That's a pretty outdated concept, Alice. A woman doesn't need to tolerate her husband's infidelities."

"We marry for life in my family."

"Not in mine. Some things are not acceptable."

"You accept a great deal if you want a happy home. Men have needs."

"I never denied Sean his needs, as you so quaintly put it."

"It's more than just sex, Cleo. It's the boredom. They need change."

"Is that what Francis told you. He needed a little change?"

"If you want a happy home, you overlook it. It means nothing to them."

"Was your home so happy for having tolerated Francis's behavior?"

Alice poured tea for us both, holding the strainer just above the rim of the cup. "I was respected."

"Not by your husband." I was instantly sorry. I remembered Francis mostly with fondness, but not once did I ever hear him speak to Alice gently. It was always, "Get me this" and "Find me that." Never once did I hear him praise her except for a good Sunday dinner, and then a perfunctory and predictable "Good dinner, Alice," generally followed by a discrete belch.

With no question of divorce, Alice had stayed with him. Helped him go up the ladder of success by pinching pennies, keeping her house so clean it was a showpiece despite the cheap furniture and having baby after baby with him. Never denying him his needs. And still he wandered. Not quite blatant, but never entirely discreet. The way of a man.

"When a woman can point and say, 'These are my children, this is my house, this is my husband,' she is respected. Francis wasn't an easy man, but he did love me. And Sean loves you."

"Sean said that?"

"Not in so many words. But he's not happy."

"You mean he's not happy with me?"

"That's not what I mean. He's unhappy he's caused this . . ." She hunted for the word. " . . . this disturbance. Trust me, I'm his mother and I know it."

"I'm glad it makes him unhappy."

"He wants your forgiveness."

"I gave it to him once before. I'm not sure I have it in me to do it a second time. Besides, I'm not sure he does want my forgiveness."

"I know my son." As if we were discussing what to have for dinner, Alice sipped her cup of tea. Then set it down in the chipped saucer. "Would you and Sean please go talk to Father Pete? He's a good confessor and surely can help get you two back on track."

"Alice, I'm going to tell you what I'm sure Sean already has. Father Pete is a million light years away from being able to help us. He's ninety if he's a day, and celibate."

"That has no bearing."

"No, in your world, of course not. But even so, he's not even a counselor."

"Marriage counselor you mean? Well, maybe not by license, but he's counseled many a couple into remembering their vows."

The word *vows* pained me, knowing my own breaking of the marriage covenant, knowing the words of the marriage service say nothing about tit for tat. Keep thee only unto him unless he screws his secretary. I shook a little more sugar into my cup of tea and kept my eyes on the process. Could I have ever imagined that I would so deliberately break my vows? Was it deliberate or liberating? And yet, when I thought of Ben, thought of what we had done together, I didn't get any sense of retribution, of imposing some kind of punishment on Sean. It was a separate thing altogether. Beyond the physical act, there was an ineffably sweet memory of fulfilled emotional need. Sitting here at a small kitchen table in a rented cottage with my mother-in-law, I was filled with fear, terrified that I would imbue my relationship with Ben with qualities which were born of my marital turmoil, and hence, not to be trusted. How could I ever know if what I felt for Ben was real or the product of anger, disappointment, and the willing arms of a new friend?

"Alice, I promise that we'll get counseling. But I don't think I can live with Sean right now."

Thirty-two

The slamming of car doors announced the return of the beach-goers. Lily and Tim were first through the door, throwing themselves around me as if it had been two weeks, not two days since they'd seen me. I wondered how much they had gleaned from the inevitable conversations my sisters-in-law would have had, conversations with no names mentioned, oblique references to the situation their brother and his wife were in, trusting that children are blissfully uninterested in adult conversation. Slipping into specifics accidentally.

"Is Daddy coming tonight?" Lily leaned one bony bottom-cheek against my thigh.

"I think we're going home tonight, Lily May. How about a night in your own bed?"

I expected protest. The kids loved being at the beach with their grandmother. Instead, Lily nodded and wordlessly went off to change out of her suit. Tim, Lily's shadow, followed her out of the kitchen.

"Do you know where Sean is?" I directed the question to Alice, but Margaret answered, "He's at Ma's house."

"I suppose I should be grateful."

"Cleo, he's there because he thinks you want him out of the house."

202

"He might have gotten that impression." I tried to scroll back and see exactly what I'd said yesterday. Yesterday. It seemed like a year had passed since Sean and I had stood on the rocking edge of the raft. "I would have liked to discuss it with him first."

"You know the address." Margaret scooped up her smallest child and left the kitchen. Siobhan followed, arms full of wet towels, one child's sandal dangling off her index finger.

Alice got up from her chair and reached for the broom, sweeping the sand brought in by her family into a neat white pile centered on a black square of linoleum. I bent down with the dustpan and she swept the sand into it. I was pained by Margaret's words, feeling a little like she was somehow mad at me.

It seemed like I had been living in a car for the past year, the return trip to Providence having begun at ten this morning, the final leg, coming back from Narragansett, taking place at five in the afternoon. Now the beach traffic was horrible, creeping along like some dying caterpillar. We watched each red light change twice before reaching it. Each time I put my foot on the brake pedal to stop yet again, I felt like I was moving farther away from home instead of closer. I felt something akin to panic in my chest, afraid suddenly that if I didn't get home soon, I would never get there. Even though I told myself that the worst had already happened and not getting home before dark wouldn't change anything, I had the sense that something bad was happening. I needed to be home.

Finally we broke through the bottleneck and sailed up Interstate 95. My house was dark, the driveway empty. Grace had come and claimed her SUV. The blank windows reminding me that Sean was gone. We three walked in the house by way of the back door. I flipped on the overhead light in the kitchen. "Where's Daddy?" Lily asked. Her tone of voice seemed less like a question to me than an accusation, and I knew that I was deeply tired.

"He's at Gramma's house. Why don't you call him and see if he wants to have scrambled eggs with us."

Lily ignored me and went to her room. Tim made the call, young enough to have missed the implication of Sean's not being home, of his being at his mother's, of having to invite him to join us.

"He's coming in a minute." Tim struggled to reach the wall phone hook. "Can I watch TV?"

"Just till dinner." I pressed my palms flat on the butcher block surface of my counter, stilling their tremble. I fought back a strange feeling, like that upon entering a fun house. You know you're about to be terrified but you aren't sure by what. The rational mind knows it's a creation of human hands and not real, only the deeper primal part reacting with heightened senses. I heard Sean's car in the driveway, the shutting of the heavy car door, his foot on the wooden back step. He knocked on the back door. He knocked.

I could see him through the kitchen door window, looking away towards the neighbor's house as if he was uninterested in whether or not I would come to the door, looking casually away like a salesman. I opened the door, standing aside to let him in. "It wasn't locked."

"I wasn't sure I should just walk in."

"It's your house."

Sean was wearing a light jacket against the evening's damp and shrugged it off now, hanging it on the hook beside the door. "Where're the kids?"

"Tim's watching TV, I don't know where Lily is. Her room, probably." Suddenly it was like any other evening, Hi, honey, I'm home. Except that Sean didn't kiss me hello and I'd never before had to open the door for him. We were stiff with one another. We had so much to say, but the subject of our metamorphosed world was momentarily prohibited by the presence, sudden and loud, of the kids.

Watching Sean with the kids, I tried to conjure up my feelings for him, tried to recall how I had felt about him a bare month ago. All I could remember was that in the past few months he'd begun to want to make love a little less often and I hadn't given it much thought. If I had I would have said that it's natural, he's getting older and the randy young man I'd married is almost forty. Did I imagine that I'd looked at his slowing down as a good thing, an indication that I could stop worrying about him so much?

I couldn't dredge up any moment when we'd been more than parents and problem-solvers together. Partners, not lovers. I watched Sean roughhouse with the kids and couldn't remember a single time we'd played together. He'd had his business and I had my writing. He begged off going to the Performing Arts Center downtown, convincing me to take his mother instead. I couldn't talk him into going to most movies and he said he really didn't like dining out. He had to do too much of that in his business. Sean hadn't wanted to go to the lake, either. Now I knew why.

It couldn't have always been like this. What had we done together when we were courting or when we were childless newlyweds? When he worked for his father and the responsibility of the business wasn't directly on his head? Was I so angry now I had censored out every sweet moment of our life together?

I stayed in the kitchen and began breaking eggs into a bowl. I remembered what we did, we had Sunday dinner. Each of those first Sundays of our marriage stands out in my mind as one day. The warm smell of cooking, pot roast most often. Alice's house thick with the noise of Sean's grown and half-grown sisters. The girls' various boyfriends, carefully vetted by the family. Alice McCarthy teaching me how to roll out a piecrust. Thinking of those sweet days, tears fell into the egg mixture and I sniffed back the overwhelming fear I was going to lose this family.

Once Sean and I had argued about going on a Sunday. He hadn't wanted to, had wanted to go with some friends to the car races in Seekonk. I remembered what I'd said, aghast at the idea of missing a Sunday. "But, Sean, we can't disappoint your mother. She's expecting us."

Sean had looked at me with amused derision. "You mean I can't disappoint you."

I beat the eggs with a fork, wondering why it was that I could only remember arguments, not laughter. I poured the eggs into the overheated frying pan and had to quickly lift it up to prevent them from burning.

* * *

We ate in silence and I wondered what had possessed me to invite him over. It had seemed at the time that we all four needed to sit down together one last time before Sean and I sundered this small family into visitation days. I could feel the tension in my cheekbones, as if I'd pressed a drama mask to my face and wore it too tightly. I wanted the salt, just at Sean's hand, but didn't ask for it. The kids were oddly quiet and I wondered what sixth sense of theirs kept them so. Lily challenged me, hopping down from her seat without clearing her plate.

"Lily. Your plate." Sean spoke before I could and the sound of his voice woke me up from the silence.

Lily dragged herself back to her seat at the kitchen table and picked up her plate, messy with half-eaten eggs and toast. Tim followed her, dropping a little egg against the side of the garbage pail. They went to catch up on all the missed TV from their sojourn at the lake, and suddenly Sean and I were facing each other over the cluttered family table.

Stacking Sean's plate on top of mine, I got up and went to the sink. Sean gathered glasses and balled up napkins and followed me there. As I turned away from the sink, Sean suddenly caught me, holding me against him, pressing my head against his shoulder. "Just for a minute, then we can talk." Sean held on to me.

The dammed-back love should have burst forth then. I should have been overwhelmed by it, been able to let go of my anger and become resolved to save our marriage. Instead, I was chilled. It was Sean believing that I would forgive him again if he could just charm me. If he could just touch me.

Instead, it was as if I had received a fatal diagnosis. I was freed by the unassailable knowledge that, no matter what sort of life support or treatment this marriage would get in the next few months, it wouldn't survive anyway. I let Sean hold me as long as he wanted, until he realized I wasn't responding.

"What do you want, Sean?"

"Tell me what to do."

"Fire Eleanor."

"I can't."

"Then what do you expect from me?"

"I don't know, Clee. Some time, maybe."

"Your mother wants us to get counseling again."

Sean's lip curled upward a little. "I know. Father Pete. Jesus."

"Have you been to confession?" Some inner devil prompted me.

"Have you?" Sean replied, blue eyes under shaggy brows looking right at me.

"Wipe the table off." I handed him a damp sponge.

He stood there, sponge in hand. "I mean it, Cleo, can you tell me you're so innocent?"

"What are you talking about, Sean?" I wanted my voice to come out derisive, but to my own ear it sounded fearful. Ben, who knew me for such a short time, could hear nuances in my voice, knowing instantly when I was upset. Certainly Sean would hear the conflict in my heart, where my own innocence was compromised.

"You and that guy, Benson Turner. Lily said you really liked him."

"We all did. He's a nice guy." I took the unused sponge away from Sean and bent over the table.

"How nice?"

It would have been so easy then. So easy to fire off my one silver bullet and kill this marriage dead. The one thing holding me back in that razor sharp moment was the thought of losing Alice's advocacy. I knew that she would always consider me her daughter-in-law as long as her son was the one behaving badly. But no matter what the circumstance, Alice McCarthy would not forgive me for doing the same. Alice's world was built on a code of behavior which allowed much for men and little for women. Too long in my life without one, I needed the comfort of the woman who had become a mother to me.

"Just nice. Let it go."

Thirty-three

When Sean and I decided to get married it seemed a rapid decision. We'd been together since my junior year of college, we'd spent every waking moment we could in each other's company. We'd been sleeping together since the first week we had known each other. I was a virgin. He was not. I felt both awkward and ashamed of my inexperience and yet immensely educable and willing. We had not, however, spoken of marriage until I had a scare. I was late. Three weeks late. I couldn't go to my mother, so I went to his. I'll never forget her reaction, it seemed so counter to the anxiety and fear I was feeling.

"He'll do right by you. Don't you worry. No son of mine will do otherwise." She held my face between her hands with their short nails and rough cuticles. She kissed me, a benediction of three kisses. Cheek, cheek, and forehead. "I would love to have you in my family."

For the first time I actually hoped I was pregnant. When I wasn't, as it turned out, we moved ahead with marriage plans anyway. But it was always those three little kisses which signified to me my acceptance into the McCarthy family.

We proceeded to divorce with a similar sense of urgency. We had allowed Sean's first affair to equal a false alarm. On Sunday morning I woke up to know that this second affair was more than that. The difference this time was Sean's reluctance to abandon it. Our conversation last night had never provoked any regret or intention to reform from Sean. He had wanted me to accept at least partial responsibility by admitting to sleeping with Ben. Without any real evidence, Sean had intuited something of the truth. Perhaps it was my unwillingness to forgive him again. I was stronger in knowing that I was, to someone else, still lovable. I didn't have to view Sean's infidelity as my fault. I wasn't fat and ugly or a shrew. My fault was simply trusting Sean when I shouldn't have. I woke up late on Sunday morning and knew that I wanted to be freed from having to care about it anymore. It was too much of an effort to sustain the illusion of trust for a man who so clearly couldn't be trusted.

I called Sean at his mother's and asked him to meet with me. Then I called Grace.

After I had Tim I had a tubal ligation. I was tired of being pregnant and was happy with two children. I didn't admit, even to myself, that I didn't want ever again to give Sean an excuse for wandering because of my being pregnant. I still blamed myself for his weakness. We never told Alice about the operation, as Old World Catholic as she was, it would have been a mistake. We let her believe that we were very good at rhythm. Or maybe she guessed and knew enough to keep her mouth shut. I supposed she allowed Francis his wanderings because of her own inadequate birth-control method. Better he wander on the unsafe days than have yet another child. I imagined a lot I knew nothing about. Having to tell Alice now that I intended to divorce her son made me think more about keeping that other sin from her.

Grace wouldn't agree to take the kids for the afternoon until she'd extracted from me the whole of my last two conversations with Sean. She prompted from time to time but generally let me tell it as stream of consciousness, hmmming and okaying in a way which didn't interrupt my narrative flow but let me say the thoughts which had been voiced only in my head for days. It was like going to a psychiatrist. Eventually I came back to the conclusion I'd woken up with and felt validated.

"You're doing the right thing, Cleo. What will you tell the kids?"

Like being patted on the back and then punched. "I don't know. That's part of what we'll talk about."

"On the agenda, then?"

"Something like that."

Grace came and collected the kids. I spent some time reading through the manuscript and making changes, but it was not a successful distraction. My own thoughts kept bumping up against the imagined thoughts of my characters. My real drama sucking the wind out of my imagined drama. The mantel clock in the living room chimed several times, and seemed to come no closer to four o'clock, when Sean said he'd come over. The nauseous feeling settled into my gut and I wished this was over.

This time Sean didn't knock. I deliberately waited for him in the living room, giving our discussion the more formal setting it required. I sat in the left-side wing chair, Sean sat in the one opposite, our little seldom-used fireplace between us. We might have been sitting for a portrait.

All of a sudden Sean began to cry. I'd never seen him cry before except when his father died, and then that was a dignified, quickly extinguished silent moment. Now he cried. Great rolling tears cascaded down his unshaven cheeks and his hands went to his face. "Cleo, I'm so torn."

"How so?" My voice was dispassionate despite my instinct to go over to him and hold him as I would any crying child.

"I hate what I'm doing to this family, but I can't help it."

What he said was so true. He couldn't help it, and by his admission it was easier for me to press on. "Sean. It's for the best. We could get counseling and prolong the agony, but I think that what we had has been dying or dead for a long time now. You've proven it."

He'd collected himself by now, dragging out a handkerchief to wipe away the proof of his weak moment. In an instant he assumed his businessman's persona. "You're right. What do we do first?"

"Decide what we're telling the children." Now it was my turn to cry.

In the corner of his eye, a lingering droplet nearly spilled over, in answer to my own sudden weeping.

Somehow we got through the necessary parts of the conversation. We would talk to the children together, explain that even though we both loved them, Daddy also loved someone else. I'd left the room for a little while after that. Then we regrouped and decided to begin the divorce proceedings before we talked to Alice. I think we were both afraid she'd talk us out of it.

We had gravitated back into the kitchen and I made us each a sandwich, some part of my mind marveling at my ability to perform such a mundane act. I handed Sean his sandwich, he got up and got us napkins. In the brief silence of our eating, I imagined that some sort of wall had been breached, or passed through like a ghost in a movie. We'd come to some other land where we could eat in comfortable silence and get on with our lives. Sean felt it, too—not exactly a peace, probably more a truce. We'd behaved. We had not screamed or accused or uttered invectives today.

We had uttered the word divorce. It was the first time I'd thought of divorce as something real, concrete, and with actions and rules of its own. Saying the word had breathed it into life, a golem of massive proportion. At the same time I felt suddenly weightless, not freed, exactly, more like coming to terms with an inevitable death. It would come, and in some ways, it would be all right.

"I should go." Sean stuck his plate into the dishwasher.

"What about the kids? Grace should have them back in a little while."

"I can't tonight. I don't have the emotional chops to go through it right now. Tomorrow night. After work."

"I'd rather do it tonight, Sean."

"Cleo, I need twenty-four hours to adjust to this."

"Sean, don't imagine this is going to change overnight. Don't think sleeping on it is going to change my mind."

"No. Of course not. Or mine." In the end he agreed to come in the morning.

I stood at the back door, holding the doorknob in my hand as Sean hefted a black garbage bag full of things he needed to take with him. As he passed by me, he stopped and kissed my cheek. It was such a natural act I don't think it even registered immediately. Then Sean set the bag down and took me in his arms, kissing me with full force of passion, as if to test my resolve.

"Don't, Sean. Don't ever do that again." I shut the door behind him.

Thirty-four

⟋

I just wanted to hear his voice. Just for a minute, just long enough so I could prove to myself I hadn't imagined him. I sat in the slowly darkening living room, half-listening for Grace to come with the kids. Judging if I had enough time to make a quick, dangerous phone call. I sat in the slowly darkening living room and pretended I was on the porch of the cabin, waiting to see Ben's light appear. Every night I had watched Ben come out of his cabin, lift the chimney of the lantern, and put a match to it, the soft yellowish light making a tiny beacon of welcome at a self-proclaimed hermit's home.

I heard the car door slam and I knew I had waited too long.

Grace stayed, wanting details, of course, but having to wait out the kids and their bedtime before getting any. Lily was particularly hard to maneuver, suddenly clingy and interested in being in the kitchen with the women. I finally lost my temper with her—"It is time for bed, now go!" My nerves were raw and I no longer had any patience with stubbornness or with negotiation.

Gathering her dignity, Lily walked away. Then, as she reached the archway, she turned and with cool knowingness asked, "When is Daddy coming home, and why is he living at Gramma's?"

I caught Grace's expression before she could quickly settle it into a mask of detachment. "Daddy and I will talk to you and Tim about that tomorrow."

Not satisfied, but recognizing she wouldn't get any more out of me, Lily nodded as if to let me know she'd hold me to that promise. She reminded me of her grandmother. Not Alice, but my mother.

"Was it okay?" Grace asked after the kids had finally gone to bed.

"I wouldn't put it on my top-ten list of things to do on a Sunday afternoon . . . but, yes, I guess it was all right. We've got our cards on the table."

"I know a great lawyer."

"I do, too."

The golem stank up the room.

I knew that Grace wanted a reenactment but I couldn't give it to her. For her benefit, I assumed a façade of weary but handling it. I wasn't in the mood for sympathy or encouragement and I knew that Grace, no big fan of Sean's in the first place, would dish it out until I broke down. I really only wanted to be alone, to have some time to examine the events and my feelings by myself.

Eventually Grace left and I lay down on the couch in the den, wrapping the pink and mauve and white afghan Alice had made for us around me. It was hot and humid outside, but I was cold in my house. I lay on my couch, wrapped in my mother-in-law's afghan, and allowed fresh tears to come. The kids couldn't hear me sniffling and at this moment I didn't have to be strong for Grace's benefit, or anyone else's, either. The only person I would have wept in front of was Ben, and he was so far away.

It was almost eleven o'clock. Oddly, it wasn't the divorce I thought about, it was the urgent need to talk to Ben. It was like a craving for something I hadn't known I was addicted to. I sat up and wiped my eyes and scolded myself for letting go. I would tell Ben that I'd made my decision, that I was divorcing Sean and that soon my life would be smoothed out.

I pulled the desk phone onto my lap and impulsively dialed his number. I was proud of myself. I wanted nothing more in those few quiet and solitary moments than to call Ben and tell him how I'd awakened from the nightmare of trying to save the unsavable. That I'd stood up on my own hind legs and stopped being grateful to Sean for lending me his family. I needed to hear Ben's voice to still my false euphoria. The phone rang unanswered, and when Ben's recorded voice invited me to leave a message, I hung up.

I was flushed with relief. By the third ring it had occurred to me that I didn't want Ben to get the idea that my choice had anything to do with my feelings for him. There mustn't ever be a hint that he should somehow feel responsible for my emotional well-being; if he thought I'd been able to cut loose from Sean because I thought I had him to go to, I'd die. Even if it might be true.

Sitting there with the silent phone on my lap, I realized that I needed to be as separate from Ben as I was from Sean. I needed to have time to let the marital bitterness wither into neutrality and the sweet feelings I had for Ben grow up naturally if they were to survive. I needed distance to see if what I felt for Ben was more than a summer fling. I had to step outside of myself and my problematic world long enough to see things from Ben's point of view. The last thing he needed was an emotionally dependent woman while he still struggled with his own problems. We hadn't exactly said we wouldn't talk to each other, but as my mantel clock in the other room chimed midnight, I allowed that maybe we both needed a little time apart.

If what we had felt for each other was real, it would wait. If what we had was a product of our separate unhappinesses, born of our wounded spirits, then it would dissipate like the morning mist, beautiful but temporary.

Thirty-five

❧

S ean got to the house even before I could get dressed. I realized
that we were going to have this conversation with the kids early
enough that he wouldn't be late for work. I supposed that was better
than being squeezed in between appointments.

It looked to me like a weak imitation of Christmas morning, the
kids all tousled and rubbing sleep from their eyes, anticipating surprise, a little nervous. Except that Sean was dressed in full business
regalia, suit, tie, and watch, which he kept looking at as we herded
the kids away from the TV and into the kitchen. Sean removed his
navy blue jacket and carefully hung it across the back of the extra
kitchen chair. I pulled my housecoat belt tighter around me and
plugged in the coffeepot. It was raining lightly—I only noticed as I
looked out of the window over the sink. I was suddenly nostalgic for
the rain on the roof of the cabin, thunderous applause against the
shingles, cascading off the slope of the porch overhang. This rain,
against which we were well protected, seemed citified and unremark-
able.

I pulled a box of cereal out of the cupboard. Ben was probably
even this morning introducing his musical theme for this brand to the
ad agency. The kids liked Ben, he was comfortable with them. I saw
them playing in the water together, laughing over Trivial Pursuit. I

squeezed my eyes shut at the suggestion my mind wanted to enjoy. Until our lives were recalled from our particular hells, I dare not think in terms of future. Ben needed to confront his past and I my present before I could think of a future together, even in the most abstract way. Echoes of my midnight resolutions forbade me to dream.

"Why didn't you sleep here last night?" Lily stood beside Sean, who was sitting in his accustomed place at the kitchen table.

He reached around and pulled her to him, but Lily wouldn't be assuaged by a mere hug, she wanted answers. "Are you guys getting a divorce?"

Lily's question put paid to any illusion our troubles had been handled discreetly.

"Why do you ask that?" Sean still held on to Lily's arm.

"I heard Auntie Margaret say you were."

Sean and I looked at each other over the top of Lily's head, allied for the instant in annoyance at Sean's older sister.

I squatted down beside Lily and grasped Tim's hand which had a sticky spoon in it. "Well, Daddy and I are—"

"Going to take a little time away from each other."

"Sean?"

"You know how you and Katy sometimes fight a lot when you've been together too much?" Sean named Lily's best friend.

Lily nodded.

"Well, Mommy and I need to be separate for a while."

"Sean, that's not what we—"

"Cleo. It could be. It should be."

I stared at him, disbelief and anger somehow blended with a kind of relief, as if an impending amputation was now a series of painful operations. I didn't envision a different outcome, only a more protracted journey. "We'll discuss this later."

The coffee was ready and I stood up. I kissed both children and went to pour it. Tim went back to eating his cereal. Lily went to her chair. No one spoke. I set the coffee in front of Sean and glanced at Tim. Two tears of equal weight trickled down his sleep puffed cheeks. He kept spooning cereal into his mouth, chewing with slow deliberation, as if he had to think how to do it. Staring into his bowl, he let the tears continue their journey until they clung to either side of his little jaw, suspended for an instant before dropping into his cereal.

"Sean, why did you make them think this is temporary? Like a vacation?"

"Look, what good would it do to hit them with the big one when this way we can all get used to the idea first?"

"You've talked to your mother."

"Yes. Yes, I did. What of it?"

I could see Alice's hand in this sudden volte-face.

"I know what she wants. She wants me to be like her, putting up with your little mistakes and keeping a Catholic house."

"That's not fair, Cleo."

"What do you want, Sean? Leaving everyone else out of it, what do you want?"

"To do the right thing by the kids."

"That wouldn't have included staying faithful to me?"

"Stop it, Cleo."

"Why do I get the feeling you prefer separation over divorce because that way you don't have to commit to Eleanor? The classic, my-wife-won't-give-me-a-divorce excuse." I was grasping at straws, my words voicing a thought I hadn't actually formulated until this minute.

I watched the choleric pink color rise above Sean's crisp white collar, grow brilliant at his ears and flush his face, except around his nose, where the skin faded to ashy white. It was like watching a movie transformation of Jekyll and Hyde. Instinctively, I stepped back.

"I think you're the one ready to throw the baby out with the bathwater, and I have to ask myself why." Sean grabbed his jacket from off the back of a chair and slammed out of the house.

I stood alone in my kitchen. Only the noise of the TV in the den disturbed the quiet, so sudden and so deep.

"Mommy, why are you and Daddy mad at each other?" Tim had come back into the kitchen. I wiped vague tears off my cheeks with the back of my hand and then licked my thumb and rubbed the traces of his off Tim's cheeks then pulled him onto my lap.

"Grown-up reasons." I saw Lily out of the corner of my eye, standing in the doorway. "You both must understand that this has nothing to do with you. We both still love you, we'll always love you. Parent love doesn't go away." Unaccountably I thought of my parents and imagined that if it doesn't go away, there are times when it simply never forms.

"Is he still going to live here?"

"No, sweetie. That's what separation is."

"Is he still going to coach my team?"

"I'm sure he is."

Lily shoved herself onto my lap, one knee now for each child. The three of us, like a portrait. I'd title it *The Restructured Family*. Sean had left me alone with the kids to make explanations without deep revelations.

Lily squirmed, her bony bottom hurting my leg a little. "Daddy's screwing another woman."

I managed to hold back my surprise. "Another thing you heard Auntie Margaret say?"

"No. Auntie Siobhan."

"Do you know what that means?" Hoping she didn't.

Lily very much wanted to appear sophisticated and worldly in front of her brother. "I guess so."

"It means he's got a girlfriend. Something married men aren't supposed to do."

"Doesn't he love you anymore?"

I had no answer for that.

Thirty-six

Life, even life in crisis, finds its own routine. It is impossible to sustain flash point. It happens, action, then reaction, then stasis. In other words, life goes on. Alice and Sean's sisters came home from the beach. I took the kids school shopping. Sean completed his move in with his mother, but came every week to mow the lawn, then to rake the leaves, then to put the storm windows on.

We formalized the arrangement, defined visitation and finances and then stood back to see what we had wrought. We were like spectators at a bull fight, anxious to see the next choreographed stage of the fight. The matador hadn't been brought in for the kill yet, but the picadors were tormenting the bull.

Separation made our marriage neither fish nor fowl. It served only to give everyone but Sean and me false hope that life would go back to what it had been, with Sean on a longer leash and me still part of the family. In theory we were to examine and rebuild our life, with the aid of a high-priced therapist. In practice, we just built new lives, the hub of our defeated marriage at the center, threads here and there crossing which would always keep us connected, but not close. By the end of October I knew that it was too fragile; an arrangement which gave me nothing except ties to a man who loved someone else.

I think even Alice got a little weary of pretending we'd get back together. She stopped asking me to have dinner with them when the kids went to her house on Friday nights. She gave up manipulating accidental "meetings" between Sean and me. It was important to me to retain Alice's love, but I couldn't do what she wanted.

"Will you come to Frances's birthday party?"

"I'll come by late."

"You two can certainly eat a bit of cake in the same room."

"Alice." She simply didn't understand how painful it was for me to be in the same room with Sean, knowing that in the next hour he'd be off to bonk his mistress.

"Why ever not?"

"I'm uncomfortable." I drew on a therapist's term.

"Baloney, you make yourself uncomfortable by not forgiving him."

I stood up and kissed her forehead. "I have to go."

I knew that every time I had a conversation like that with Alice, I was digging a chasm I would soon not be able to cross. Eventually she would stand on the other side of it. After all was said and done, Sean was her son, I was the outsider.

I stood to the side of Tim's bedroom door. I could hear him, at two in the morning, flying a little plastic airplane over his head, making little puttering noises. I knew that if I looked in, I would see his other hand clutching a newly resurrected baby blanket. Tim's sleeplessness had gone unabated despite all the suggestions of his pediatrician, his therapist, and his grandmother. I sighed and went in. Sometimes simply lying down with him helped. I was already exhausted by worrying about Lily's behavior. It was unnerving how certain miscellaneous misbehaviors could add up to what the school guidance counselor called acting out. More than once since September I'd been called to school. Lily had been picking fights with girls she barely knew. She'd been hanging out in the girls bathroom instead of going to art class. Lily had thrown food at older kids at another table during lunch. The list went on and on.

I'd found my limited supply of makeup in her backpack. Unrepentant, Lily shrugged, "I needed it. You won't let me buy my own."

"Lily, you're in fifth grade."

"Everyone else has makeup."

She quickly discovered that saying, "Daddy lets me" was guaranteed to get a reaction out of me. Tiring of that, she grew more subtle, more silent, and I worried that she, my chum and boon companion, was drawing away. Lily began to remind me of my mother. Cold and undemonstrative. I fought the idea that genetics would come to bear on this child and prayed that she would outgrow this as she would come to accept that her behavior wouldn't change anything.

The good news was that my novel had sold and now I was left with the task of refining and reshaping the rough bits. I nearly went down on my knees in relieved thanks when it sold for enough to insure that I could manage alone financially. In the worst-case scenario, I could buy Sean's share of the house if it came to that, although I had a good lawyer and it might not.

Not a day went by when I didn't think of Ben. I played the CD and listened to his music and remembered with masochistic delight moments of our brief association. I thought about him at his wife's bedside, holding her hand and then holding mine. I heard the plaintive rise of Stash's tenor voice against the underscoring bass line and remembered lying next to Ben on the raft at noon, and in his arms that last night. I took little pauses in whatever I was doing, suddenly smitten with memory. I sat staring out of the little window in my office and saw not my small city backyard but the expanse of lake water shimmering in the early day.

But I didn't call him. Or write, although I phrased out messages in my head all the time. I stuck to my resolve that it would be unfair to both of us. Distance and time hadn't lessened my feelings, the memories were no less poignant, but I was hyper-aware of my own vulnerability and emotional fragility right now.

Ben didn't call me. On good days I imagined him wanting to, thinking of me, resisting the same temptation I resisted, and for the same reasons. On bad days I thought he'd probably forgotten all about his summer companion.

"Mom, come quick, it's Ben on TV!" Tim shouted from the TV room and I made an ungraceful dash from the kitchen.

Tim had been flipping channels, and randomly selected *Entertainment Tonight* just as they announced their cover story: "Startling Discovery Made in New Hampshire Nursing Home." An old film clip of Ben and Talia working their way through a crowd of fans was visual backdrop to Mary Hart's voice announcing the teaser for the second time. I wiped my wet hands on my jeans and sat next to Tim to watch all the other stuff which would fill in the half-hour program before they got to their "cover story." Three times they teased me with the "mysterious appearance . . . thought to be dead . . . former rocker with the . . ." each time with the same brief clip of Ben, Talia's arm linked through his, coming through this throng of clamoring people. At second look I realized they must have just been married when this was shot. Dressed in a deep blue suit, Talia carried flowers cradled in the arm not holding Ben. In the two seconds of broadcast history, I saw what had drawn Ben to her, her smile and the sparkle in her eyes. Ben had eyes only for her and seemed oblivious of the crowd of well-wishers surrounding them. I sat through "News Briefs" and seven commercials before they got to the story.

I listened to every word reported by Mark Steines, suddenly afraid that what I heard would go counter to what Ben had told me, some detail which would change my understanding of him.

Someone newly hired at the nursing home had made the connection between Talia Judith Turner and Talia Brightman, and had recognized Ben coming to see her. Steines rehashed the year-and-a-half-old story of Talia's apparent drowning. "At a news conference the next day, doctors reported that Miss Brightman had dived or fallen from a swim raft, hitting her head on a submerged rock.

Unconscious, she had somehow gotten caught beneath the raft and drowned. Her husband, former Interior Angles member Benson Turner, had resuscitated her, but she was later pronounced brain dead." More video of Talia, with and without Ben. "It was widely known that Turner and Miss Brightman had been estranged at the time of the accident. Although an investigation was made, no charges against Turner were ever filed."

I felt myself flush, Ben had never said anything about an investigation. He'd said that they had been apart, not estranged. I had to believe that this was a reportorial flourish.

We watched the rapidly changing clips of Ben, from his Interior Angles days to his obscurity and then rebirth as Talia Brightman's husband. Except for hair and sideburns, he really hadn't changed in thirty years. In the fast-moving kaleidoscope of images, I could see that his features had simply evolved from sharp angles to mature lines. He hadn't changed enough to become anonymous. To those who remembered him from his public days, Benson Turner was easily recognizable.

"It has always been believed that Miss Brightman had died shortly after being taken to the hospital." Cut to a random shot of the exterior of a hospital. "Sources say that Benson Turner has always claimed his wife died in the accident." Cut to current shot of Ben, moving rapidly from the car to the back door of the nursing home. A close-up revealed to me his jaw hardened with determination not to be drawn into answering any questions.

Why are they doing this to him? I shook my head and covered my mouth in horror at the invasive questions of the gathered reporters.

"Why have you kept this secret?" "Why have you let the world think she's dead?" "Mr. Turner, did you push her?" The paparazzi clamored like children begging for a treat.

Mark Steines concluded the segment. "Benson Turner has not made any statement regarding the discovery of his wife's survival. Efforts to contact him today have been unsuccessful. Doctors would not comment on Miss Brightman's condition but an inside source reports that she is considered permanently brain-damaged with no hope of recovery."

The program closed with a clip of Talia in concert, eyes closed and her whole body moving with the sounds emanating from her flute. She seemed enraptured by her own music, oblivious of the audience. The deliberate juxtaposition of this video against the report of her living death was very moving and I felt myself cry inside for her and for Ben.

"Mommy, did you know Ben had a wife?" Lily had joined us.

"Yes, honey. I met her one day. I mean, Ben took me to see her."

"Did she talk to you?"

"Tim, she can't talk to anyone. She's in a kind of deep sleep."

"Why did he tell people she was dead?" Lily demanded, clearly angry about it, although I wasn't sure whether she was angry about the report or at Ben for not telling her his secret or at me for keeping it.

"That guy got it wrong. Ben never said that, he just hasn't said that she's alive." I tried then to explain to my children what Ben had explained to me about permanent vegetative states.

"Could that happen to me?" Tim sat on the floor and pressed his hands against his head.

"It's why we tell you to wear a bike helmet, and not to swim alone." Might as well make a lesson of it. I pulled him to his feet and hugged him. I reached for Lily, but she slipped away.

I stared out of my window and finished the dishes. Poor Ben. Just exactly the kind of thing he dreaded had happened. I wiped my hands on a towel and picked up the phone. My heart still did its pounding in my chest, but this was appropriate, this is something I could do legitimately. This wasn't about us as lovers, but as friends. *At the customer's request, the phone has been disconnected.*

"Oh Ben." I hung up the phone. "Don't go incommunicado on me now." I tried the number again, thinking maybe I'd dialed it wrong, simultaneously hunting through my purse for the bit of napkin it had been written on long ago, certain both that I knew the number and that the napkin was long since lost. The electronic voice once again told me that Ben had disconnected his phone. It made sense, of course. Hadn't Mark Steines said efforts to reach Ben were unsuccessful? Did I think that Ben would expect my call? I hung up again and went into my office. Ripping a sheet out of a notebook I wrote a quick note to Ben.

"I'm thinking about you . . . call me if you want." I didn't know what else to say. I was afraid to commit to paper all the tumbling thoughts in my head, afraid that I would end up writing a chapter instead of a message of support. "I'm so sorry your secret got out. Let me know if there is anything I can do." I held the tip of my fine-point pen over the notebook paper and wondered how to sign it. Sincerely? Your friend? Love? In the end I simply sketched my signature and folded the paper into one of my last engraved envelopes. I addressed it to Ben at the Cameo Lake post office and stamped it. The engraved return address caught my eye: Mr. and Mrs. Sean X. McCarthy. With a bold scribble, I blocked out the first line and wrote: "Cleo Grayson."

"I'm going to the post box on the corner, answer the phone if it rings." Halfway down the block, I wished I'd put on a jacket. The late-October air was winter-chilly and I could see my breath. I dropped the envelope into the post box and wondered how long it would take to get to Cameo Lake. I imagined the lake as it was in July, then imagined it as it must be now, past peak foliage season, still and quiet. Had Ben gotten electricity yet? Had all the lake people gone, leaving him alone? Was he even there? I didn't walk home right away, but kept going around the block, tormenting myself with thoughts of Ben. I kept thinking, has he wondered what's become of me?

"Mommy, Auntie Grace called." Lily called down from her room.

I knew that she'd seen *ET.* Grace was an unabashed celebrity watcher. Her bathroom was littered with *People, InStyle,* and *Vanity Fair.* "Did you see it?" Grace demanded without preamble.

"Yes."

"Why do you think he's kept that secret all this time?"

"I suppose because he was afraid that what just happened would happen."

"He should have known this would come out." Grace managed to sound sympathetic and cynical at the same time.

"He didn't want her to be a sideshow."

"Well, she is now. This is the kind of thing the supermarket rags love. Photographers will be climbing in the windows of her room."

"Oh, Grace, I hope you're wrong. Ben couldn't stand that."

There was a pause in the conversation, an unusual thing for Grace, while she analyzed my remark. "You got to know him pretty well, didn't you?"

"We did get to be friends."

"Have you called him?"

"I tried. His phone's disconnected." I knew then that Grace was running the odds in her head. The odds that there was something more to this friendship of mine.

"Did you know about Talia?"

Now I paused, running my own odds against Grace reading more into my answer than I wanted. "Yes. Please don't ever tell him I told you." I was slightly nauseous, knowing I had betrayed a trust, but I knew that Grace would know it if I lied.

"I see."

"No, Grace. You don't see. We got to a point this summer where we shared the painful things in our lives. That's all." I was glad that this conversation was taking place on the phone.

"Well, the cat's out of the bag, so now we all know."

"I wrote and asked him to call me."

"Cleo, can I give you a word of warning?"

"If I said no, would you stop?"

She laughed, not put off by my words. "Keep away from Ben or the spotlight will fall on you."

Thirty-seven

Halloween was on a Sunday night this year. A school night, and the school party, which took the place of trick-or-treating for the younger children, was early. It was Sean's weekend so he was the attending parent. I felt a little left out, especially since I usually volunteered to help with the party. Half of the fun for me was dressing up, usually as a witch, sometimes as a gypsy, once as a ballerina. I helped to oversee the apple bobbing or bean bag toss, making sure every child got a prize. My favorite party was the one last Halloween, when I was part of the haunted house—very zombie-woman. Someone had taken my picture, and when he saw it, Sean hung it on the refrigerator with Magnetic Poetry words spelling out: "Because I'm the Mummy, that's why." It was still there. When I remembered that this would be the last year for Lily to attend, as next year she'd be in the middle school, I grew even more sorry I couldn't go with her.

I'd spent a long time making their costumes, turning Lily into a flamboyant movie star by making good use of a horrid bridesmaid's dress from 1982. I made a sweet little bat cape for Tim, complete with batwing shape and a felt hood. Lily moued and Tim struck a super-hero pose as I took half a roll of film of them dressed up.

"After the party can I go trick-or-treating?" Lily didn't look at me as she asked this, but fussed with the strap on her shoe.

"No." That sounded abrupt. "I mean, it will be too late."

"No it won't." Lately Lily argued everything and I couldn't be sure that it wasn't preadolescence or something more insidious.

"You can knock on Mrs. Webster's door and the O'Callahans on your way to Gramma's."

"The party is so babyish . . ."

"Lily. Take it or leave it, or you can hand out candy here."

"Everyone else—"

"Lily!"

Buttons pushed, Lily left the house with her brother in tow, trooping to their grandmother's to wait for Sean. It was no secret that Sean spent most of his time with Eleanor, but he kept up the pretense of living with his mother. I supposed that, come the finale to this drama, this playacting would work in his favor.

It seemed very late, long past the time I knew the party ended. Long past when I expected them back. I called Alice.

"No, they weren't planning on coming back here. They were going to drop the kids off at your house. I'm sure that's what Sean said."

"They?"

Stillness on the other line, then, "Yes."

"I see. Did *they* mention other plans?"

"No. Well, they might have said something about going to Eleanor's neighborhood. I'm sure everything is fine."

"How can you say that?"

"I'm sorry, Cleo. I don't really know what to say." Alice hung up quickly, leaving me to simmer in frustrated anger. I knew that Eleanor was insinuating herself into Sean's life from every angle, but thus far I hadn't considered that Alice had met her. That Alice might be verging on accepting her as part of Sean's life, like she had accepted Francis's philandering.

I had a flurry of trick-or-treaters come by, mostly children of people I knew. A few parents got out of their cars to say hello, that weak

I-know-something-bad-is-happening-but-I-won't-ask-about-it sort of hello. I kept the conversations Halloween-centered. A small group of teenaged trick-or-treaters descended and effectively cleaned me out of the rest of my candy. I shut off the porch light but left the front door open. Sitting on my stairs to the second floor, I could see the street perfectly through the storm door but was invisible to anyone there. Across the street most of the porch lights were out, universal announcement "We are out of candy" to those still wandering the streets of Providence at nine o'clock on a school night. I was getting pretty angry. From my vantage point I could see car lights when they turned the corner, but car after car went by.

Finally, I picked out the headlights of the Volvo. As it pulled up alongside the curb I got up from the stairs and went outside. I stood on the porch as the backdoor opened up and the kids emerged. As the interior light went on I could see both Sean and Eleanor. Sean and Eleanor dressed in costume. In three strides I was at the car and shooing the kids into the house. "I need a word with your father."

"Night, Dad, night, Eleanor." Much too friendly for me, much too comfortable.

I went around to Sean's side of the car. "Where have you been?"

"We took them to Eleanor's neighborhood to trick-or-treat."

"Was that your idea or Lily's?"

"They needed some real trick-or-treat experience."

"Sweet Mary Mother of God, how stupid can you be? You let Lily manipulate you into doing something we both agreed they shouldn't do?" I was spitting angry.

"Cleo, my neighborhood is a very safe one. You don't need to worry. They had a good time."

I stared in at Eleanor, dressed as the Bride of Frankenstein, the makeup contorting her smug smile into a freakish parody of friendliness. "This is none of your business, Eleanor. My children aren't your concern." I know my voice was loud in the quiet street and I was momentarily embarrassed.

"Cleo, don't make a scene out here." Sean was fingering the keys and I knew then he'd drive away before I could say another word.

Make a scene. I wanted to heave a rock through his window. I wanted to scream epithets at them both. I didn't. As I had ever done, I didn't make a scene.

I stepped away from the car. The kids had lingered on the porch and I was glad of my control.

Lily was in the shower and Batman was in bed when I confiscated their bags and dumped it all into the garbage. I'd replace it with new stuff tomorrow. They'd be mad as hell, but they'd get over it. The fact is that this went way beyond taking chances with our kids, it was Eleanor's latest volley in the war for their affection. Convincing Sean to give them a forbidden treat, letting Lily get her way. Getting Alice's tacit approval.

I could hear Tim in his bed, making airplane noises as I, too, lay awake in my bed, wondering how much longer I could take this.

Thirty-eight

Grace was right. At least about the supermarket rags. I stood in line and stared with fascinated horror at a blurry photo of a recumbent figure in a hospital bed. It might have been Talia, it might have been an alien. The banner headline read: TALIA BRIGHTMAN ALIVE BUT BRAIN DEAD, HUSBAND KEEPS YEAR-LONG VIGIL. A different tabloid read: POLICE INVESTIGATE MYSTERIOUS ACCIDENT, BENSON TURNER SUSPECT.

I turned my face away, as from a car crash. I wondered how long Ben could keep a low profile with these sorts of things being written. The tabloids had indeed latched on to the story. One expressed it as romantic, Ben Turner's bedside vigil and all. The other spun it as an unsolved mystery—how did she fall and who was responsible? Both were determined to keep the story alive as long as Talia was.

In the week since I'd sent the letter, Ben hadn't contacted me. Part of me wasn't surprised, most of me was very disappointed. I only wanted to say I was thinking of him, I only wanted to hear that he was all right.

Halloween past, Thanksgiving loomed. The first official "family" holiday to be contested on the field of emotional football. Without any family of my own, the holidays had never before needed planning. For nearly twenty years it had been simple, Alice had as many as could gather at her house. Sometimes all the daughters and their husbands and their many children descended from all parts. Sometimes the husbands kept the daughters from coming, proclaiming other family obligations, and only two or three of the daughters would come. But always the McCarthys were there, the mainstay family. Sean was the only son, lived closest in proximity, and had a conveniently orphaned wife. No other claims on holiday visits could be made. There were Margaret, Mary Alice, Siobhan, then Frances, named for her father after all those sonless pregnancies, then Sean, apple of his mother's eye and delight to his sisters, followed by a last stillbirth and finally, late in life, the baby, Colleen, never in the world a more spoiled little girl who managed to grow up selfless and sweet.

To them, I was another daughter, another sister. Sean and I had been so young, barely in our twenties when we married, that it seemed to all of us I had always been a part of the family. It was this which kept me tied to Sean.

Only Colleen remained unmarried, a career Navy nurse stationed in Bethesda. She was coming home on leave for this Thanksgiving and in honor of that fact the whole family had earmarked the date last March, in the time before my world fell apart. Each of us women promised to bring our specialties, mine being the pumpkin pies. Alice would only have to cook the turkey and set the massive dining room table. Her current house had been chosen as much for its old-fashioned formal dining room as for its proximity to us.

The kids, numbering now eleven with Margaret's surprise fourth baby, ranged in age from the six-month-old baby to a fifteen-year-old girl, Margaret's oldest daughter, Rachel. The children would sit together at the collapsible metal table and folding chairs in the adjacent living room, separated from the adults only by the low mahogany room dividers on either side of the wide archway where Alice kept her display of the children's school pictures. The furniture would be pushed aside for the occasion. The combined volume of the

SUSAN WILSON

two rooms would be loud. Some child would cry, some adult would get angry at another and then, just as quickly, forget about it.

That had always amazed me about Sean's family. They argued right out loud. In mine the arguments were stifled, then drowned in alcohol. *Don't make a scene.*

Even the year Francis McCarthy died, the Thanksgiving celebration went on as before, but the absence of the Patriarch, as we jokingly referred to him between ourselves, subdued us. The laughter was still loud, but the arguments were stilled. That was the year Sean was elevated to Francis's position at the head of the table. Alice remained at the foot, closest to the kitchen. I sat on Sean's right and the sisters and brothers-in-law alternated around either side. There were twelve of us that year, but I can't recall who was missing.

I remember it as a moment of mythic significance, when Sean held the familiar carving knife, the bone-handled knife carried over from Ireland by Francis McCarthy's father. There was a moment's hesitation, like a child might take when he first attempts to do a man's task. Then the long blade of the knife touched the crisp brown skin of the turkey and the first cut was made. Sean looked up from his task and looked at me, a proud, slightly self-conscious smile on his face. An overwhelming comfort suffused my body and I felt as though this was where I had always been. Where I would always be.

"Joanie and I are having a gathering of loose ends."

"And I'm a loose end?"

"You're *at* one, aren't you?"

"Grace, whatever are you talking about?"

"Surely you don't have Thanksgiving plans?"

It was a continual source of amazement to me just exactly how perceptive Grace Chichetti could be. I don't know how she could have known before I told her that the kids would have dinner at Alice's, with Sean. I suppose it was a logical assumption, but I might have said we were spending the day together, to hell with the McCarthy traditions. Evidently Grace assumed there was little chance of that. I asked her anyway.

"How do you know I wasn't planning on having you and Joanie to my house for dinner?"

"Because you live in a state of denial and you haven't mentioned the holidays once since you got the official separation. Please note: Thanksgiving is next week."

"I know that. I've been busy."

"Okay, let's say it's that. Now, for the record, will you come?"

"Yes." I hurried to qualify my answer, "but only for dinner, I'm to have dessert with Alice and the clan when I go pick up the kids."

"With Sean?"

"God, no. He'll have left by that time. Alice is unhappy about things, but growing more tactful. She's pretty much given up getting us in the same room"

"What about Eleanor?"

"Who?" I couldn't help myself.

"You know who. What are her plans?"

"Oh, you mean Bride of Frankenstein."

My story of the Halloween argument had struck Grace as funny. As I described Eleanor's own big blond hair raised into a pyramid on her head it suddenly struck me that way as well.

What I didn't say to Grace was that Alice had not specifically said Eleanor wasn't coming. But in my heart of hearts I knew she'd never allow that to happen, at least not while there was a chance, in her view, of our reconciling. As long as our divorce wasn't final, Alice held out hope like a weapon.

Thanksgiving morning I tumbled my kids out of bed and made them a real breakfast. Alice's dinners were always at two o'clock. I knew the kids would be so hungry at noon, they'd be both grouchy and picking at the pickles and olives, stuffed celery and pitted dates until they'd be full by the time dinner was served and everything piled on their plates would go to waste. So I made them French toast, scrambled eggs and bacon and hoped that that would hold them until dinner. We ate breakfast in the TV room just off the kitchen, watching the Macy's Thanksgiving Day Parade. Just as Santa and his reindeer appeared on the screen, the phone rang. Automatically, Lily jumped up to answer the kitchen phone.

"Mom! It's Ben!" Lily called as matter-of-factly as had it been Grace or Alice on the phone.

I was on my feet and into the kitchen in a shot. The thumping of my startled heart threatened to deafen me. I know my voice was a little tentative as I spoke. "Ben?"

"Cleo, hello."

I was nearly speechless. "Ben. How are you?"

"The better for hearing your voice."

"No, tell me if you're all right or not."

"You mean with my newfound celebrity?"

"Something like that."

"I've had better PR."

"Stop kidding around."

"Cleo, I'm all right. I'm keeping a very low profile, and an unlisted number, which I want you to have."

I scrambled around looking for a piece of paper within reach of the wall phone.

"And how are you, how are the kids doing?"

"We're okay. I won't bore you with the details, but Sean and I are separated, the kids are beginning to accept it, and my mother-in-law insists I forgive him."

"Can I see you?" It sounded blurted, as if he hadn't planned on saying that. "I mean, if you want to."

I made sure the swinging door between the TV room and the kitchen was shut. "Ben, is that a good idea?"

"No, probably not, but that doesn't stop me from wanting to see you."

I felt a rise of tears, "I can't think of anyone I would like to see more."

"I have to be in Boston in a couple of weeks. Could you come up for the day? Or maybe we could have dinner?"

I appreciated Ben's subtlety, he wasn't asking for more than what our friendship had been based on.

"Lunch would be best. Yes, I could do that." Yes. Now I could. All the holding back, the fear that to speak to him or see him would be corrupted by my state of mind, had dissipated with the first words out of his mouth. He was Ben, my lakeside friend. We were friends, irrespective of our personal upheavals, not because of them. Even as I thought that, I knew it wasn't quite true. Our personal upheavals had formed us into the people we now were.

"I've got to go. I'm having dinner with Talia's parents and I'm only halfway there."

"How is Talia?" It seemed so odd asking that, as if all the publicity would have affected her somehow.

Even over the poor-quality pay phone, I could hear him sigh. "We're losing her slowly. We're losing the battle against the contractures in her legs. She's starting to draw into a fetal position."

"Oh, Ben. I'm sorry."

"Cleo, I wish it was over." It was a cry from the heart. I knew what he meant, and that he meant it in the most loving way.

"I know, Ben. I know. It will be, and you'll have done everything you could have for her."

"Almost everything." His voice was suddenly hardened and I knew he meant he hadn't stopped her from jumping. He pulled himself back from that abyss quickly. "Cleo, give the kids a kiss for me and have a nice holiday. I'll see you in a couple of weeks."

"Ben, I'm glad you called. I was worried." I felt a little shy saying it, but it needed saying.

"Thank you."

Thirty-nine

Bathed, dressed in their best non-jeans pants, hair restrained in a barrette for Lily and combed into submission for Tim, my children made their way down the street and over two blocks to have Thanksgiving with their massive family. I was still in my grungy jeans and sweatshirt, flour and bits of pie dough stuck here and there. Grace and Joanie had said three-thirty was early enough. I had a couple of hours to get myself presentable and the pies for both occasions done.

Ben's unexpected call had cheered up a day when I had fully expected my primary emotions to be depression, alienation, and grumpiness. I actually hummed as I rolled out the pie dough. I had our date to look forward to, two weeks hence, and it felt like spotting a life ring while drowning in a choppy sea.

Typical of Grace, she filled their second-floor flat with the homeless waifs from her classes. Students whose families were too far away to make going home feasible, foreign graduate students who enjoyed the American feast without completely getting into the conceptual significance. Besides the turkey, there was an array of vegetarian, Chinese, Turkish, and Greek foods on the trestle tables built with sawhorses and doors. Lacking enough chairs, many of us stood or sat on the floor in a quintessentially sixties fashion to eat. It was loud, crowded, and lively. At some point I cornered Grace and whispered that I'd heard from Ben, that he was pretty much okay. I left out the part about going to Boston to see him. I had no use for a lecture today.

I enjoyed meeting the students and sampling the odd array of foods, but it wasn't my tradition and I was glad to slip away. On my way out Grace caught my arm. "If you talk to Ben again, tell him I'm thinking about him too."

"I will."

It was a nice evening, brisk and dry. No wind. I parked the minivan at home and walked to Alice's with the pies in the special basket Sean had given me one Mother's Day. They were heavy and cumbersome, but still I liked the idea of arriving on foot, Thanksgiving basket in hand. Off to Grandmother's house I go.

I recognized the variety of minivans and Hondas Sean's siblings drove. I picked out Connecticut, that was Frannie; Rhode Island times two, Margaret and Siohban; Pennsylvania, Mary Alice; and a rental car, must be Colleen's, I thought. I felt a slight flutter of nervousness in my chest, it would be the first time I'd been in the whole company since Sean and I split. But I trusted Alice's welcome and thought I could depend on my sisters-in-law to be happy to see me.

Sean's blue Volvo was in the driveway. The pies felt very heavy at that point and I didn't stop to grumble about his being late to leave. I knew it would be hard for him to pull himself away from the gathering, so I kept moving toward the back door with a tolerance I might not have ordinarily felt. As I approached, the back door opened and Sean quickly stepped out. Automatically I handed him the pie basket. Reflexively he bent to kiss my cheek. I let him. Then we both stepped back, remembering ourselves.

"Mother sent me out to look for you."

"I'm not late, am I?"

"I think she harbors hope that if we're left alone for a few minutes we'll ... well, I suppose the correct word is reconcile." He made a sound through his nose which might have been derision, or maybe it was just against the weight of the basket, which he then shifted to the other hand.

"Is that what you want, Sean?"

He shook his head sadly, not looking at me but beyond, toward the street. "No, not really."

"Me either." Even to myself, I sounded like a little kid.

"Cleo, you have to understand something. I'm happy. I haven't been for a long time and it's not that putting you through all this hasn't been painful to me. But, I know that it's best. We haven't made each other happy for a long time."

"Sean. I wasn't unhappy."

"No. But I was." Sean hefted the basket and opened the screen door to let me go in first.

I didn't move. "You bastard. How did I make your life so unhappy?" Sean's words were so hurtful to me that I felt physically weakened by them. "Tell me how?"

"Cleo, look, just drop it. We can't go into it right now." He stood there, the door still held ajar. "Are you coming in?"

"Yes. Yes I am." I pushed past him, bumping the pie basket painfully against my hip.

The kitchen was exactly as it had been every other Thanksgiving in my twenty-year memory of McCarthy holidays. Redolent of cooking, half cleaned up, half still filled with the dinner dishes which couldn't fit into the dishwasher, voices loud and cheerful coming from the dining room, laughter. I stood in the dining room archway. The evening's dark was warmed by the light of the chandelier over the massive, cluttered dining room table, a perfect setting for this close-knit family. With Sean's words I understood for the first time that I stood outside of it. I was in danger of losing my place in the family. The only family I had.

A voice chimed in above the din and clatter of china dessert plates being distributed. A high-pitched unfamiliar one, laden with abrasive Cranston vowels. Eleanor's voice. I realized that Alice was coming to me as I stood immobilized in the archway. The look on her face was a blend of regret and stubbornness. I could tell that this was not her idea, but that she had capitulated to Sean's demands as she always had when it came to the favored only son, and would defend her right to do so.

"Why didn't you tell me she was here?" I might have been speaking to Alice, facing me, or Sean, still behind me. Neither one said anything. I knew then that Alice had sent Sean out to warn me and he had lacked the guts to do so. Picking a fight instead, so as to ratify his contention I was hateful. "What did I do to deserve this?"

Alice had taken hold of my wrist, as one would a naughty child. "Cleo, come have dessert with us."

I shook her off with a wrench of my arm. "At the very least they should have been out of here before there was any chance I would arrive."

"Cleo. Sean is my son. He doesn't have to leave at all."

I felt as though I'd been slapped. "No, but Lily and Tim are my children, and they do." I pushed past Alice and walked past the table, now terribly silent. I did not look at any of them, I strode past as if I were walking through an empty room into the big front parlor, which was set up as the children's dining room. I caught my children by their hands and sent them to fetch their coats. It was an interminable five minutes. I smiled at the gathered innocents, the myriad cousins, assuring them they bore no fault. I loved them still.

Not one of the adults spoke, just kept their eyes on their empty dessert plates and their hands on their wineglasses. They had never been shy about entering into each other's marital arguments before, but somehow something had shifted. A daughter-in-law is no match against an only son.

As we made for the front door Alice did come to me and repeated, "Stay, Cleo. Please. Have dessert with us." Sotto voce, a more gentle hand on my arm, she said, "They'll be leaving in a few minutes. Stay."

I shook my head, not trusting my voice, opened the front door, and walked out, one child gripped in each hand. Lily started to protest but I shushed her with enough vehemence that even she knew not to whine.

Not since the beginning of this drama had I felt so wrenched. I could almost hear the tearing of my emotional fabric. My ties to the family had been sundered and now I stood on the other side of the chasm.

Forty

Sean came to the house the next day. I saw him coming, my pie basket in his hand. He knocked on the back door and I was slow to
unlock it.

"Can we talk for a minute?"

"Come in." I took the basket from him and set it on the table
between us. We were forced to look through the tall fixed handle, and
I was reminded of a confessional. Sean moved the basket.

"My mother is very hurt by your walking out yesterday."

"Your mother is hurt? How does she think I feel?" I stood up,
outraged at Sean for putting forth such a patent lie.

"Look, I know it was a bad idea to be there when you came, but
my mother had nothing to do with that. We would have left in a few
minutes anyway."

"Your mother sat that woman down at her table and fed her. In
my mind that means she's accepted her."

"What if she has?"

I had no answer for that. "Just leave, Sean."

"Can I see the kids?"

"They're still in bed. Come back later."

"No. Cleo, listen to me. Eleanor is in my life. I don't know if it will
last, I just know that I'm trying as hard as I can to make this easy."

"Easy for whom? Certainly not me. Certainly not your children. Easy for you. As always, Sean. What's best for Seannie is best for everyone. Even for your mother. It's easier to turn on me than make you leave your doxy at home."

"My mother loves you . . ."

"She has a funny way of showing it."

"Cleo, she does. She always will."

"You once said *you* would always love me. Love changes, doesn't it?"

"I can't talk to you."

I pressed my hands flat against the wooden surface of the table-top. "It's over, Sean. We both know it. We should never have prolonged the dying with futile efforts at life support." Even as I spoke them, the words made me think of Talia Brightman and Ben's nearly year and a half of watching her die.

Sean got up from the chair. He hadn't removed his tan overcoat and I noticed a grease stain near a buttonhole. He looked fat and rumpled and a little remorseful. "Shouldn't we wait until after Christmas?"

"No, I'm giving you your freedom and for Christmas giving you to Eleanor."

"And what do you get?"

I smiled, feeling suddenly empowered and in control of my life. It was a kind of bliss, knowing that, as painful as the next few weeks might be, as contentious and difficult, I had asserted my own will into this situation and I was now free. "Sean, I get my life back."

Even as I closed the door behind Sean, I felt comforted by knowing that Ben and I had reconnected. By freeing myself from the confines of this blighted marriage, I was launching myself into new waters, at once still deep, and unknown. Ben was to me in this moment like the raft, midway between shores. A safe place to rest.

I knew it was only a matter of time before Alice came to see me. She didn't knock. I was in the office, thumping on my laptop. I heard the back door and knew without a doubt Alice had arrived. "I'm in here!" I saved my work and got up from the desk chair.

"Cleo, you can't give up now."

"Alice, it isn't giving up, it's acknowledging the end." I led her back into the kitchen and put the kettle on. "It's a dead issue. He loves Eleanor. Although my money says he'll eventually cheat on her, too."

Alice sat on the chair Sean had used and kept her hands folded as she leaned her arms against the table. She didn't say anything, and when I turned around I saw that she was weeping.

I knelt beside her and took her hands. "Alice, Ma, it doesn't have to mean we can't be friends."

"No, Cleo. That's not it." Abruptly she pulled away from me and reached for a paper napkin. She blew her nose. "I'm just sorry I didn't have the courage you have. I slapped Francis across the face when I found out about him. I told him I must never catch him cheating again. But I knew, I knew he was doing it. I was the laughingstock of our parish. For the sake of the children I stayed. I could have left. But I stayed."

"Alice, where would you have gone?"

"I had relatives who would have taken me. There was only me and the first two girls then. My sister would have done." As she spoke, Alice regained her composure and waved me off to mind the boiling kettle. "Of course, if I had gone, I wouldn't have my others. They were and are more precious to me than anything."

"You were right to make your decision the way you did. But I need to keep to mine in my way."

"You don't love him at all?"

"Not right now. I'm very angry with him."

"But you still wear your ring." Did she imagine that this oversight meant something, that there was some subconscious hope left for this marriage?

I looked down at my left hand and stared at the wide gold band as if I had never seen it before. It had never even occurred to me to remove it. I did so now, tugging a little against the snug fit. I set the ring down on the kitchen table and rubbed the vacated finger. "Not anymore."

Forty-one

A lice had agreed to have the kids come to her house on the second Tuesday of December. I was nearly honest with her, I was meeting a friend in Boston. We would have lunch and I would be home by seven. I was a tyro liar and the effort not to blurt more detail was difficult. I thought it very obvious, my avoidance of any pronoun to describe this "friend." It was a mark of her regard for me that Alice didn't ask who it was I was meeting. I left the impression that the lunch had something to do with publishing. My work was a mystery to Alice and I counted on her not to ask questions.

The kids were unconcerned with their mother's day away. Any day they could go somewhere besides home after school was a good one. Lily did lobby for going to a friend's house instead, but lately her selection of friends had bothered me and I said no. She sulked but got over it.

I hadn't waited for Sean to join me to tell the kids we were moving ahead with the divorce. The three of us were eating a pickup dinner of canned clam chowder, squeezing in a family moment before homework, when I simply told them.

"You need to know that Daddy and I are getting a divorce."

"Is that like the Separation?" Tim always made it sound like a proper noun.

"Not exactly. It means that Daddy and I aren't married at all anymore."

By this time both kids had had enough counseling and easy-reader books on a "Children's Guide to Divorce" to understand intellectually what was going on. And I had enough instinct to know they'd need more reassurance of our love for them than ever. To that end I gathered them into my arms and told them that none of this meant they weren't the most important thing in our lives."

"Except for the new baby." Lily had, as always, pulled away from me, and she faced me to deliver this bomb.

"What new baby?"

Adding to the potency of her revelation, Lily folded her arms across her chest. "I saw the test thing in Eleanor's wastebasket."

I wasn't going to ask when Lily had been in Eleanor's bathroom. "How did you know that's what it was?"

"TV."

"So what color was it?"

"It wasn't a color, it was an *X.*"

"Do you mean like a letter *X,* or a plus sign?"

"A plus sign."

I felt a slow heat rise from my waist to my armpits to my neck. So classic. "Do you suppose Daddy knows?"

Lily shrugged.

I kept trying to figure out how Eleanor's pregnancy would affect our divorce. Primarily it assured me that it would happen. Secondarily, I knew that I needed to get certain financial and territorial considerations locked in. I called my lawyer immediately and she was on the job. My second call was to Grace—there was no way I could keep this tidbit to myself.

"Cleo, if this wasn't so serious it would be funny. Sean's kids tell his first wife his mistress is enceinte. Too bizarre."

"I have more bizarre for you. I'm going to Boston to meet Ben next week."

"Is that a smart thing to do?"

"Just for lunch, Grace."

"I repeat. Is that a smart thing to do? He's being pursued by paparazzi, you don't want to be on the cover of the *Enquirer,* do you?"

"Might boost book sales." I wasn't going to let Grace cast a shadow across the only thing which had been keeping me from despair in the past week. "Besides, the press is tired of all that. It's blown over."

"Be careful. And tell Ben hello for me."

"I will, Grace." I was grateful that she hadn't lectured me further. I wouldn't let the doubts about the wisdom of this meeting gain any foothold. I had only allowed the sweet anticipation of it to grow.

"And, Cleo . . . despite what I maybe have said about him, Ben is a good man, and you deserve a little fun."

I smiled into the phone and could barely get out my goodbye.

Eleanor's pregnancy was like the sound of a handful of dirt on a casket. Although I had declared the marriage over, news like this, whether true or not, rattled me. Sean had yet to tell me about it, and I swore the kids to silence. Lily might have been mistaken. To myself, I acknowledged that Eleanor was playing what she thought was her trump card. Her timing was good, though, even if her imagination was limited. At four in the morning I wondered if Eleanor's attraction for Sean was that she was young and fertile. Had I damaged my marriage in some way by refusing to have another baby? Had that decision somehow been construed as a primal punishment? In the dark hour before dawn I wondered if that had been my way of getting even with Sean. I had made that choice, thinking that it would prevent him from wandering. Awake and cold in my uncompanioned bed, I probed my intentions for some subconscious malfeasance in making that choice.

Driving into Boston, I realized how nervous I was by the several mistakes I made finding my way into the city. I knew where I was going, but suddenly nothing seemed familiar. I parked the car in the garage under the Hynes Auditorium and decided to walk to Copley Square rather than take the "T." Despite being dressed as if going to meet an editor, black from head to toe, wearing my good wool coat, I felt as though I wore an aura visible to any passerby. *Woman going to meet special man, see me glow.* We were to meet on the portico of Trinity Church, that much we decided on Thanksgiving. After that we'd find a place for lunch. I imagined something intimate and quiet, we had so much to say to one another.

It was cold, a damp breeze against my cheeks hinted at snow later in the day. I had listened to the forecast last night with fear that the whole expedition would have to be called off because of the weather. When the day arrived cloudy but snowless, I'd seen it as a sign of God's blessing. I leaned back against the brownstone wall of the church and waited. I waited long enough to begin to worry that I'd mistaken the place, then long enough to worry that he wasn't coming. Sharp bits of snow began to fall. For the first time I wished that I carried a cell phone. I didn't dare leave the portico to find a pay phone in case he came along at just that minute. Anxious tears began to rival the sharp flakes stinging my eyes.

"Cleo!" Ben came striding up to me from across the square. "I'm so sorry I'm late. The stupid car quit on me again. I ended up on the bus."

I stood where I was and watched him come. I felt the tears transform from anxiety to joy. Ben wore a green ranger's parka but no hat. He looked out of place in the city and wonderful to me. I hadn't intended on throwing myself into his arms like a schoolgirl, but he bear-hugged me like a boy. Everything was familiar about him, despite the winter clothes and strange setting. His scent, his spontaneous laugh, his keeping my gloved hand in his. When we finally settled down and I looked at him, I saw that he'd grown a goatee. "I like it." I reached up and touched the short beard hairs.

"A feeble attempt at incognito."

We headed for Newbury Street, moving quickly through the lunchtime crowd. We were lucky enough to find a table for two in a small coffee shop, although Ben hesitated just a little as it was in the window. "Oh, screw it, I've become just a little too paranoid." He held my chair out for me and then went to hang up our coats. Coming back to me, he commented, "You look lovely and you've grown out your hair, I like it."

"I suppose I have." It wasn't really a conscious decision, but I had let my wavy hair grow out. For so many years I'd kept it short and under control.

We had so much to say, it was hard to begin. I saw Ben looking at my bare left hand and I nodded. And told him my marriage was over. I told him about Alice's reaction, about Lily's behavior and Tim's sleeplessness, I even told him about the baby. For a long time I talked, and I began to feel self-conscious, but Ben kept me going until I was depleted. At the end my sandwich was untouched as was his and I felt as if I had lanced a blister and all the poison had flowed out. I took a cleansing breath and laughed, "Ben, you shouldn't encourage me to use you like a father confessor."

He was leaning against one fist, watching me as I talked, his collie brown eyes full of interest and concern and a little hint of amusement, as if looking at me was giving him pleasure. No man had ever looked at me like that. Not Sean, not really—he had looked at me with lust, or by habit. Not my father. He had never looked at me with interest, only with annoyance.

"Ben, will you tell me what's happening with you?"

"I grew a goatee."

"Seriously, how bad has it been since the press found out?"

"Very invasive. I came very close to moving Talia out of the convalescent home because the press were camped out on the lawn. Fortunately, it got cold and they gave up. What's difficult is that they've made this discovery just as she's reaching, well, for lack of a better word, the end. They know, just like vultures, that the end is near and it's worth waiting around for the big finale."

"Ben, you sound so . . ."

"Cynical? Hard? Flip? I am. I'm at the end of my rope, Cleo. I envy you. You've come to a conclusion and it's over and done."

"Not entirely."

"You know what I mean. I never know from day to day how much longer my life is going to be on hold. I'm so fed up with the whole thing, I wish it were over." He suddenly covered his face with his hands and then ran his fingers through his hair in a gesture so familiar to me. "I don't mean that. I'm just very tired." He looked tired, his summer tan gone, and pale and faint circles lay beneath his eyes. I should have seen it immediately but I was so happy just to see him, I hadn't noticed.

I took his hand away from his face and held it, glad for the small table, glad to give him a moment to let down his guard. I knew what he meant, though. In some faint parallel way, I, too, had been waiting for a death. Now that the clock was ticking down on the life of my marriage, ticking toward that day when the courts would pronounce it dead, I understood the peculiar limbo of being not quite free. I didn't do bedside vigil, but every day some new reminder of its termination struck me. I could only equate my divorce with the loss of his wife metaphorically, but because of it I did understand his ambivalent feelings and his quiet cry from the heart that it would soon be over.

"Can I ask you something?" I still held his hand and the question which clogged my throat needed asking in order for me to reconcile what I'd heard on the television with what Ben had told me.

"Of course. Anything."

"The report on *Entertainment Tonight* said something about an investigation."

"Actually, it was a routine inquiry, but, given who we were, it seemed more newsworthy to the media to call it an investigation. I'll show you the clippings someday." Ben slowly withdrew his hand from mine. A waitress hovered nearby and he caught her eye.

I needed more. I realized that Ben never finished the details of his story, he moved me ahead in it only by increments and only prompted by my questions. I was always left puzzling out the details. "They said she drowned. I thought she'd broken her neck."

"Talia struck her head on the rock and then somehow slipped under the raft's edge, pinned against the rock. I heard her go over, heard the splash. You remember that I told you it was very dark out. I dived off after her, but jumped off the other side. My splash, my swimming, would have masked the sound of her own, so I never thought that she hadn't struck out for shore. When I got there and she wasn't on the beach, I realized what had happened. I swam back but I couldn't find her at first. Then I did. Do you know how hard it is to get help out on an island? I had to chose between breathing for her and calling nine-one-one. We had to wait for the emergency people to find the harbormaster. Now the doctors tell me that it probably wouldn't have made any difference anyway after so many minutes underwater. The only thing I accomplished by getting her breathing again was to prolong her dying."

"Ben, you did the right thing. Don't ever go down that road."

The waitress reappeared with lunch-hour-rush efficiency to set the bill in front of us. It had begun to snow in earnest and I knew that I'd have to leave as soon as we were done. I had one more question that needed answering.

"Have you been able to work on the concerto?"

"No. I haven't touched it since you left." Ben gave me a little amused smile, "Would you believe that there's been a rebirth of interest in Interior Angles? They want us to do a reunion CD."

"Will you do it?"

"No. At least not soon." He suddenly reached across for my hand, his thumb rubbed at the empty place on my ring finger and he looked into my eyes. "Cleo, I can't take on anything more right now. I'm tapped out. It won't always be this way, but for now, I've got to stay where I am and see it to the end." His thumb pressed on my finger.

"Ben, you know I won't do anything to complicate your life."

He looked at me with an odd half-smile, "Oh, no, Cleo. You're the light at the end of my tunnel."

Forty-two

It was snowing in earnest by the time Ben walked me back to my car. We joked a little about ducking the paparazzi, but I know Ben was relieved that no one had followed him here. "They've been hanging out at the boat launch, long-range cameras, the works. I haven't felt this invaded since my IA days. Fortunately, the public's attention span is about four weeks, so it really has blown over. They just keep tabs on Talia and you can't imagine the ploys they use to get information. One of the reasons we came to the conclusion she needs to stay where she is, is because of the small town. The staff knows everybody so it's well nigh impossible to slip in pretending to be a staff member."

"Someone tried that?"

"That's how they got that picture, the one splashed all over supermarkets around the nation."

"How awful."

"Well, we're dealing with it, and they've apparently lost interest in following me. Although eventually they'll be back."

I knew he meant when she died, but I made no comment.

At my car, Ben took my keys and unlocked it. Then opened his arms to me and I went to him, for the instant completely unambivalent and uncautious. I buried my face against the soft flannel of his worn shirt and then lifted my face to meet his kiss. It is possible to go weak-kneed. We didn't pretend that this kiss was a simple farewell. The passion behind it was a little frightening. I thought that I would die if it stopped, or if it didn't. We whispered our passion to each other. Then finally stood apart. I was breathless and he was flushed. We laughed a little, to feel so adolescent.

The sound of someone walking by startled us both and Ben quickly turned me to face the car, and away from the lone business-man. As the sound of the footsteps died away I knew that we were in dangerous waters. That this was the wrong time to be together.

"Ben, some day, some day soon, we can be together. But," and I grasped his ungloved hands, "for now, I think we need to be . . . I can't . . ." I was trying to say what had been at the root of my silence before, we needed to wait for our separate stories to conclude before we could begin our own. "I don't want to confuse compassion with passion."

"Do you think that's what this is?" He moved an arm's length from me. "I know the difference. Sometimes I do want your compas-sion—but, Cleo, what I feel for you is not so one-dimensional. That isn't the only thing I want from you." Without meaning to, I'd hurt him with my caution.

"That's not what I'm saying. I think that I love you Ben. But until I'm clear of the confusion in my life, I can't explore this possibility without dragging the burden of that confusion along." I grasped the edges of his jacket and pulled him back to me. "And until you are clear of your burdens, neither can you."

He had no rebuttal, only took me back into his arms and we stood against my car for a long time, just holding each other as if it might be the last time.

Finally Ben opened my car door for me. "It's snowing, and you should go."

"How are you getting back?"

"I'm staying in town."

I felt the weight of squandered opportunity.

"Cleo, I'm here when you're ready."

"It won't be long."

"Just promise me you'll be there when I'm ready."

* * *

The snow was making the drive challenging enough that I needed to concentrate on my driving, relieving me of thinking back on the last hour. I wanted nothing more than to turn around and follow him home, but we both knew that my instincts were sound. What hurt was the look on his face, at once disappointed and accepting. We knew we were doing the right thing. Beyond even the chance of being the target of the paparazzi, we had to keep out of each other's lives until we could come together unencumbered.

Except that our resolve and the rightness of it did nothing to allay the grief of such a decision.

Forty-three

Christmas morning dawned mild and damp. Lily and Tim were up, as I expected, at dawn. I heard them whispering as they gazed at the array of gifts. Sean and I, in some understandable urge to compensate for the upset we'd inflicted on them, had gone overboard with gifts. We bought them both new bikes, and I could hear their excited voices and the rustle of paper as they tried to extricate the bikes from the pile of boxes. This was the moment when I usually nudged Sean awake, "Hear that? Santa's been here." He'd yawn and kiss me, "Merry Christmas." I'd have to poke him one more time to get him up.

I threw back the covers and pulled my old URI sweatshirt on over my nightgown, determined to be happy. Determined to make this day as close to normal as possible.

"Mom! Mom! Mom!" A duet singing out the glories of Santa. I plugged in the percolator and sat in the big chair beside the tree to dole out the presents.

"Mom, you have to wear the Santa hat." Tim was a stickler for tradition.

"I don't know where it is." I didn't mention that I had seen the red and white fuzzy hat in the box of ornaments and left it there. Sean always wore it on Christmas morning as he passed out the gifts.

"Can you guys wait while I pour a cup of coffee?" I didn't wait for an answer but fled to the kitchen. Nothing felt normal.

A sharp tap on the backdoor window startled me into spilling a little coffee. Sean's face was framed between the curtains on it, a little self-conscious smile. I felt myself grow cold and I set my coffee back down on the counter. Through the glass I could see that he'd come alone and so opened the door to him.

"Merry Christmas, Cleo. I know I should have talked to you about this before but"—Sean had kissed my cheek, and still stood very close to me as he whispered—"I woke up before dawn and found myself listening for the kids. You can throw me out, but I wish you'd let me be here for a little while. Just till they finish opening presents."

"What does Eleanor say about this?" Sean had moved in with her once the divorce papers were filed. He still hadn't confirmed to anyone that she was pregnant and I was beginning to think Lily had been wrong. I had every right to ask, but held back with an odd sense that even between illicitly formed couples, there was a right to privacy.

Sean still stood close. "She's still asleep."

"Help yourself to the coffee." I moved away from him and slapped on my happy face to convince the children this was all right. Their delight at seeing their father was almost painful. An odd thing happened then. Maybe it was the Christmas spirit, but suddenly it *was* all right. It was actually more than all right. It was like intermission at a very long and draining opera.

Stockings were emptied, boxes were opened, wrapping was strewn into every corner of the living room. Lily handed Sean the box with the gloves in it which I had gotten for them to give to their father. Always Sean and I had waited to exchange our gifts until after the kids were done. Like an empty place at the table, there was a fleeting moment to recognize that this year we weren't. I started gathering the debris. Sean went and got a trash bag.

We looked so normal amidst the mess, two pajama-clad children, one rumpled and unshaven dad with the Santa hat, which I'd suddenly found, and one mom still in her nightshirt and uncombed hair.

I should have taken a picture. "I'm making French toast. Will you stay?"

Sean looked at his watch. "I'd better not." He looked at the kids and then shrugged. "What the hell. Just let me call her."

He was smart enough to call from the phone in my office, out of earshot of any of us. When he came back he had that tense jaw I always associated with annoyance.

The devil in me forced the question. "She's not too happy about this, is she?"

"What? No, Eleanor's fine with this. She understands."

Somehow, even though the breakfast was lovely and we all laughed at old stories, the atmosphere had been sharpened by his remark. He was very loyal to his girlie. Sean left right after breakfast, promising to be back to collect the kids by noon.

"Dad, Mom, can't we ride our bikes to Gramma's?"

Sean and I passed one of those silent, what-do-you-think looks over their heads. "I guess so, if it's all right with your mother."

"Sean, why don't you meet them here on foot and walk with them?"

"Sure. I'll have Eleanor drop me off."

The sharp end of the spear. Eleanor would be there, of course. And I would not.

Grace and Joanie once again opened their holiday to me. I was a little surprised to find myself the only guest, but was all the more touched by the gesture. I brought the holiday pies, they did the rest. I had waited at home until the last minute, fussing with straightening up, making the pies, staying close to the phone in case Ben called. Hoping for a reenactment of the Thanksgiving call. I'd sent him a card, signed by all of us. I stuck a little note inside which said I was thinking of him. I was trying to bring to bear all the purported skill of my writing abilities to convey that I loved him, and that I was sorry for making him wait without actually writing those words. I hadn't gotten a card back and I tried to shrug it off. He was busy, distracted.

It was such a comfort to be at Grace and Joanie's University Avenue flat. It smelled of proper Christmas dinner, and their little artificial tree sparkled with twinkle lights and silver ornaments. Here and there were handmade ornaments my kids had given them, clothespin dollies and construction-paper stars. Under the tree, in gracious display, were several open boxes holding sweaters and various articles of winter wear. It seemed to me that the girls were planning a winter vacation by the look of their gifts to each other. I caught sight of a small box with my name on it beside several with Lily's and Tim's names written on Joanie's handmade gift tags.

Dinner was ready and we ate before opening gifts, true grownups. Joanie had provided us with an outstanding feast and we all ate well and drank too much wine. By the time we pushed ourselves away from the table and went into the living room, I was feeling quite unguarded. So it was without embarrassment I wept when, after oohing and aahing over my gifts to them, I opened my present and found a beautiful scarf and an invitation to be their guest at the Cameo Lake Inn the next weekend.

"You'll love the place in winter. We'll rent cross-country skis and go all over the frozen lake." Grace was so excited about her brilliant gift, she didn't notice the tears which ran unchecked as soon as I saw the words *Cameo Lake*. All of a sudden all the world shrank into what those words held for me. Finally Grace realized that my silence wasn't speechlessness but a true meltdown. She put her arms around me and let me have at it. Joanie excused herself with a kiss on the top of my head and went to visit her mother. Grace hugged me to her large body and rocked me like a child until she began to demand what had set me off. "Is it because that's where you found out about Sean?"

I shook my head and used the end of my sweater as a tissue.

"Then what is it?" Grace reached for a tissue box. "Oh, I know. Ben."

I nodded and took the box from her. Very slowly I told her about everything, coming at last to the decision made in Boston to stay apart until we were totally free. "I think I may have hurt him, although he agreed it was the best thing."

"You nincompoop." Grace physically moved me away from her and stood up, hands on hips, ready to lecture. "The man all but says he loves you. Why hold him at arm's length? Don't you deserve a little happiness, Cleo Grayson?"

"What if it's only a product of our situation? Because of all that's happened."

"You mean rebound love?"

"Yes."

"Cleo, you fell for him a long time ago. Not since Sean's affair. You don't even know it, but you've been falling for Ben Turner for six months."

"What if the divorce is because I fell for him?"

"Take it from me, Cleo. It ain't. You want to divorce Sean because he's a cheating schmuck. Don't you trust your feelings for Ben? Go get him. Come with us Friday and go get him."

"How can I? It wouldn't be right. Don't forget, I cheated too." The wine had loosened up all my fears and emotional confusion, all my anguish and deep seated guilt.

"Apples and oranges." Grace sat back down next to me and looped me close. "What did your parents do to you that you don't think you deserve some happiness?"

Forty-four

*A*nd the snow lay round about, deep and crisp and even.... The words of the Christmas carol were so apt as we drove up from the bare ground of Providence to the winter-white landscape of the White Mountains. A fresh snow had fallen the day before and even as our headlights led us on to our destination, new flakes were brilliant in their beam. We passed through the village of Cameo Lake, its familiar brick and clapboard buildings were still decorated for Christmas. It was like seeing a playmate all dressed up. Even the Dairy Bar, long since closed for the season, sported a big wreath and a SEASON'S GREETINGS banner on the door.

The Cameo Lake Inn, on the West Side of the Lake, was an imposing nineteenth-century mansion, the summer home of an industrialist with a yen for the Alps. A pair of New Yorkers had bought and converted the house to an inn thirty years ago and never looked back. We arrived in time for the single seating of dinner and I knew then just why Grace and Joanie made this an annual visit. The five-course meal was fabulous and retiring to the small fire-lit parlor afterward was heaven.

"This is wonderful, guys. Thank you so much for my Christmas gift."

Grace reclined on a Victorian settee, looking for the moment more Rubenesque than ever. "We couldn't think of anything that you needed more than this."

She was so right. Christmas night, when he brought the kids home, Sean finally laid his unexploded bomb at my feet. "Eleanor is pregnant."

It was all I could do to act surprised. I had, for once, had the advantage and been able to digest my feelings about this new wrinkle in an otherwise shredded fabric, so I turned the table on him. "How do you feel about that?"

Sean smiled, and to his credit, didn't seem to look at this as the hook which would snare him. "I guess I'm happy about it. I never thought I wanted more children, and the idea of raising a second family is pretty weird. But, I guess that I would have eventually been doing that so, as I'm forty now, it's a good thing to start."

"So, what you're saying is that you intended all along to marry her?"

He shifted uneasily on his feet. I noticed that the stain was still on his overcoat and I gestured to him to take it off. He shrugged off the coat without question, still wondering how to answer me. I headed into the basement with his coat and waited for him to follow me.

The basement was divided unevenly into halves, my laundry side and his workbench side. I took down a bottle of stain remover and went to work on the grease stain. Sean wandered over to his workbench. It had been so long since he used it that it was in fair order. Even so, Sean picked up various tools still on the bench and hung them on their proper hooks. "Would you mind if I left this stuff here? I don't have a basement where I am and there's no room in Ma's."

"I guess so." I took a wet cloth and rinsed out the remover. The wet mark would dry and I was pretty sure the stain was gone.

Sean finished hanging the hammer and screwdrivers and wrenches left out from his last project. "Cleo, I didn't intend that things would go this far."

"I know, Sean."

*   *   *

I was afraid that Grace would badger me about going to see Ben. I was unwilling to commit myself to a when and how. I would call him. Give him some warning and let him tell me if he wanted to see me. Every time I thought about making that call, I felt my insides contract with nerves.

That first day we went out and rented skis, and spent the morning keeping to the well-marked trails surrounding the inn. Afterward, Grace and Joanie were content to entertain themselves while I went back out to explore more of the trails. We met again at dinner, then spent the night soaking in the hot tub and playing cards with other guests.

Joanie had gone up to bed and Grace and I stayed for one more sherry in the parlor. The fire had gone to dull embers and the room was growing chilly.

"Have you called him?"

"Not yet."

"It's only nine o'clock. Call him now."

Buoyed by the sherry and Grace's stage directions, I went to the alcove with the pay phone. My hand actually shook as I dropped the coins into the box. *At the customer's request this phone number has been disconnected.* I heard the coins drop into the return slot and imagined that I'd dialed the old number. I ran upstairs to get my address book and rechecked it. I hadn't. He'd disconnected his phone again.

"I guess things must be heating up for him to do that again. It was an unlisted number." I flopped back into the armchair, noticing that someone had come in and plumped up the dying fire.

"So go over there tomorrow." Grace heaved herself up from the settee, "I'm going to be too sore to ski, and there are, as you know, great trails around the lake. Don't be obstinate, Cleo. Has it ever occurred to you that Ben might need you right now?"

I parked Grace's big car at the top of the driveway and snapped on the skis. The day was one of those perfect winter days, almost windless, azure sky and not a cloud in sight. It was deeply cold, but so dry it felt comfortable and I thought maybe I was overdressed in vest and jacket. It wasn't difficult to pick out the lay of the road to Grace's cabin. The trees outlined a clear trail. I glided along, enjoying the sensation of effortless trail breaking in the powder that had recently fallen. The bare branches of the deciduous trees made strong shadows in the snow through which I skated, light and dark, light and dark. The little bit of wind sang in the pines, and without the birdsong of the summer, the woods seemed very quiet. Just as I came into sight of the cabin ahead of me, the bright red flash of a cardinal against the snow-covered roof caught my eye and I was unaccountably reminded of the first time I'd seen the cabin. How I'd sat in the car and wondered if I was doing the right thing. A cardinal had called for a mate, I remembered, his piercing whistle distracting me from myself.

I worked my way around the corner of the cabin to see the lake. It was breathtaking. As far as I could see, Cameo Lake was under snow. The deep freeze of the past few weeks had frozen the lake entirely and the recent snowfall had laid a layer of untouched white on the surface, making it a white desert. Not a track showed. And, except for the top of the ladder, poking up out of the snow like a periscope, the raft was invisible.

I stood leaning on my poles and gazed across the lake at Ben's cabin. It looked so tiny, tucked in snowdrifts which came up to the sills of the windows. I hesitated. Maybe I should only look at Ben's cabin and move on. Maybe I should just leave him alone. I stood leaning against my poles and looked across the distance which in summer had come to seem so close. The white expanse seemed so much wider without the way station of the raft. I wondered, Should I just go back? But I didn't. I slid down the embankment and started across the lake.

A thin whisper of chimney smoke had beckoned me.

By the time I reached the midway point of the nearly invisible raft, I realized that mine weren't the only fresh tracks. I also realized that I was very visible, a dark speck on a white surface. I paused in midstride to unzip my jacket. I was close enough now to hear the sound of a gas generator and I knew that Ben had gotten his electricity. The sound of it was loud enough to block out the sound of an approaching snowmobile. I was startled by its sudden appearance, and more so by its even quicker departure. The photographer's camera pointed at me like a weapon. I remained rooted to the spot, uncertain whether to keep going or retreat. Until I stepped onto Ben's shore, no one could associate us, I might be just a random skier crossing the lake. Once I touched Ben's shore, I would become part of the tabloid story.

I saw his cabin door open up and then I knew what to do. Ben came down from his porch, no coat or hat, unlaced boots. I thought he was going to run out onto the ice and I started skiing as fast as I could toward him. I called out a warning to him about the photographer, but he waved his hand in a dismissive gesture. We met just at the shoreline in a quick embrace. Ben bent to release my feet from the skis and picked them up under his arm. "Cleo, that idiot raced off too fast to get a really good shot." And with that he kissed me. It wasn't a kiss of passion, it was a kiss of solidarity.

Inside the cabin I knew immediately what was happening. "You've brought her home, haven't you?"

"Yes. It was time."

Forty-five

The sound of the generator was an odd background noise to the quiet drama unfolding inside the cabin. Ben took my coat and hung it on a peg beside the door. He didn't right away speak to me, only held my face between his hands and looked into my eyes, as if to assure himself that, unannounced, I had really come to him.

I wanted to apologize for doubting the trueness of our relationship, I wanted to ask him if he wanted me to leave. I wanted to know if he could love me. Everything I wanted to ask was answered in the look in his eyes, then his gentle lips on my forehead. Stay.

Then I could hear a snowmobile over the sound of the generator. I pulled away, but Ben only smiled. "That's Jeremy. He's our private nurse."

Two days before, the doctors had told Ben that Talia had succumbed to pneumonia. She had been slowly withering away and the news was almost welcome. "I promised her that I'd bring her home. Right from the beginning, when there might have been some hope, I whispered to her every day that I would bring her back here."

"You kept your promise."

"The thing is—" Ben lifted a kettle off the stove and poured water into our teacups—"we never resolved our argument. I've spent a year and a half imagining how we could. That night she told me she was in love with someone else. She told me not to touch her. In the time since, I've touched her every day and I've had a thousand variations of that argument which would have ended differently. The only thing I am sure of is that she did love this place. The only certain thing was that she would want to be here.

"I tried to find out who the lover was. No one has ever come forward to say, 'Hey, Talia Brightman was going to run away with me.' No one has shown up grieving. Even after the hoopla last month, no one has come forward for a fifteen-minutes-worth of fame."

"Are you saying you doubt what she said?"

"Sometimes."

I sipped the tea and tried to imagine the cruelty of someone to tell such a lie. "Ben, what would you have done if things had happened differently?"

"I would have given her her freedom."

Jeremy, the middle-aged African-American I remembered from my visit to the nursing home, came from Talia's room and the two men left me to confer in the living room. I tidied up the cups and wiped down the counter. I didn't listen, but I could hear. Things were drawing to a close. Without the life-support and breathing apparatus, it was only a matter of the clock of life winding down. Talia was drowning again, this time in her own fluids. I breathed the only prayer which came to mind, a plea to let God take her quickly and let Ben get on with his life.

Ben came back into the kitchen and sat down. I stood behind him, my arms around his neck. I kissed the top of his head, where the little bald patch was, and then lay my cheek against it. "Do you want me to go?"

"No. Please don't. I like knowing you're here."

"I'll have to call Grace and let her know where I am, but your phone is out."

"No, just another unlisted number. It is amazing how persistent these people are." Ben caught my hands and kissed them. "Cleo, thank you for being here. I don't know how you knew to come, but I'm glad you did."

"You can thank Grace Chichetti."

I made the phone call brief, telling her where the car was if they needed it and how Ben was. Grace said they would get a ride to pick it up, and I wasn't to leave Ben's side. "I love you, Grace."

"I love you, too. In a Platonic kind of way."

I've never been good at waiting. So I made cookies. Then I foraged around until I came up with ingredients for dinner, hot dogs and beans. I straightened up the living room and kitchen. Jeremy came out and we sat together, making small talk while he ate. Then Ben came out and we sat quietly while Jeremy performed some nursing task. Ben only picked at the dinner I set before him. Then they both went back in and I sat alone in the darkened living room until I fell asleep.

Entering my sleep like a dream was the sound of a piano, the familiar motif crossed and blended now with something new and I awoke to hear what would become the solo flute passage in Ben's homage to Talia. I knew then that she was gone.

Epilogue

The orchestra has risen to greet the conductor. He shakes the hand of the principal violinist and then raises his arms. They begin the first chords of Mahler's Fifth Symphony and I try to focus on the music, on the faces of the musicians, trying to loosen up the listening muscles with a familiar and powerful piece.

The audience is appreciative but anxious to hear the featured piece, a new, never-performed concerto by a man whose music is more usually associated with rock concerts than symphony orchestras. The conductor, without an introductory word, gives the downbeat.

Instantly Ben's familiar motif begins and I am plunged into memories so thick I choke back tears. At first the low instruments, the tubas and double basses, the baritone horn and dark tympani, explore the theme. Then the cellos and bassoons imitate and embroider. Finally, the flute, a lone voice above the crowd, begins to sweetly sing the melody. I did not really know Talia Brightman. I have not heard her work, listened to her CDs, so I do not think of her. I think of the birds calling in the thick woods around the lake. I think of the hum of a mosquito and the splash of a trout breaking the surface of the water. In my mind's eye I see the dawn and feel the dirt beneath my running feet. I close my eyes and feel Ben's touch.

Her passing had been peaceful, he said, her breathing increasingly shallow, fading like the last note in a song, slowly diminishing. He'd lain with her in the hospital bed, holding her and talking with her until he involuntarily fell asleep. When he woke, she was gone and the long months of waiting were over.

"Are you all right?" I'd asked, studying his face.

"Yes. I think so." He squinted past me, watching the dawn breaking over Grace's cabin. "I think that I'll be okay. I've been mourning Talia for such a long time that I don't feel a difference in the intensity yet."

"But now you can heal."

The second movement of the concerto is the adagio, a slower, contemplative movement which evokes so clearly the gentle rocking of the raft. I think of his grief, spread out over eighteen months, mourning the loss of his love long before she died. Ben told me that he mourned more fully the loss of Talia's love long before the accident. Her withdrawal from his life. He mourned for the death of their passion and their life together. Seated in this small auditorium, listening to Ben's music, I realize that I, too, have been in mourning for the loss of love. What Ben and I have now we appreciate all the more. We both know how fragile love can be.

The final movement is amazing to me. I had never heard even a fragment of it and am delightfully surprised at its brightness and joyful sound. The flute is playing against the mimicry of a viola, back and forth; in a kind of jazzlike one-upsmanship, they seem to challenge each other. At last they blend and the last note fades away, diminishing into the silence of the spellbound audience and I feel the goose bumps prickle my arms. The conductor teases us and keeps his arms aloft until the reverberations die completely. He brings them down and the audience erupts. I am so proud.

Finally, reluctantly, Benson Turner rises from his seat beside me and takes the stage. He shakes hands with the conductor and is embraced by the flautist, then bows to the audience in a remarkably humble acknowledgment of our applause. Ben catches my eye and winks. I give him the thumbs-up.

Sean and I, we let something go. It wasn't Eleanor's fault. It was ours. But, in letting it go, we have both found something which has become precious to us. My kids have a new baby brother. I am both a first wife and a second. Alice has made room at her Sunday table for Ben and me.

Grace reaches across Tim and takes my hand. "Isn't it wonderful?"

She might mean Ben's music or my life. I nod, too full of emotion to say anything aloud, but she knows I think that, as always, she's absolutely right.

$(10, ^{\checkmark}5/16)$

NNS   NC